Ju. Owed

by

Dave P. Fisher

DOUBLE DIAMOND

Washington

Novels by Dave P. Fisher

The Poudre Canyon Saga

Where Free Men Gather
White Grizzly
The Men from Poudre Canyon
We Never Back Down
Shifting Trails

Individual Titles

Jury of Six
Zac Doolin's Gold
The Turning of Copper Creek
Virgil Creede
Beyond Raton
Bitter Grass
A Man for the Country
The Hanging of August Miller
The Outlaw Hunter

Short Story Collections

Bronc Buster – Short Stories of the American West

The Auction Horse (humor)
They Still Do That (cowboy poetry)

Outdoor Sporting Fiction

Cold Blows the Tundra Wind
Code of the Bush

Old Family Secrets

Adam looked at Elwood. "Uncle Elwood, do you know of any enemies the folks had?"

Elwood slowly shook his head.

"Anyone who would want to kill them?"

Elwood replied, "No. I can't think of anyone around here who would do such a thing."

Cordell looked from one to the other, "Old family secrets?"

Elwood's eyes suddenly widened and he took in a gasping breath.

"What's wrong, Uncle Elwood?" Adam asked.

Elwood shook his head, panic widening his eyes. "I have to go." He left the brothers at a fast walk.

"How strange was that?" Cordell asked.

"Very strange," Adam answered.

Fallon watched his uncle growing smaller in the distance. "He looked like a man who just got the answer to a puzzle."

Cordell looked at Adam and then Fallon. "Old family secrets?"

"It wouldn't be the first time in history," Fallon commented.

"But, the folks never had any old secrets," Adam protested.

Fallon gave his brother a sober look. "We don't actually know that."

Justice Owed

Chapter 1

The flames leaped high into the night sky as the fire eagerly consumed the structure. Its wooden frame and walls, baked dry by the Arizona sun, cracked and roared engulfing in minutes the house belonging to Ryan and Tessa Monroe. The house was far enough from the other homes in the Tucson residential district that they were not ignited by the flying sparks and brands.

Men rushed to the scene from all directions carrying buckets, shovels, and a variety of tools in hopes of stopping the fire. The volunteers of the Tucson Hook and Ladder Company in the year 1881 had nothing more to work with then the general public did. The intense heat thrown off by the fully involved house was evidence enough that any effort to put down the fire would be futile. The best they could do at this point was to stamp out any additional fires resulting from it.

The Monroes had moved to Tucson with their three young boys ten years before and took over a closed mercantile. Ryan, now sixty years of age, and Tessa two years younger, had become stellar members of the growing community and town. Ryan was involved in civic groups and Tessa active in the church. Their generosity and good nature made them a wide array of friends.

Fear raced through the hearts of the men who watched the last of the wooden frame crash to the ground in a shower of sparks and flame. The question in every mind was had Ryan and Tessa escaped? No one had yet to see them and that instilled fear that they were at the bottom of the hellish inferno.

Bank president Elwood Boone rushed to the scene in his hastily thrown-on clothes. He stared in wide eyed terror at the licking flames and red glow of what had been his sister's and brother-in-law's home.

Bill Quinn, chief of the Hook and Ladder Company, stepped up beside Elwood and put his hand gently on his back. "I'm sorry Elwood, it was gone in a blink. There was nothing we could do."

Elwood felt as if he were in a dream. Maybe he was still asleep and this was a nightmare. He turned his head slowly to look at the chief. The man was flesh and blood, this was no dream, but it was a nightmare. "Has anyone seen Tessa or Ryan?" he asked, his voice quivering.

Quinn shook his head. "No," he replied in a pained voice.

Elwood rubbed his hands across his face. "Oh, my God, oh, my God," he whispered. Then, he began to weep.

It was mid-morning before the remains of the house had cooled enough for Marshal Clay Scott to investigate the scene. Wearing leather gloves and carrying a shovel he stepped his way carefully through the warm debris, pushing smoldering bits of wood out of his way with the shovel. A crowd of the curious had gathered around to look at the disaster and watch the marshal.

Bill Quinn walked into the charred remains. "Morning, Marshal."

Scott turned to look at him. "Bill."

Quinn shook his head. "It went so fast."

Scott flipped a smoldering board out of his way with the shovel. "These bone dry houses usually do."

"Unfortunately, yes."

Scott continued to look at the debris as he talked. "I take it no one has seen the Monroes."

Quinn shook his head, "No. That means . . . "

"They're in here somewhere," Scott grunted with a tone of indifference, "or, what's left of them, if anything."

Quinn gave the marshal a sidelong glance. It was no secret that Clay Scott and Ryan Monroe did not get along. Over the years Scott had become arrogant in his power and bullied where he could get away with it. He was often challenged by Ryan, who had no fear of him, at town council meetings over his tactics.

There was also the fact that Ryan's youngest son, Cordell had been in trouble a lot and Scott hated the young man. Ryan and Scott had frequently gone toe-to-toe over Cordell, who had left Tucson three years before at age seventeen. Rumors of his gunfighting and reputation as a bad man were the talk of the town. Cordell was not liked by most but Ryan was, so exceptions for his son were made.

A clutter of burned wood surrounded a ten foot deep cellar that had been dug under the kitchen. A slanted door outside had led down into it. The wooden steps were charred, their usability uncertain.

Scott held up his arm toward Quinn. "Watch it, there's a cellar here."

Scott stood at the edge of the hole and stared down into it. Wisps of smoke drifted up out of the hole as they scanned the bottom. Scott's wandering gaze stopped as he stared hard at a spot on the bottom. "Get the undertaker, I found them."

Quinn looked over the edge of the hole and saw parts of two bodies under a scattering of burned wood. He turned to obey the marshal's instructions.

"Bring a ladder too," Scott called back to Quinn. "I don't trust those steps."

Scott was standing above the cellar when the undertaker, with Quinn riding beside him, pulled a buckboard to the edge of the charred ground and stopped the horses. The horses shied away from the smoke smell as the undertaker clipped the end of a rope to one of the horse's headstalls and the other to the iron ground anchor that he dropped to hold them.

Quinn jumped off the seat and pulled a ladder off the wagon bed. One of his volunteers ran toward him and took up the opposite end of the ladder. They carried it to the cellar and lowered the ladder in. The undertaker followed, stepping his way carefully though the debris.

Scott nodded toward the undertaker, "Hiram."

Hiram nodded, "Marshal. So, what have we got?"

"Two bodies at the bottom there."

Hiram looked down in the hole. "Yes, I see them."

Scott stepped down the first rung of the ladder. "Let me check it first."

"I'll get the canvas and rope to bring them out with." Hiram walked back out to the buckboard.

Scott reached the bottom of the ten foot square cellar and stepped carefully around the bodies. He flipped the partially burned boards and debris off the bodies. They were both face down, but not badly burned indicating that they had either been in the cellar when the fire started or fell through the collapsing floor to their deaths. The fact there was debris on top of them indicated they had ended up in the cellar before the frame came down. He rolled each body over, it was Ryan and Tessa.

Quinn called down to Scott, "Is it?"

"Yeah, it's them."

Hiram returned to the cellar. "Here, Marshal."

Scott looked up as Hiram dropped the canvas and rope down to him. He then climbed down the ladder.

Hiram looked at the scorched faces of the bodies, "Such a shame, they were good folks."

Scott only grunted as an acknowledgement. "Too bad they didn't do a better job raising their kids."

Hiram looked shocked at the marshal, but then there had been no love lost between Clay Scott and Ryan Monroe. "They had one out of three that went bad. No one's perfect, Marshal."

Scott snorted. "Let's get them wrapped up."

The two men rolled the bodies onto the canvas tarps and tied them around with the rope.

Scott looked up at Quinn. "Get a couple of men over here to pull on these ropes."

Quinn called out for men to help. Several responded and hurried to him. Scott tossed the rope ends up and guided the bodies against the ladder as the men on top pulled them up one at a time. The bundled bodies were carried to the buckboard.

Scott and Hiram climbed out of the cellar. Scott brushed the soot off his clothes. "Let me know if anything looks unusual about them."

"They died in a fire, Marshal."

"I don't know that for a fact, Hiram. It looks kind of suspicious to me."

"How so?"

"Both dead in the cellar. Could be a murder-suicide. I never did trust that Ryan Monroe."

Hiram's mouth turned down in an angry frown. "That's a horrible accusation to make, Marshal."

"Just do it. I need to be out of town for a couple of days, you can give me a report when I get back."

"If that was the case, who started the fire?"

Scott cast a hard look on the undertaker without answering.

"Fine, I'll do it," Hiram agreed as he walked back through the debris to his buckboard.

The crowd had gathered to watch the bundles laid in the wagon bed. Elwood stood staring in shock knowing the bundles could only be his beloved sister and Ryan. His eyes followed the wagon as the horses pulled it away.

Quinn walked up beside Elwood. "Sorry, Elwood. I truly am sorry."

Elwood coughed to clear his tight throat. "I need to send word to Adam, and wire Fallon to come home."

Quinn nodded. "Yes. What about Cordell?"

Elwood shrugged, "I have no idea where he is. I'll let Adam track him down."

Elwood read the disapproving look on Quinn's face. "I know what folks think of Cordell, but they're wrong. He's a good young man, just a little wild. He was always respectful to his folks and to me and Ruth."

"I never said otherwise, Elwood."

"No, but you thought it."

Quinn patted Elwood on the back and walked away.

With help the bundled bodies were carried into Hiram's work room, unwrapped, and lifted up onto the work table. The men helping him turned a shade of green and quickly departed the room. Hiram closed and locked the door.

He peeled the burned clothes away from each body. There were burns of varying degrees, but he could not see anything resembling wounds. "Murder-suicide indeed," he grumbled aloud. "That arrogant fool. Just because Ryan would stand up to him. As if Ryan would murder a woman as beautiful and wonderful as Tessa."

He knew the Monroe sons would need to be gathered before a funeral could be held. It would take a few days as the oldest boy, Fallon, lived in Austin, Texas. Considering the fire damage to the faces there would not be an open casket service. That gave him some time to prepare the bodies and make the funeral arrangements with Elwood.

Chapter 2

Elwood Boone staggered into his house like a drunken man and flopped down into a sitting room chair. He buried his face in his hands and remained motionless letting the pain sweep through him. A stifled sob escaped his hands.

Ruth stepped softly into the room, her feet soundless on the rug covered floor. "Elwood?"

Elwood lifted his face from his hands and looked at his wife. "Marshal Scott found them."

A tear slid down her cheek. She knew if Ryan and Tessa were alive they would have come directly to them. "In the fire?"

Elwood nodded.

Ruth moved across the room and bent over her distraught husband, wrapping her arms around him in a sympathetic embrace. "I am sorry."

He was unable to answer as he released another sob.

"I loved Tessa as my own dear sister," Ruth replied in a soft voice. She then sat down in the chair next to him.

"Hiram took them."

Ruth nodded.

Elwood straightened his back and sniffed. Pulling a white handkerchief from the pocket of his suit coat he wiped his eyes and blew his nose. "I must pull myself together."

"It is all right to grieve, dear."

"There is much to do and it will not get done with me blubbering here like a child."

Ruth knew her husband was emotional and often wore his feelings on his sleeve. She saw no harm in that. He wept when he was in pain. When their only son Seth died while they were still in Texas he was incapable of doing anything for days.

"It will all get done, Elwood. I will talk to the ladies at church about arranging the service and lunch."

Elwood ran his fingers through his gray hair and nodded. "I will take care of Hiram's services."

"What about the boys?"

"I will send a wire to Fallon and drive out to the ranch to tell Adam."

"And, Cordell?'

Elwood was silent for several seconds. He had taken to Tessa's boys as his own, particularly to Cordell as he was Seth's age. He acknowledged that Cordell was a fighter, in and out of trouble until he left town. Along the way he picked up a reputation as a bad man. Much of the town saw him as the black sheep in a well-respected family. He defended the boy, the same as Ryan did, the same as he would if it had been Seth. "Adam will know how to get word to him." Elwood stood up. "I'd best get to it."

Ruth gave him a worried look. "It is twenty miles out to the ranch. In this heat and your emotional state it might not be a good idea. One of Adam's hands might be in town, you can send a message out to the ranch."

Elwood did not relish the long drive in the hundred-plus-degree heat. "You may be right. I will see if there is another way to get word out to Adam." He bent down and kissed Ruth on the cheek then left the house.

Word had spread fast through the community that the Monroes had been found dead as a result of the fire. Ryan and Tessa had been an integral part of the growing community, loved and respected by all. Losing them was a painful blow to all who knew them, a tragedy of epic proportions.

Little was known about the Monroes prior to their arrival in Tucson from Texas ten years before. They had taken up the store right off and blended into the community. The most anyone knew is they had raised cattle in west Texas. Ryan had told stories of fighting Apaches and had moved his family north for their safety. No one asked questions beyond that.

As Elwood walked through the town he was greeted by well-wishers and condolences. The bank employees would not expect him to come in that day. He wasn't sure what to do next as his mind was in a fog. There was no sense in talking funeral arrangements with Hiram right now, he would be busy. Tomorrow would suffice for that.

He walked by the Monroe store to see the usually propped open door closed and locked. A pain wrenched at his heart. As he approached the store he saw a wagon stopped in front and then a man, looking confused, walked around from the backside of the building. He recognized the man, it was Roger

Simms, the Delaney Ranch cook.

Roger spotted Elwood as he returned to the front. He waved at the banker, "Where is everyone?" he called out good naturedly. "I need supplies, but no one seems to be around."

"I guess you haven't heard," Elwood replied in a choked voice.

Roger's smile dropped off. "Heard what?"

"Ryan and Tessa were killed last night when their house burned down."

Roger's mouth dropped open and then closed, "Oh, Lord, no."

Elwood nodded. "The marshal found their bodies in the cellar."

"Oh, I'm sorry, Mr. Boone. Has anyone sent word up to Adam yet?"

"No. They only found the bodies this morning. Will you take the message back?"

"Yeah, sure. Actually, one of the boys rode his horse in with me. I'll have him ride back with the message for Adam."

"That would be good. Save me the long trip. Thank you."

Roger studied Elwood for a moment. "You don't look so good Mr. Boone, you should go home and rest."

"Yes, it has been a trying night and day. I must send a wire to Fallon first."

Elwood began to walk away when he stopped and turned back to Roger. "Oh, ask Adam to find a way to reach Cordell, will you?"

"Sure. You might want to start by sending wires to the Marshal's Offices in Tombstone, Bisbee, and Benson. Cordell might be around one of them, or if they see him, they can give him the word."

"Is he around these parts?"

"Last anyone heard anyways." He didn't want to tell Elwood that the trail word had it that Cordell killed a couple of Mexicans down in Black Water on the border. He was likely heading north again putting distance between him and Mexico.

"I will do that, thank you."

Adam rode into the ranch yard beside his father-in-law, Red Delaney. It was late and darkness had been over the desert for an hour. They pulled up at the corral behind the two houses and wearily dismounted. They led the horses into the barn where Red lit a lantern.

As they stripped the tack off the sweat streaked horses Laura hurried into the barn. "I saw your light."

Adam smiled at her, his face covered in dirt and dried sweat streaks. The smile faded as he took in the distressed look on his wife's face. "What's wrong?"

Red turned to look at his daughter. "Laura, did something happen?"

Laura drew in a shaky breath and let it out. "Oh, Adam," she began to cry.

Both Adam and Red became instantly alarmed. "Laura, what?" Adam asked in a voice reflecting his anxiousness.

"Ma and Pa were killed in a fire last night." She put her hand over her mouth and cried.

Adam stood in shock, not quiet comprehending the statement. "What?"

"There was a fire last night, their house. They

. . .," she took in a shaky breath. "They both died in it."

"Oh, my God," Red whispered. As well as being related through the marriage of his daughter to Adam he had been good friends with Ryan and Tessa.

Adam stood stone still staring at Laura. He swallowed and tried to form words without success. Laura threw her arms around him and they embraced.

"Who told you?" Red asked.

"Brad rode in from town with the message. Uncle Elwood had talked to Roger. He sent Brad back with the message and then I talked to Roger when he returned."

Adam let go of Laura and stepped back. "What did he say?"

"He did not know much. Only that Uncle Elwood said there had been a fire last night. Their house burned down and they were killed in the fire."

Adam stared at the barn wall behind Laura. "I'll need to head in there and talk to Uncle Elwood."

"I want to go too," Laura said as she wiped her hands across her face. "It is too late tonight though."

Adam absently shook his head. "No, you're right. We'll take the buggy first thing in the morning."

It was a long and restless night for Adam and Laura. Adam finally fell into a fitful sleep from pure exhaustion as a result of his day's labor. Laura was up with coffee and breakfast made when the blue and orange streaks of dawn promised another hot June day.

Adam walked out of the bedroom and into the kitchen. Laura looked at him, his face was drawn and weary making him look ten years older than his twenty-two years. He had taken the news hard.

They ate in silence, eating more from necessity than desire.

Adam sat over his empty plate and cup. He rubbed a hand over his whisker stubbled jaw. "I'd best go shave and look a little more presentable." He stood up and walked out of the kitchen.

An hour later the two were headed down the ranch's dirt road to Tucson in the buggy. Laura knew her husband was a quiet, mild mannered man not given to idle chatter, yet she engaged him as much as possible in talk. They both needed to talk to alleviate the sorrow and questions over what had happened. Three hours later they pulled up in front of Elwood's and Ruth's house.

Elwood and Ruth opened the door at the sound of the buggy and walked out to greet them. The women hugged, then Ruth hugged Adam. Elwood shook Adam's hand. "You will stay with us until the funeral, I trust?" Elwood asked.

"If it's convenient for you," Adam replied.

"Of course it is," Elwood said with feeling.

"We wouldn't hear of it otherwise," Ruth added.

"Thank you," Adam gave a slight smile.

"Let us go inside, I will make lunch," Ruth said.

Adam and Laura followed the elderly couple into the house.

As they sat around the table Elwood explained that he had wired Fallon. "I was not sure how to locate Cordell, but Roger suggested I wire the Marshals in Tombstone, Bisbee, and Benson so if he passed through there they could notify him to come home." He knew that all the marshals knowing Cordell was not a good sign. He cast a nervous eye on Adam, then Laura, and added, "Roger had heard Cordell was in that part of the country possibly heading this way."

Adam nodded. He had heard the stories as well about Cordell shooting two Mexicans down on the border. He knew his younger brother was a fighter, but he never killed unless it was in self-defense. The problem was he had a tendency to hang out in places where he ended up having to regularly defend himself. He had been involved in a shooting in Tombstone the year before and Marshal Virgil Earp had given him his walking orders.

Adam coughed, "There's quite a network among those who work and ride the trails and the towns. Word gets around fast. I'm sure Cordell will get the message quick enough."

"Is there still animosity between him and Fallon?" Ruth asked.

Adam nodded, "Like coal oil and water. Two opposite personalities, neither tolerant of the other."

Elwood shook his head, "That is too bad. Brothers should get along. I was very close to my brother . . . until the war."

Adam knew that his uncle's younger brother had gone off to fight for the Confederacy and never came home. Elwood had known a lot of pain in his life, yet he persevered. "Yes," Adam agreed. "It should be that way. Maybe someday."

Chapter 3

The man sat in the hard chair working his fingers nervously around the brim of his derby hat. Sweat trickled down his face disappearing under the stiff collar encircled by a black tie. His face was twisted in anguish as he pleaded with the stone faced lawyer sitting across the desk from him. "Please, Mr. Monroe, please."

Fallon Monroe glared at the man through cold blue eyes. He let the man snivel on as he rested his chin on his knuckles and elbow on the chair arm.

"It wasn't my fault. I didn't do it. If you don't help me I'll go to prison. That judge will send me up for twenty years, don't you understand?" He stopped talking and set his pleading eyes on Fallon.

Without moving from his position Fallon spoke with a voice as cold as his eyes. "You're good. Pleading eyes, whining tone, sniveling. If you were a puppy you might win me with the eyes, but it's the whining . . . I hate a whiner."

The man continued to stare at him.

Fallon dropped his hand and leaned back in his chair. "The bottom line is you lied to me. I hate being lied to, especially when the prosecuting attorney comes up with eye witnesses that I never knew about all saying you stole that money. You made a fool out me in front of the judge, in front of the whole courtroom."

Fallon leaned menacingly forward in his chair glaring hard at the man. In a voice low and icy he seethed between his teeth, "The only thing I hate worse than a sniveling whiner is a liar, and the only thing I hate worse than that is a sniveling liar who makes a fool out of me in court."

The man's mouth dropped open as he gaped into the angry face of his attorney.

"Get out of my office. I am no longer representing you."

"But, but . . . Mr. Monroe. I need you to get me off."

Fallon stood up and walked around to the other side of the desk. He grabbed the man by the back of the jacket in a hard hand and jerked him up out of the chair. "I said get out of my office!"

Fallon rushed the man across the small reception room, opened the door and physically threw him across the hall. He slammed hard into the opposite wall. He fell to the floor, rolled over and stared at Fallon, holding his hands out in front of him in terror.

"I hope they hang you!" Fallon shouted at him. He slammed the door and turned back into the reception area buttoning his suit coat to cover the holstered .45 on his hip.

He looked at his secretary who sat calming scratching an ink pen across a sheet of paper. She had not looked up or shown any interest in the eviction of her boss's client. It wasn't the first time he had physically tossed someone out the door. Without looking she said, "I take it you did not like him."

"He lied to me," Fallon shouted.

"That is news, Mr. Monroe? Most of the people who come in here lie."

"I'm sure you overheard our conversation."

"They overheard all the way to the capital building, Mr. Monroe."

Fallon took a deep breath. He was angry over the lying client, but then he seemed to always be angry. Bitterness seemed to be a constant companion, along with frustration, and a longing to be anywhere but in Austin, in an attorney's office.

He closed his eyes and took another settling breath. "I'm sorry. I didn't mean to yell at you."

"It is alright. I am used to it."

Fallon sighed. He didn't mean to take his frustration out on her. He asked in a calmer voice, "Do I have any more business today?"

"Just this telegram that came for you while you were in . . . conference." She handed Fallon a sealed envelope.

He took it and tore open the end sliding the telegram out. He read it. He froze in place as his mouth dropped open and read it again.

The woman looked at him, "What is it Mr. Monroe? You look shocked."

Fallon lifted his eyes from the paper to look at her. "My parents were killed in a fire last night."

"Oh, how horrible! I am so sorry."

Fallon nodded as he tried to think. "Yes. Cancel all my appointments for the next week."

"Yes, sir. I will rearrange your court dates as

well."

"Thank you. I'm going home to pack and grabbing the first train to Tucson."

Cordell Monroe rode casually down Allen Street. The Tombstone street was steady with activity. He pulled up to the hitchrail in front of the Campbell and Hatch saloon and stepped out of the saddle. Spinning a rein around the rail he looked around him, slipped the loop off the hammer of his Colt, and stepped up on the boardwalk.

The door to the saloon was propped open against the heat of the day. He moved in, slowly scanning to his right and left as he made his way down the narrow long room. On his face was a slight mischievous grin, what his mother used to call impish, framed by several days of whiskers. His blonde hair hung out from under his hat, reaching past the neck of his shirt in the back.

A billiard table at the far end of the room in front of him was surrounded by several men watching a game. The curved polished bar was to his left. Three men were lined up at the bar, their boots on the brass rail, and their reflections in the wall mirror. Cordell took a spot towards the straight end of the bar, leaned his elbows on the polished wood and propped his dusty, worn boot on the rail.

The barkeep stepped up to him wiping his hands on a clean bar towel.

"Beer." The young man's grin widened. He jerked his head toward the game, "Big match?"

"Morgan Earp and Bob Hatch playing for the Tombstone championship," the man chuckled.

"What do they win?"

"Five dollars and a vacation in scenic Tombstone, Arizona."

Cordell laughed. "That's worth fighting for." He then leaned his head forward and peered at a large glass jar behind the bar. "That jar full of frogs?"

"Yup. Bob figures he can tell the weather by the way they croak."

"Can they?"

"They say it's hot and dry in June," the barkeep laughed.

"Oracles."

"Something like that."

"I think you'd do better with some dancin' girls in here rather than frogs though."

A fourth man leaning on the bar around the curve was caressing a filled whiskey glass between his hands. He set his liquor dulled eyes on Cordell. "Why don't you give us a dance? You look like a girl with that long hair."

Cordell gave him a humorless smile. "Anyone as ugly as you ought to be in the jar with them frogs."

The man stiffened, "What did you say?"

"I said you were as ugly as a frog, but I take that back."

The man sneered, "You'd better."

"Yeah, you're too dang ugly to be a frog."

The men in between them quickly got out of the way.

The man stepped away from the bar. Standing unsteadily he hovered his hand over his belted pistol. Cordell straightened up and stood casually watching him; however, his hand was near the Colt and his eyes were alert to the man's movements.

A tall, heavy set man turned from watching

the game and marched with purpose toward the poised men. "That's enough of that," the man shouted as he approached them.

The oncoming man went directly up to the stranger and stuck his mustached, strong face into the man's. "You've had enough, get out."

The man glared at him for a full second than turned on his heels and stormed out the door.

"And you better not be lingering out there either," the mustached man called after him. He then turned to face Cordell. "Monroe, I thought I told you to stay out of here."

Cordell grinned. "Actually, Marshal, you told me to stay out of the Oriental, you never said anything about Hatch's."

"Don't get smart with me."

"I didn't know you meant the whole town." Mischief played in Cordell's eyes.

"You kill a man in my town, you get your walking papers, permanently."

"It was self-defense. I was cleared."

The marshal looked at the barkeep. "What was this about, Stan?"

Stan gestured toward the door, "That one started in on this fellow. They exchanged insults. The usual stuff, Virgil."

Virgil Earp looked back at Cordell. "What do you want in here?"

"A beer. I'm thirsty and the water ain't fit to drink for a hundred miles around."

Virgil glanced at the beer on the bar. "You're a young man Monroe with your whole life ahead of you, why don't you behave yourself?"

"I didn't do anything."

"You've got an older brother that's an attorney if I'm not mistaken. Why don't you take after him?"

Cordell snorted, "We don't get along."

"Well, you ought to. At the rate you're going you might need a good attorney sooner than later."

"I suspect he'd work to get me hung more than to get me off."

Virgil shook his head. "Drink your beer and head out." He started to turn back to the game when his deputy walked in holding a message.

"What's up?" Virgil asked.

Cordell looked at the man, it was Virgil's brother, Wyatt.

Wyatt gave Cordell a hard eyed look. "I saw you come in here. Why are you back?"

"Because it's the only place between Bisbee and Benson to drink something that won't kill me or put me in the outhouse for three days."

"Did you shoot anybody yet?"

Virgil replied, "Almost, but I cut it off."

Wyatt shook his head and then narrowed his eyes at Cordell. "Where have you been the last several days?"

"Down on the border catching wild cattle. Sold some to a rancher down that way."

"You have anything to do with those Mexicans who were killed in Black Water? I heard your name tied to it."

"They were banditos. They tried to rob me of the money I made selling the cattle."

"Your cattle or have you been out with the Clantons and McLaury's rustling cattle?"

"Why would you ask me that? I might get into

fights, but I'm no outlaw. I catch my own cattle, I don't steal 'em. In fact the last time I ran into Ike Clanton he got tough with me and I threatened to shove my boot up his rear end. I've got no use for that outfit."

Wyatt snorted, "Ike Clanton always was a yellow belly."

Virgil pointed at the paper in Wyatt's hand, "What's that?"

"Message for Monroe. His uncle is trying to find him." He handed the paper to Cordell. "You best get for home."

Cordell stared at the message, shoved it in his pocket, and headed out the door.

"What was that all about?" Virgil asked.

"His folks were killed in a fire up in Tucson."

Chapter 4

The two wooden coffins rested on the ground to either side of the twin graves. Adam stood solemn and stiff, his face a mix of shock and grief. To his right stood Laura, her left hand in the crook of his arm. With her right hand she pressed a white hanky to her nose, her eyes red from crying. To his left Fallon stood staring at the coffins with the look of a haunted soul. He had not come home in three years and Adam knew that guilt raged through his brother's mind.

Dozens of mourners were gathered around the graves. Red stood beside Laura as they waited for Reverend Morse to speak. Elwood and Ruth were together at the entrance to the cemetery as Elwood was unable to bring himself to stand beside the coffin holding his sister. Cordell had stayed at their sides for moral support and his own reasons.

Reverend Morse stepped to the head of the open graves and began to recite the burial prayers. Once the proper rituals were conducted he spoke freely. "We are gathered here today to lay to rest, Ryan and Tessa Monroe, two beloved members of our community. There are few here today who have not felt the friendship and generosity of these wonderful people. It is with heavy hearts that we recall the tragic accident that claimed these two people. Devoted husband and father, devoted wife and mother. Rest in peace Ryan and Tessa you will be missed." He then recited the 23rd Psalm.

The gathered sang Amazing Grace and fell to silence at the end. The reverend was the first to quietly walk away. One-by-one those in attendance departed.

Red turned to Adam and shook his hand. "Sorry, Adam. Take as long as you need attending to matters."

Adam nodded, "Thanks, Red."

Red turned his attention to Fallon and put out his hand. "Good to see you again, Fallon."

Fallon shook his hand. "Same here, wish it were under more pleasant circumstances though."

Red nodded, "I understand. Come up to the house before you leave."

"I'll see what I can do."

Red gave his daughter a hug and then walked away from the graves.

The gravediggers slid ropes under the caskets and began to lower them into the graves.

Laura turned her head away. "I do not want to see this part Adam."

Adam shook his head. With Laura's hand on his arm they walked toward the cemetery entrance. Fallon walked beside Adam.

Fallon looked ahead. "Uncle Elwood said he couldn't bear to stand up here."

"He's taking this real hard," Adam replied.

Fallon frowned. "Well, look what the

tumbleweeds blew in."

Adam then saw Cordell standing behind Elwood and Ruth talking with them. "Looks like one of Uncle Elwood's wires found him."

"Some marshal must have let him out of jail," Fallon jibed with a sneer.

Adam tensed, but did not reply.

"He couldn't stand up here with his brothers?"

Laura squeezed Adam's arm to keep him from responding to Fallon. Adam pursed his lips, but said nothing. He didn't want to see a fight between his brothers on this day.

Cordell looked past his aunt and uncle and watched his brothers as they approached.

When Adam and Fallon reached them Elwood was quick to apologize. "I am sorry, but I just could not stand up there and watch."

Adam put his hand on Elwood's arm. "It's okay, we understand."

Adam extended his hand to Cordell. "Glad you got the message."

Cordell shook his hand. "I was in Tombstone when Marshal Earp handed me Uncle Elwood's message."

Fallon scowled at Cordell. "Through the bars?"

Everyone fell silent as they tensed at Fallon's cutting remark.

Cordell met Fallon's frigid eyes with a matching expression. "No, we were having tea when the butler brought the wire in on a silver platter."

Fallon looked his brother over. "You wore a gun to our parent's funeral?"

Cordell reached out and pushed back Fallon's suit coat revealing the holstered pistol. "What's that, a barn shovel?"

"At least it isn't out in the open making me look like an outlaw. Why didn't you stand up there with your family?"

Cordell's voice turned several degrees icier. "Because I didn't want to soil you and all those perfect citizens with my black sheep presence."

"Why don't you get a haircut you look like . . ."

"Stop!" Adam snapped. "For the love of God, can't the two of you be civil to each other for five minutes, even on our parents' funeral day?"

Cordell looked sheepish. "Right, sorry Adam." He bowed his head toward Laura and Ruth. "Sorry, Aunt Ruth, Laura."

Laura smiled at Cordell. "It has been so long since we have seen you Cordell, will you stay with us for a while?"

"Thank you, I'd like that."

"Good." She cast a chastising glance at Fallon.

Fallon reached his hand out to Cordell. "Glad to see you could make it."

Cordell shook his hand with no great feeling exchanged between them.

Adam wanted to derail the tension. "I could use another hand out on the ranch if you're interested in a steady job," Adam said to Cordell.

"Thanks, I might take you up on that one day."

Hiram approached Clay Scott who was walking toward the cemetery entrance alongside his wife and eighteen year old daughter, Charlotte. Hiram nodded toward the women, "Afternoon, ladies."

They greeted him in return.

"Marshal, I have something to show you."

Scott glanced at him without stopping. "*Later.*"

Hiram stopped walking and let the marshal and his family go on ahead. Clay Scott had become a rude and arrogant man. He would tell the Monroe boys and the heck with Scott.

Scott's wife threw a dagger look at him. "That was certainly rude, Clayton."

"I have an office. He can see me there."

Scott looked ahead to where the Monroe brothers stood with Elwood and the women. He paused for a second, made a face, and then continued walking toward them. In a low voice he growled, "Cordell Monroe," as if he had tasted something rotten.

"*Attempt* to be civil, Clayton," Heddy Scott snapped.

The Monroes stopped their conversation when the Scotts met with them. Scott nodded tersely at Adam and Fallon, who nodded back. No friendship existed between the Monroes and Clay Scott.

Scott tipped his hat to Laura and Ruth and shook Elwood's hand. The women all exchanged hugs.

Charlotte smiled warmly at Cordell.

Cordell smiled back at her and lifted his hat. "Afternoon, Charlotte. It's been a long time. You have been well I hope?"

Charlotte's smile beamed back at him. "Yes, I have been well, thank you for asking. How have you been, Cordell?"

"Holding my own. You certainly are looking nice today."

Charlotte spun lightly side-to-side. "Thank you."

"What are doing these days?"

"I am learning to be a nurse by assisting Doctor Smith. I do so admire Clara Barton."

"Yes, a fine woman."

Scott could barely control his rage as he scowled at Cordell, his face and neck turning dark red. "Heddy, take Charlotte home."

Heddy cast an irritated glance at her husband. "As soon as I pay my respects, Clayton."

After greetings had been exchanged with Heddy and Charlotte they turned from the group. Charlotte cast a coy look back at Cordell as they walked away.

Charlotte whispered to her mother, "Cordell used to be such a little rascal in school."

Heddy glanced back over her shoulder "He still is a rascal, dear." She grinned and added, "A very handsome rascal."

Charlotte smiled, "Yes."

Scott locked a rage filled glared on Cordell. "Don't even think about it, *Monroe*."

Cordell gave the marshal a wide eyed innocent look, "Think about what, Marshal?"

Scott ground his teeth and seethed, "You know full well *what*. No daughter of mine is going to be associated with a saddle tramp gunslinger. You're riff-raff Monroe, nothing more."

Elwood snapped, "Now see here . . ."

Fallon cut Elwood off mid-sentence with an

angry response. "No one calls my brother riff-raff. If you weren't the marshal, I'd knock that swelled head off your shoulders."

"Try it."

"Stop!" Adam pushed in between Fallon and Scott. "You have no call to bad mouth my brother, Marshal. I think it's time for you to go on home."

Scott's face turned red enough to explode. He ground his teeth together, but said no more. He spun on his heels and stormed off in the direction his family had gone.

"How rude!" Ruth said with an angry lift of her chin.

Elwood sputtered, "That man is getting to be too much. I intend to speak to the town council about replacing him."

Everyone then turned their attention to Fallon who stood with his fists clenched and breathing hard.

Cordell chuckled, "I didn't know you cared about me, big brother."

Fallon shot an angry look at Cordell. "Shut up Cordell, you're a mess."

"We can't all be suit wearing lawyers, fancy pants."

"Don't call me fancy pants, you little snot."

"Children!" Adam broke in.

Both men stopped. Fallon looked at Adam. "No one talks to a Monroe like that."

Adam gave him an incredulous look. "Except his brother."

Hiram had been standing back waiting for the row to end. With Scott gone he walked up to the group.

Adam turned his attention to Hiram, "Sorry

about that Hiram, a little family problem."

"That's quite alright, I heard what the marshal said." He then coughed, "I have something I want to discuss with you boys." He glanced at Laura and Ruth.

Adam understood that Hiram had something to say that he didn't want to expose the ladies to. "Laura, it's awful hot out here, maybe you should escort Aunt Ruth back to the house where it's cooler."

Laura picked up on the hint knowing Adam would tell her later. "Yes, it is awfully hot. Shall we, Aunt Ruth?'

Ruth threw Elwood a look that said she expected to be filled in when he got home. Elwood gave a slight nod.

As the two women walked away the men stepped in closer to Hiram. Hiram began hesitantly as he searched for the proper words. "The bodies were found in the cellar of the house, they were not too badly burned as a result of being below the level of the fire. We moved them to my workroom so I could prepare them. At first I didn't notice it. Then, while cleaning the bodies I found a hole on the side of Ryan's head. I attributed it to striking something sharp as he fell through the floor. Then . . ." He stopped, twisting his face as he struggled with the words.

"Yes, Hiram, go on," Adam coaxed.

Hiram looked at each of the men in turn to see them intently focused on him. "And then, I found a similar hole on the side of Tessa's head. I thought it was too much to be a coincidence, so I went into their skulls." He put a hand in his pocket and pulled out his closed fist.

His voice was shaking, as was his hand, when he held it out and opened his fist. "I found these."

On Hiram's hand rested two pieces of lead crushed into a mushroom on one end. The men all stared speechless at the objects.

Cordell was the first to speak. "They're spent bullets."

Hiram nodded. "One in each head. They were killed by these, not the fire."

"I don't understand," Adam said as he stared at the pieces of lead.

"They were shot," Cordell said.

Adam shook his head. "Wouldn't the bullets have gone all the way through? Are you sure Hiram?"

Cordell put his hand on Adam's arm. He knew his brother had little exposure to violence and didn't understand. "If they are light loads they will mushroom like that, Adam and not exit."

Elwood's mouth had dropped open in shock as he stared at the bullets and taking in what Hiram was saying. "What about the fire?" he asked.

"A ruse," Fallon answered.

Elwood looked at him, "A ruse? I don't understand."

"They were murdered," Cordell answered, his tone turning angry. "The fire was to cover it up."

Elwood opened and closed his mouth and then whispered, "Why?"

"I've seen this before," Fallon explained. "The one who killed them set the house on fire believing the evidence would be destroyed in the fire and the fire blamed for the cause of their deaths."

"They just never counted on the bodies not

burning," Cordell remarked.

Fallon nodded his agreement.

"But, who would want to murder two nice people like them?" Adam asked.

"That fool Scott suspects it might have been a murder-suicide and wanted me to let him know if I found anything unusual," Hiram said with disgust.

"What?" the men all shouted at the same time.

"That's the stupidest thing I've ever heard," Fallon snapped.

Adam suddenly turned angry, "For crying out loud, anyone who knew them would know better than to come up with a fool idea like that."

"Scott never liked Pa," Cordell said. "You could expect something like that from the likes of him."

"They were two old people who sold dry beans and penny candy," Adam remarked. "Who would want to kill them?"

"Maybe it was a robbery," Hiram suggested.

Fallon shook his head, "If it was a robbery it wouldn't have happened at home, it would have been in the store."

"That means someone flat murdered them," Cordell said with a chilled tone.

"But why?" Fallon asked to no one in particular.

Adam looked at Elwood. "Uncle Elwood, do you know of any enemies the folks had?"

Elwood slowly shook his head.

"Anyone who would want to kill them?"

Elwood replied, "No. I can't think of anyone around here who would do such a thing."

Cordell looked from one to the other, "Old family secrets?"

Elwood's eyes suddenly widened and he took in a gasping breath.

"What's wrong, Uncle Elwood?" Adam asked.

Elwood shook his head, panic widening his eyes. "I have to go." He left the brothers at a fast walk.

"How strange was that?" Cordell asked.

"Very strange," Adam answered.

Fallon watched his uncle growing smaller in the distance. "He looked like a man who just got the answer to a puzzle."

Cordell looked at Adam and then Fallon. "Old family secrets?"

"It wouldn't be the first time in history," Fallon commented.

"But, the folks never had any old secrets," Adam protested.

Fallon gave his brother a sober look. "We don't actually know that."

They all stopped and stared at each other with questioning expressions.

"I think we need to start looking for some answers," Cordell said.

"And anyone who might have known them back in Texas," Fallon added, "because this is not adding up at all."

Chapter 5

As children, any questions regarding their mother and father's lives before they came along were steered away. There never had been any answers. As children they accepted that, as adults they now wondered why. The Hueco Tanks ranch north of El Paso was all they knew until the folks suddenly sold it and moved to Tucson. It was entirely possible something in those unanswered questions might be a factor in their murders.

Three years ago, Adam and Laura married and Fallon moved permanently to Austin. Cordell followed his wild streak and left town at the same time. What might have developed during the past three years was a guess as none of them had been home. Their parents may have made an enemy during that time, although they now believed it went much further back than that.

The brothers left directly from the cemetery to talk to as many people as they could about their parents. They agreed to split up and discover what they could. They figured it would be the old timers who might know something about them when they first arrived in Tucson ten years ago. It was a long shot hoping someone knew them in Texas, but it was worth a try. They would meet later at the Congress Hall Saloon to compare notes.

Their discussion before splitting up found them all amazed that they knew so little about their parents. Each wished they had sought out more information about the history of their family; however, that had always been stonewalled, and now it was a moot point. These thoughts echoed in their minds as they worked their way through the town.

Adam had gone to work for Red Delaney at seventeen. He married Red's daughter and only child, Laura when he turned nineteen. Last year, once he proved his worth as a son-in-law, Red made him a partner in the ranch.

Adam was the most respected of the brothers as he lived in the area, was married to Red Delaney's daughter, and partner in the big Delaney cattle company. He had friends everywhere. Everyone he talked to offered their condolences for his loss, then they'd scratch their heads and admit they really didn't know anything about Ryan and Tessa before they took over the store. All agreed that they were salt of the earth people though.

Cordell knew he would have little success trying to talk to the businessmen or people that considered themselves to be of a better class than him. He had made a bad reputation for himself even before he left town. He was often involved in fights, hung with a bad crowd, and had regular confrontations with Marshal Scott which earned him two overnight stays in the city jail. He confined his inquiries to the labor class who held no ill will toward him. No one knew anything about his folks except they had a store.

Fallon stepped out of the newspaper office onto the dusty boardwalk along Congress Street. He had hoped someone there might know about the folks, but no one did. He had spoken to several business people who had been friends with his parents, but they only knew them in Tucson. He was passing a bakery when he heard a familiar feminine voice call his name.

He stopped and looked around. He felt a sharp pang of guilt as a young woman approached him.

The woman stopped in front of him. "Hello, Fallon."

Fallon smiled weakly, humbled with embarrassment. "Hello, Helen." He felt a surge of old feelings flood over him. Helen had been his girl before he went off to Austin. After graduation he returned and they discussed marriage. Then there came that day, the confrontation he now wished had never happened. He had left for Austin filled with anger and indignation. Helen had become an innocent, broken hearted casualty of his animosity, fueled by self-pity. He went to Austin and never came back to Tucson or her.

Helen looked up into his face. "I am so sorry about your mother and father. It was a horrible tragedy."

"Yes, it was quite unexpected. Were you at the service?" He knew she wasn't or he would have seen her. He just needed something to say.

Helen gestured toward the bakery, "No, I was working."

Fallon looked up at the bakery sign over his

head. "Do you work here all the time?"

"Only in summer. I am still teaching school, but when the children break for summer there is no pay."

Fallon felt his throat go dry. They had spoken of marriage and now the woman he once loved was struggling to get by. He didn't know what to say as his shame overwhelmed his thinking.

A sad smile formed on Helen's lips. "I suppose you are doing well. Did you open your own office?"

"Yes, I have an office in Austin now."

"Austin. I had hoped you might return to Tucson."

He stared into Helen's face and realized that he still loved her. He had been careless, cruel, and selfish. "I . . . I'm sorry, Helen."

Tears glistened in her eyes. She nodded slightly. "You stopped writing."

Fallon took a deep breath and let it out. "I could say I was busy, but that would be a lie. I was . . . thoughtless."

Helen felt a tear escape her eye and roll down her cheek. "I miss you, Fallon."

Seeing the tear made Fallon feel even worse. He looked at her face unable to speak.

Taking his nonresponse as disinterest, Helen wiped the tear off her cheek. "I am sure you are a busy man. It was pleasant to see you again." She began to walk past him.

"Helen," Fallon choked out as she moved by. "Would you have dinner with me tonight?"

Helen turned and looked at him. "You have changed Fallon and I do not want my heart broken again." She continued to walk on.

Fallon watched her as she disappeared into the movement of people. He had been a fool to lose her. Actually, he didn't lose her, he threw her love away in order to bury himself in self-obsessed pursuits fueled by self-pity. Things could be made right again though, and he vowed to make it so. He headed for the Congress Hall Saloon.

Fallon walked into the saloon, his head more filled with Helen than the search for information. Looking around he spotted Cordell sitting at a table with a glass of beer in front of him. He stopped at the bar, ordered a beer, and then headed for Cordell's table.

Cordell slouched lazily in his chair with his left arm over the back. He looked up at his brother in silence. Fallon sat down and took a drink from the glass. He met Cordell's eyes, "Any luck?"

Cordell shook his head. "Folks don't like talking to me."

"Got that black sheep tag around your neck."

Cordell shrugged, "As if I give a care."

"I know you don't, but you should."

With a grunt Cordell started to say, "Like I said, I . . ."

"I know," his brother stopped him, "you don't care."

"You learn anything?"

"No." Fallon stared into his glass thinking about Helen and how badly he had hurt her.

"You look like a man worrying a problem. What happened, besides the obvious?"

Fallon turned his eyes up and held them on Cordell for several seconds. "I ran into Helen."

"Oh. Yeah, you did her a dirty trick."

Fallon's face scrunched up in an angry scowl, "Thanks."

Cordell shrugged, "Facts are facts. You think you're so high and mighty with your lawyer license and store bought suits, but you can be a cold hearted coyote when you want to be."

Red color streaked up Fallon's neck and face as he grew angrier with his brother. "I don't need a lecture from the likes of you."

Cordell chuckled and shook his head.

"Why are you always so hard to get along with?"

"I'm the easiest man in the world to get along with," Cordell grinned. "You just have a full time burr under your saddle, big brother. Maybe it's because you know you did that pretty girl wrong, and you know you're a coyote, or maybe it's because of the fight you had with Pa and ran off like a spoiled brat."

Fallon flew up out of his chair, his face near to purple and the veins in his neck bulging as he glared down at Cordell.

Cordell maintained his relaxed position and watched him, unimpressed or frightened.

Adam walked up to the table and studied his brothers. "I see you two are getting along again."

Cordell smiled up at him, "I'm doing fine." He pointed at Fallon hanging over the table in a rage. "He ran into Helen and is taking out his guilty feelings of being a coyote on me."

"Alright Cordell, don't prod him."

Adam looked at Fallon, "Helen, huh?"

Fallon sat back down in his chair. He glared at Cordell as he bridled his anger. His brother was right, but he couldn't bring himself to admit it.

"I'll be right back. Try not to kill each other in the next two minutes." Adam walked off to the bar.

He returned with a glass of beer and sat down. He eyed Fallon who had calmed a bit and his face had faded to pink rather than purple. "I got a lot of condolences and praise for the folks being fine people, but no one knew them before here. How about you boys?"

Fallon shook his head. "Nothing."

Adam looked at Cordell who shrugged while maintaining the same position.

"I'll take that as a no,' Adam said.

Fallon took a pair of settling breaths, took a long drink from the glass and then began to spin his glass around in circles on the table staring at it. "It stands to reason," he said. "Except for the Mexicans and Indians most people are fairly new here and come from all over. It was a long shot at best."

Cordell broke into Fallon's trance. "You're the oldest, did you ever hear the folks talk about anything before Hueco Tanks?"

"No. I've thought it to death and can't think of a single time that talk was of their past life. At least not in front of me. They always refused to answer my questions."

"Sometimes things get said in front of kids that parents don't think they hear. I can't recall anything like that though," Adam said.

"Me either," Fallon agreed. "It is strange when you put it into the present perspective. Why wouldn't parents talk about life before the children came along?"

"Because there were things they don't want

the kids to know," Cordell put in.

Adam shook his head, "I can't believe that. A mysterious past from our folks? Pa was a small cattle rancher until we moved here. Then, he ran a store."

"You ever wonder why they sold the ranch and took up a store here?" Fallon looked at Adam.

"Yeah, I guess I have. I figured it was for financial reasons."

"I once heard him tell a customer in the store that we moved here because the Apaches were a threat to the family. I recall thinking at the time that wasn't true," Fallon said.

"Pa fought off occasional Apaches to hold the ranch" Cordell said. "He loved that place and he was no more scared of the Apaches than a dog is of a cat. Then, he up and sells it to run a dry goods store? Then, he tells folks it was because we were scared of the Apaches? Why?"

The three sat in silence for several minutes trying to make sense out of what they had never considered, or had taken for granted.

Fallon continued to spin his glass in slow circles. "Youngsters never think of their parents as having lives before they came along. Obviously, they did. Ours never talked about it though. It was like they never existed before us. There was someplace and a life before us though, it's ludicrous to think otherwise."

"Pa was fearless," Cordell said, still annoyed by the reference to fearing the Apaches.

"He was," Adam agreed. "I remember one time we were out on the ranch and three Apaches jumped us. I couldn't have been more than ten. He had that old Navy Colt out in a flash and nailed all three. He was fast."

"Like a gunfighter," Cordell said as he looked at his brothers.

Adam nodded as his face showed concern over the possibility.

Fallon stopped spinning the glass and looked at Cordell and then Adam. "I don't intend to go back to Austin until this business is resolved. The mystery is too deep to leave it be."

"I guess we need to find out who did this," Adam said in a low voice.

Cordell cast a hard look at Adam. "Guess? There's no *guess* about it. We find who did this and then I intend to kill them."

Adam jerked his head around to look at Cordell. "We can't be taking the law into our own hands."

"We can and we will,' Cordell snapped at him.

"It's a job for the law," Adam argued.

"What law? *Clay Scott*?"

Fallon looked at Cordell. "You can't go shooting the place up. This is Tucson, not the border."

Cordell snorted, "Like you have room to talk. I read in a paper about Austin attorney Fallon Monroe shooting a man to death in an Austin, Texas courtroom."

"You heard right."

Adam gaped at Fallon. "What happened?"

"A man stood up in court, pulled a gun, and said he was going to shoot my client. He spent too much time talking about it. Pa had always said if you're going to shoot someone shoot him, don't talk about it, so I shot him."

"How did the judge like that?"

"He scolded me for shooting in his courtroom, but then complimented me on saving people's lives. Once things got back in order he found my client guilty and sentenced him to hang." With a shrug he added, "It's the legal system, who can figure it out."

Cordell snorted, "You're not all that much different from me even though you like to think you are."

"I'm a lot different than you are."

"Yeah, just keep telling yourself that."

Adam sighed. "You two ever stop? Sniping at each other isn't helping."

The brothers fell silent. Cordell drank down the last of his beer and started looking over the men in the room. His wandering gaze passed over the barkeep and kept moving. Out of the corner of his eye he saw the barkeep make a hand motion. His eyes came back to the man behind the bar.

The barkeep looked directly at Cordell and waved him to come over to the bar. Cordell stood up without a word to his brothers and headed across the room to the barkeep who was watching him.

Adam and Fallon looked at him as he walked away.

"Where is he going?" Fallon growled.

Adam shrugged, "Another beer, I guess."

"I hope he doesn't get drunk, we need to focus on this problem."

"Adam turned his face toward his brother and met his eyes. "You need to let up on him. It's getting petty and childish. If we don't work together on this we're never going to accomplish a thing."

Fallon scowled, "Sure."

"You're the elder brother, set an example will you?"

"With him?"

"Yes, with him. I have to say it Fallon, I think you feel guilty over Helen and are taking it out on Cordell."

Fallon opened his mouth and then snapped it shut. He pulled his lips tight together and then released a pent up breath. "Cordell and I were having problems before I ran into Helen today."

"Then, it's something else. Whatever it is you need to rein it in."

"Yeah."

"What did she say?"

Fallon shook his head. "Not much . . . she was crying."

Adam held the look on his brother without speaking.

Fallon glanced sheepishly at him. "I know. I intend to make it right."

"I hope so."

Fallon turned his attention to Cordell watching him lean over the bar and talk to the barkeep. "After we find the man who did this."

"I don't know about finding him and killing him though. That doesn't seem right."

"Well, I sure don't intend to hand him a rose."

"Then, you agree with Cordell?"

"For once little brother and I agree on something."

Chapter 6

Cordell put his elbows on the bar. "What's up, Mike?"

"I understand you Monroe boys are asking around about your folks. Before they moved here."

"You heard right. Just trying to figure some things out."

"I'm sure you have your reasons." He tipped his head to the back corner of the room. "Leroy back there might know something."

Cordell looked where Mike had gestured to a fiftyish man with a tough, weather etched face sitting at a table reading a newspaper. Cordell studied the man. "Leroy? Leroy Jackson?"

"Cattle buyer from Texas. I understand he's buying up here now."

"Leroy was with Pa at the beginning of the Hueco Tanks ranch. I don't remember him much, he left when I was little. I didn't know he was in town."

"He only showed up a couple years back. You've been gone since then. That does explain why your Pa used to share a drink with him on occasion."

Cordell continued to look at Leroy. "Yeah,

Leroy would know."

Mike swept his towel over a spill on the bar. "Go ask him."

Cordell noticed an empty beer glass in front of Leroy. "Think I will. Give me two beers."

Mike filled two glasses and set them on the bar as Cordell handed him two-bits. He picked up the glasses and walked toward Leroy's table.

Leroy looked up from his newspaper as Cordell stopped alongside him. He studied Cordell and then the glasses in his hands. He folded the paper and laid it aside as he pushed a chair out with his foot. "I never turn a man away with a free beer."

Cordell set the glasses on the table and sat down.

Leroy took a drink and then leaned back in his chair. "Hear tell you've got a reputation."

"So, I've heard."

"Heard even the Earps are scared of you." Leroy grinned.

Cordell laughed. "Virgil and Wyatt aren't scared of anything, least of all me. They've run me out of Tombstone twice."

Leroy chuckled. "That was a test. I never heard no such thing. I like an honest man. No puffed up nonsense in you."

"Reputations are made by doing, not talking."

"Sound like your old man." He eyed Cordell, "That's why you're here isn't it?"

"Word gets around."

"It's a small town."

"I didn't know you were in town. Truth be told, I wouldn't have known you to look at you though."

"You were just a pup when I left Hueco Tanks. We haven't met since you've grown up."

"I recall you worked the ranch with Pa. Is that where you met, on the ranch?"

Leroy chuckled and shook his head. "No. Your Pa and I go way back." Leroy drank the glass down to half. "You want to know why someone put a bullet in his head, and Tessa's as well, don't you?"

Cordell stared at him. "No one knows about that, how come you do?"

"It's a long story."

"I've got nothing but time."

"You might not like what you hear. Sure you want to know?"

"I want to know who murdered my folks. If it drags up matters long buried than it's time to drag 'em up."

"You aim to kill who did it?"

"What do you think?"

Leroy smiled, "Yeah, figured you would."

The two were silent for several seconds as Cordell waited for Leroy to start talking.

Leroy looked at Cordell. "You ever hear of the Winston Cain gang?"

"Stories. They outlawed across the Indian Territory and up the Shawnee Trail. They got down into Texas some."

"Ever hear of Beau Whitlock?"

"Sure, who hasn't? He was part of the Cain gang. A lot of men credit him with being a gunfighter before gunfighting was common. A pistoleer they called him."

"You ever hear what happened to Beau Whitlock?"

"He was killed down San Antonio way, so the stories go."

"He wasn't. He left San Antone, headed into Apache country to lose his name and Winston Cain. He went to raising cattle."

"Did he go straight?"

Leroy finished his beer and then nodded. "He married a woman. A waitress from San Antone, prettiest girl this side of heaven."

"I take it he left the outlaw life for her."

"He did that. She asked him to and he did it."

"You seem to know him pretty well, but what has that got to do with this?"

"He didn't stay in Apache country."

Cordell shrugged, "Okay, so?"

Leroy locked his eyes directly on Cordell's. "He moved to Tucson and opened a store."

Cordell sat silent as the impact of the statement sunk in. Tentatively he asked, "Did he change his name to Ryan Monroe?"

"When he married Tessa in San Antone and went straight, he did."

Cordell fell back hard into his chair. He stared at the tabletop and then turned his eyes up to Leroy who sat patiently watching him. "How do I know you're telling the truth?"

"Because I know all about Beau before the Hueco Tanks ranch. We were in that gang together, we left it at the same time. It's all life before Beau married Tessa Boone. Before San Antone. I suspect he never told anyone about those days so you just have to take my word for it."

Cordell studied Leroy's face and knew he wasn't lying. "Why did they leave San Antonio?"

"That's part of the long story."

"I'm listening."

"Back when we were still in the gang we robbed a bank in Arkansas that nearly ended it for all of us. The law was ready for us and we had to shoot our way out of town. We split up to escape the posse. Cain's brother, Rube was the last one I saw with the money. Well, it seems that money disappeared. Rube claimed Beau stole it. When we all come back together Cain confronted Beau about it and demanded the money.

"I backed Beau, but Cain believed his brother and pushed it. Beau told him he was crazy and to ask his brother where the money was. Cain went for his gun, but Beau got the drop on him. Beau was fast, Lord he was fast, and Cain was scared of him. He told Cain to ride away and he did. He and Rube went one way. Beau and I headed for San Antone because Beau had Tessa waiting for him there.

Beau married Tessa. Him and I changed our names since we were wanted men. We also knew Cain was vindictive and would never rest until he found us and killed Beau for stealing his money and backing him down. We all stayed in San Antone. Beau took a job with a blacksmith and I hung around working the stockyards and such. One day I was in a saloon when in walks Cain and Rube. I let Beau know and he kept his eyes open. Then, somehow they found Beau. There was a shooting and Beau killed Rube. Cain, being the coward he was, lit out.

"Beau took off on the run because a hearing would reveal his true identity. Before he did, he asked me to bring Tessa and you boys to him in Fredericksburg. I did and we all headed west. It was a dangerous time in west Texas. Comanches and Apaches were wild Indians, but Beau wanted distance between his family and the law and Cain. We stopped at Hueco Tanks. I stayed with them and we built up the ranch, caught wild cattle, and fought Apaches."

"So, what happened with the Hueco Tanks ranch? Why did they leave it?"

"Your uncle. Elwood was in San Antone when all this happened. He didn't much care for his sister marrying Beau. Beau and Elwood didn't get along while they were in San Antone, even after Beau went straight. When the shooting happened and they headed west, Tessa stayed in touch with her brother by letters. Elwood knew about Cain and why Tessa worried about him."

"Why didn't Pa just hunt Cain down and kill him if he was such a threat?"

"Your Ma had made him promise not to. She hoped they could just lose Cain in the wild country."

"How did they end up in Tucson?"

"Elwood moved to Tucson. I had left the ranch years before that, but according to Beau, Elwood offered to set him up in a store if he would move you all there. Beau was getting older, and he and Tessa realized you boys needed a better education and a community to grow up in. They took him up on it."

Cordell sat in silence trying to comprehend that his father had been an outlaw, and not just any outlaw, but Beau Whitlock.

The more he thought about it the more some of his father's words and actions made sense in light of his past. It accounted for his patience with him in his wild ways. He gave advice that was meant to steer him away from trouble, but he never accused or condemned him. He knew that if Beau Whitlock, the outlaw, could become Ryan Monroe the storekeeper, then anyone could change.

"You look a little shocked, Cordell," Leroy mused.

"It's a lot to take in all at once. What happened next?"

"Next? I had gone into partners with a cattle buyer in El Paso. About three years ago, someone opened a fancy bawdy house in El Paso. I heard some men talking about it one day and they said it was owned by Winston Cain. I scouted out the place trying to see if it really was him. One day I saw him coming out of the House, it was Cain alright, and he was dressed like a millionaire.

"Now, Cain's twisted, a few cards short of a deck. You know the type. A killer without conscience. When he got something stuck in his head, he never let it go. No doubt he still had it stuck in his pea brain that Beau had his money, and of course Beau had killed his brother. If he ever stumbled onto Beau he'd for sure kill him. Cain didn't care much for me either as I had sided with Beau, which in his mind made me equally guilty.

"I told my cattle buying partner I was going to set up an office in Tucson and headed here to let Beau know that Cain was only a few hundred miles down the road. Beau and I made a pact to watch out for each other in case Cain showed up."

"Did you ever see Cain around here?"

"No, but he obviously found Beau and Tessa though."

"How do you know it was him?"

"How do I know he's the one who murdered them?"

Cordell nodded.

"They were both shot in the head, weren't they? One shot each, execution style."

Cordell stared at Leroy for several seconds before answering. "Yes."

"Cain's style. He executed anyone he thought did him wrong, providing he could catch them unarmed. He had to have caught Beau unarmed in his house."

"If Pa was his target, why Ma then?"

"Kill the witness. For revenge. Who knows, like I said he's twisted."

Cordell's eyes narrowed as anger welled up in him. "Where can we find Cain?"

"El Paso, place called the *Desert Rose*."

Cordell sat in silence for several seconds staring absently at the tabletop. He then looked at Leroy. "Thanks for telling me the truth about it."

"You needed to know. Plan on taking a trip to El Paso?"

"First train out."

"I was planning the same trip. Figured I'd square things for Beau and Tessa. I'll ride with you if you want."

Cordell tipped his head toward his brothers, "We've got it covered."

Leroy looked at the table where Adam and Fallon sat intently watching the two of them. "Alright. Word of advice. Cain's sneaky and a coward, but he is deadly. Don't take him lightly."

Cordell stood up. "I don't take anyone lightly. Thanks again."

Leroy nodded, "Thanks for the beer."

Adam and Fallon watched Cordell as he walked back to their table. It was clear to them he had learned something and whatever it was had him deep in thought. He sat down staring at the tabletop.

"What was that all about?" Adam asked.

Cordell's focus rose up out of the deep well of his thoughts at Adam's question. "That's Leroy Jackson."

Adam stared at Leroy who had gone back to reading his newspaper. "Pa's old ranching partner?"

"Yeah."

Fallon's eyes were intently locked on the man in the corner. "That *is* Leroy Jackson. I was a little kid when he left the ranch, but I remember him."

Cordell looked at Fallon without saying anything.

"It's been years. Put gray hair on him and fifteen years and yes, that is Leroy."

"I don't recall much about him except his name," Adam said.

"You were too little to remember him. I barely remember him." Fallon continued to study Leroy, then added, "I didn't know he lived in Tucson. I never saw him around."

"He only came here a couple of years back," Cordell replied. "You've been gone that long."

"That would account for it then."

Cordell looked at Adam. "Did you ever see him in here?"

"I don't spend a lot of time in town or in here. I likely never did."

"He's a cattle buyer. I take it Red doesn't do business with him."

"Red has been selling to the same buyer for more years then we've been here. It looked like you two were having quite a talk, what did he have to say?"

Cordell leaned into the table and spoke in a low voice. "Leroy and Pa go way back, even before Hueco Tanks. Before San Antonio. Before us. Even before Pa met Ma. Back to the Indian Territory . . . back when he was . . . Beau Whitlock."

Fallon frowned at Cordell. "Leroy is Beau Whitlock?" His tone said he didn't believe it.

"Beau Whitlock, the storied outlaw?" Adam broke in. "Leroy was him?"

Cordell flicked his eyes from Adam to Fallon. "No, when Pa was Beau Whitlock."

Fallon's frown turned into a scowl. "This isn't a time for your smart mouth, *Cordell*. Can't you ever flat answer a question?"

Cordell held a cold, straight face as he locked eyes with Fallon.

Fallon looked deep into his brother's eyes and realized that he wasn't joking or smarting off. "You're serious?"

"As a bullet in the head."

Adam's mouth dropped open and then he turned angry. He glanced around the room then leaned over the table toward Cordell. Through clenched teeth he whispered, "Are you saying our father, easy going Ryan Monroe, was in reality the notorious outlaw *Beau Whitlock*? You expect me to believe something that outrageous?"

Cordell turned an icy eye on Adam. "I don't care what you believe. I'm telling you the truth."

"The truth? From who? Him?" Adam jerked

his chin toward Leroy.

"Yes, from him."

"And you believe him?"

"He knows things no one else around here would know about Pa and Ma both. About San Antonio, about Hueco Tanks, about Uncle Elwood, about their moving here. Yes, I believe him."

Adam stubbornly folded his arms across his chest and leaned back in his chair. "Well, I don't."

Cordell glared at Adam. "So, what would be so horrible if Pa had a past, he turned into a good man, a good father didn't he?"

Adam clenched his jaws and refused to answer.

"What did he say?" Fallon asked.

For the next few minutes Cordell retold the story Leroy had told him. Fallon listened as he looked back and forth from Cordell to Leroy. Adam remained in his angry, arm locked position clenching his jaws ever tighter as Cordell related the story.

At the end of it Adam snapped, "I don't believe a word of it."

"Why?" Cordell asked, "Because you don't *want* to believe it?"

Adam started to get up out of his chair. "I'm going to tell that liar a thing or two."

"Sit down, Adam," Fallon said.

Adam glared at him. "Why? Do you believe that cock and bull story?"

Fallon shifted his eyes up to Adam. "Yes."

"What?"

"I believe it. The folks did come from San Antonio, we were born there. It explains a lot of what I recall as a kid. Things I saw and heard. Why Pa was so good with a gun. Why Pa and Ma whispered together when they thought we were asleep. I have heard them say the name Cain, especially before we moved to Tucson. I didn't know what it meant."

Adam sat back down looking bewildered.

Fallon flicked his eyes to lock on Cordell's. "It explains a lot of things."

Cordell knew Fallon was referring to their father's defense of him. He refused to respond to the accusation. He turned his attention to Adam. "He knew Pa and Ma were each shot in the head. Only Hiram knew that, he hasn't even told Scott about it yet. How would Leroy know that?"

Adam began to unwind his tension. He looked back and forth to each of his brothers. He finally rested his eyes on Cordell. "How *does* he know?"

"He knows Cain and how he does things. This fits his pattern and he had that old grudge against Pa."

"So, this Winston Cain murdered them?"

"Leroy is certain of it."

Adam passed the story through his mind, concentrating on the parts about why Cain would want to kill his father. He had to admit that it made sense and added up. He was still angry over the idea that they had never known about their father's past. "I still find it hard to believe Pa was an outlaw."

Cordell glanced at him, "*Was* an outlaw. A man can straighten out his life."

"There is one sure way to find out," Fallon broke in.

"How's that?" Adam asked.

"We go ask Uncle Elwood and insist he tell us

the truth."

Adam clenched his jaws again. "Yes, and he'd better tell us or I'll shake it out of him."

Cordell's eyes flashed anger. "Uncle Elwood has been nothing but good to us. He's an old man, you touch him and I'll bust my gun barrel over your head."

Adam let out an angry breath and settled down. "I would never hurt Uncle Elwood, I'm just upset."

"Better not, that's all I've got to say."

"He said he wasn't going into the bank today, he's pretty upset. We'll find him at home." Fallon said.

Chapter 7

The brothers walked down the street in the fading light of day. Businesses were closing for the night as the owners locked their doors and headed for the Congress Hall saloon. Men smiled and greeted Adam and Fallon as they passed, but regarded Cordell with cold disdain.

Cordell snorted after being once again ignored. "Got to love this town."

Adam's thoughts were filled with the revelation of their father's past. "What if Uncle Elwood says it's all true?" he asked.

"Then, we know the truth," Fallon answered.

"I don't see why it should make any difference," Cordell said with a hint of irritation.

Adam glanced at him, "Difference about what?"

"The kind of man Pa was. Just because he had a past doesn't change the fact he was a wonderful father."

Adam was silent for several seconds before saying, "No, I guess it changes nothing. I loved Pa and that's all that should matter."

"Exactly."

"Wonderful depends on whose point of view you look at it from," Fallon said in a sour tone.

Cordell stopped on the boardwalk and faced Fallon. "What is that supposed to mean?"

"It explains why he was so tolerant of you," Fallon replied.

"You're the one started the big fight. Don't blame Pa because you acted like a horse's butt."

Fallon bit back the angry words ready to spill out. "Forget I said it."

"I'm not forgetting nothing. You meant because Pa was a bad man once he encouraged my bad behavior. That's what you meant, isn't it?"

Adam broke in, "Hey, stop it, people are staring."

Cordell gave Fallon an angry glare and resumed walking.

They reached their uncle and aunt's house. Stepping up on the porch Cordell turned to Adam. "Are you calmed down now about Uncle Elwood? I don't want to bust your skull but I will if you get mean with him."

"I've calmed down. Sorry about the way I acted. It was childish."

"You always get wrought up like that," Cordell replied. He then cast a dirty look at Fallon and knocked on the door.

The door opened and Ruth looked out at them. "Oh, come in. We wondered what happened to you after the funeral."

The three stepped inside the house and closed the door. "We had some matters to attend to," Cordell replied.

Ruth's expression turned sad. "Elwood told Laura and I about the bullets. I can hardly believe it. Who would do such a wretched thing?"

Cordell agreed. "Yes, it is unbelievable. We were looking for some answers."

"Did you find them?" Ruth asked with a look that expressed her hope they had learned who did it.

"We think so. We would like to talk to Uncle Elwood."

"He is in his office. After he came home and told us he closed himself in there and hasn't come out all day. I knock on the door and he says he is fine, he simply wants to be alone."

Cordell smiled at his aunt. "He'll talk to us."

Laura stepped into the room where they were standing. She put her arms around Adam's neck and hugged him. "It's so awful," she whispered.

"We think we know who did it, but we need to talk to Uncle Elwood first."

Laura let go of him and looked up in his face. "Someone in town?"

"No. I'll let you know after we talk to Uncle Elwood."

The brothers walked through the house to Elwood's office. Cordell knocked on the closed door.

Elwood's muffled and slurred voice sounded from the other side. "I am fine, I want to be alone."

Cordell whispered, "He's been drinking." He turned the knob to find the door locked. "Uncle Elwood, open the door."

"Is that you Cordell?"

"Yes, with Adam and Fallon. We need to talk to you."

"I do not want to talk."

"Uncle Elwood, don't make me shoot the lock out of this door."

They could hear movement behind the door, then a key turning in the lock, and the door swung in. Elwood was standing in the room holding the door knob. His hair was disheveled and it was clear he had been weeping and was drunk.

The brothers walked in past him, Adam was the last in. He closed the door and gave Elwood a chastising look.

Cordell put his hand on Elwood's arm. "You alright, Uncle Elwood?"

Elwood nodded as he stumbled back to his chair and sat down. He looked up blurry eyed at the three of them as they focused their attention on him.

"I'm drunk you know," Elwood whispered. "I rarely drink."

"Today's been pretty rough," Cordell replied with sympathy.

Elwood nodded. "You want answers don't you?"

All three nodded that they did.

Elwood waved his hand over the room, "Pull up a chair."

Adam and Fallon moved chairs closer to Elwood and sat down. Cordell continued to stand.

"Tell us about Beau Whitlock," Cordell said.

Elwood gave Cordell a surprised look, then picked up his half empty glass and took another drink. He looked back at Cordell.

"I talked to Leroy Jackson today. He told me a lot. Should I believe him?"

Elwood's head wavered slightly side-to-side and his words were slightly slurred. "Leroy was your Pa's best friend, if he said it, he would know. I didn't like him though, in fact I didn't like your father either. I thought Tessa was making a huge mistake by marrying that outlaw."

"So, Pa *was* an outlaw?" Adam asked.

Elwood nodded. "His name was Beau Whitlock in those days. He was a desperate and notorious outlaw. What Tessa ever saw in him was a mystery to me. She married him in spite of my objections."

"What happened after she married him?" Fallon asked.

"He stopped being an outlaw and took a job in a blacksmith's shop. He changed his name to Ryan Monroe. I kept telling Tessa to expect him to revert back any day. I did not believe he had really changed. Then, one day two men came from his past. They attacked him and he killed one of them."

He made a sad face and shook his head, "I was not very nice to Tessa, telling her 'I told you so.' Tessa stuck up for him and claimed he was only defending himself. Beau, or Ryan he was then, took off. I thought he had deserted her."

Elwood took another drink and stared out the window for several seconds. "I told her to stay with Ruth and me, for the sake of you children. The next thing I knew she was gone. I got a letter from her months later, from El Paso. They had settled on a ranch there."

"That's what Leroy told me," Cordell said in a soft voice. "He was the one following Pa's instructions to bring us to where he was holding up."

Elwood looked up into Cordell's face. "I was wrong about him you know. He hadn't run away at all, he was making a safe place for you to go. He was not running from his responsibilities and family, he was running from his past, for their sake. I started to see him in a different light."

"How does Winston Cain come to play in

this?" Fallon asked.

Elwood drank down the last of the liquor in the glass and reached for the bottle. Adam stood up and took the bottle and glass away from him. "You've had enough of that."

Elwood nodded and sank back into his chair. He was silent for a moment and then scrunched his eyes closed and began to sob.

The brothers allowed him his emotion in silence.

Elwood took a deep breath and began. "Winston Cain knew Tessa even before your father did. He had come around the café where she worked and tried to make her his girl. She despised him and would give him no attention. That made him angry. Every once in a while he came back into town looking for her. She refused to give him any time at all."

"Did Pa know about that?" Cordell asked.

"No. When Tessa fell in love with Beau, er Ryan she made me swear to never let him know about Cain. It wasn't until after she married Ryan that she learned that Cain was the leader of the gang he had been in. She told him about Cain then."

"Leroy told me Cain came looking for Pa to kill him for a past wrong."

"I don't know about that. I do believe Cain came looking for Tessa and found her married to Ryan. I think that was what the shooting was over."

"And why they escaped to Hueco Tanks," Adam concluded.

"Yes. I learned later that Ryan did not like the idea of Cain remaining a threat, even though they were a long way from San Antonio. He wanted to go after Cain and finish him off. Tessa made him promise not to pursue him. She feared Cain and the possibility of him killing Ryan. She only wanted to keep the family as far away from that vile man as possible."

"So, Pa never went after Cain," Cordell concluded.

"No. He made the promise and stuck to it."

"What brought them to Tucson then?" Adam asked.

"I did. I was working at a bank in San Antonio. I was offered a better position at the bank in Tucson as the town was growing. Ruth and I moved here. We felt you boys needed a better life than in the wilderness. The owners of a store vacated it and the bank took it over. I wrote to Tessa asking her and Ryan to move up here for the sake of you boys and take the store. They did it. Ryan and I became friends. He was a good man. I had been wrong about him."

Elwood stopped talking as his bottom lip began to tremble. He fought a losing battle for control of his emotions. He buried his face in his hands and spoke through his hands. "Three years ago Tessa told me Leroy had come to town to let Ryan know that Cain was living in El Paso."

He lifted his face from his hands and sniffed. "Tessa was afraid, but Ryan didn't think Cain could ever find them after all these years. We were all cautious and watching just the same, in case he came to Tucson."

"So, you think Cain did find them?" Fallon asked.

"It had to be him, no else would ever do such a horrible thing. How he found them I have no idea."

"Leroy is certain it was Cain, it was his style," Cordell said.

Elwood's chin began to tremble again. "If Tessa had let Ryan hunt him . . ." he broke down in tears.

"This would not have happened," Cordell finished the sentence.

Elwood bent over his knees shaking all over in wracking sobs. "Oh, my dear Tessa. That monster shot her in the head. Oh, my God, my dearest Tessa." He sobbed uncontrollably.

Cordell placed his hand on his uncle's trembling back. "We're going to kill him for this, Uncle Elwood."

Cordell looked at his brothers. "I think we know the whole truth now."

Fallon stood up. "There's a train to El Paso in the morning."

Adam added with a tremble of rage in his voice, "And we're going to be on it."

Cordell studied Adam. "Are you sure? You were talking against killing Cain earlier."

"That was before I knew what he was."

"Make sure Adam, because once we set out on this there's no turning back."

"I'm sure."

"Alright then. I'm heading over to see Hiram. I don't want him telling Scott about the bullets."

"Why not?' Adam asked.

"Because I don't want that fool interfering with what we intend to do with Cain."

Adam nodded his agreement.

Fallon opened the office door to find Ruth and Laura outside the door with concerned expressions.

Ruth looked past the brothers into the room. "We heard . . .," she stopped as she saw Elwood bent over in the chair sobbing. "Oh, my poor Elwood, he has taken this so hard. So broken hearted."

"He told us everything," Adam said.

Ruth nodded. "Yes. I told him he must tell you boys the truth, all of it, about your father."

"He told us about Winston Cain."

"Yes, that horrible wretch."

"Between what we have learned from Uncle Elwood and Leroy Jackson we are sure Cain did it," Cordell replied.

Ruth gasped, "Oh no. Tessa had so feared he would find them. Ryan did not believe he would."

"Apparently he did."

Laura took ahold of Adam's arm and drew his attention to her. "What is going on? Who is Winston Cain?"

Ruth took in a settling breath and stiffened her resolve. She looked at each of the brothers. "What are you going to do now?"

Cordell looked her directly in the eyes. "Leroy told us where to find Cain."

"He is in El Paso," Ruth said.

"We know. We're going there on the morning train."

Laura searched Adam's face with a look of fear, "Why are you going to El Paso?"

"To kill Winston Cain," Adam answered.

Laura's eyes opened wide, "Kill him! What are you talking about?"

Adam looked down at Laura's upturned face and fear filled eyes. "There is a history behind Pa. A man named Winston Cain, who was part of that history, murdered Ma and Pa. He's in El Paso and the three of us are going to kill him for it."

Laura's face blanched, "You cannot go killing people like that."

"He's not people, he's an animal. A blood thirsty, murdering animal."

"Then, let the law take care of it. Tell someone in authority. You can't do this."

"There is not enough proof to convict Cain of the murders. It is only something certain people know about. He murdered them and he is not getting away with it."

Laura gaped at him. "You need to tell me every bit of this."

Adam took Laura by the arm. "We will talk in our room." They walked away from the group.

Cordell looked back in the office to see Elwood still bent over. He had fallen into a drunken sleep and was snoring. He glanced at Ruth, "He was drinking."

"He does not do that often."

Cordell walked back into the room and took ahold of his uncle. He lifted the small man from the chair and carried him like a child. "I'll put him in his bed." Cordell carried him up the stairs with Fallon and Ruth following.

He laid him on his bed. "Aunt Ruth, I'll let you undress him."

"Of course, thank you for carrying him up here." She looked at Cordell and then Fallon, "Are you all going?"

"Morning train to El Paso," Cordell answered. He shifted his eyes to Fallon, "All three of us."

Cordell and Fallon left the room leaving Ruth to tend to her husband. Reaching the bottom of the stairs Cordell turned to Fallon. "Are you up to this?"

Fallon glared at him. "Say what you mean."

"It might not go easy. I know what a refined gentleman you've turned into." His voice reflected sarcasm.

"While you were still figuring out how to use the outhouse I killed two Apaches when three of them tried to get into the cabin while Pa was out working the ranch. So, don't go acting like you're the only one who has any sand in this family. Don't *ever* doubt my loyalty to this family, you little snot."

Cordell held his brother's eyes. "You'll have to convince me of that."

"I made a mistake in turning my back on the family, but I won't let this go."

Cordell nodded slowly still holding his brother's eyes. "You might turn out alright yet."

"I don't care what you think or your opinion of me."

"Now, you sound like me, better watch out."

"Shut up, Cordell."

"There's no guarantee of the outcome of this. As long as you're making things right you

might want to have a talk with Helen and make things right with her before we leave."

Fallon felt the anger blow out of him. "Yes, before we leave in the morning."

"You do that. Right now I'm going to put my horse up at the livery."

Chapter 8

Seven o'clock in the morning found the family sitting around Ruth's table as she and Laura served up breakfast. Adam had put his suit back on for the train trip. Fallon was wearing his suit from the day before. Cordell was dressed as he had been when he arrived in Tucson, with the addition of a buckskin jacket to cover his gun.

Elwood was leaning over the table with a mug of hot coffee clamped between his slightly shaking hands. His face was splotchy red and his eyes swollen. It was evident by his posture that he was a man in misery, both body and mind.

Conversation was nonexistent until Elwood spoke in a cracked, weak voice. "I apologize for my behavior yesterday."

Everyone looked at him without comment.

Elwood could not bring himself to look at any of them. "I am not a drinker and I know I made a fool of myself."

"It's alright, Uncle Elwood," Cordell said softly. "You had a pretty rough day."

"Yes, but it does not excuse my poor behavior or drinking to excess. I have shamed myself."

"You're human," Cordell said. "You have no need to apologize."

Elwood smiled slightly. "Thank you. What are you boys going to do now?"

"We're taking the train to El Paso this morning."

Elwood nodded and then turned his face toward Cordell. "Cain?"

"Yes. He's not getting away with this."

"I expected you would. I am sorry that you had to learn about the past in this way."

"A past can't be hidden forever," Fallon commented.

"No, I suppose not. It is a hard way to learn of it though. I am sure it came as quite a shock to you."

"Actually, no. It made a lot of things fall into place," Fallon replied.

Elwood glanced at Fallon, "You had wondered about things, I suppose."

"It's better to know the truth."

"And it changes nothing about our family as far as we are concerned," Adam put in.

Laura looked at Adam and nodded agreement.

Cordell smiled at Adam pleased with his comment after the way he had responded to the news the day before. Adam acknowledged his brother's look with a nod.

With breakfast finished the brothers went out on the front porch to talk among themselves.

"How is Laura with this?" Cordell asked

Adam.

"She has her reservations about us doing this, but understands the circumstances. She would rather we let the law handle it."

"The law can't handle it," Fallon said. "There is no way to build a case against him."

Adam agreed. "She knows, she just doesn't like it."

"Not everything is black and white," Cordell said. "Some things are gray and you have to handle matters yourself if they are to be handled at all."

"That's what I told her. She understands."

"I'm glad you're not going to have family difficulty over this," Cordell remarked.

Adam shook his head. "I guess it's something that needs to be done."

Cordell looked at Adam's beltline. "Did you bring a gun?"

"Yeah, I wore it on the road. It's in the room."

"Wear it," Cordell said. "I'm going to see Hiram."

Fallon poked his thumb over his shoulder. "I have something to do."

"Train's leaving at ten," Cordell reminded him.

"I can tell time," Fallon snapped. He walked away.

"Meet at the depot," Cordell called after him.

"Where is he going?" Adam asked.

"To see Helen, probably. Do you want to get our tickets at the depot and we'll meet you there?"

"I'll take care of it. I left my horse and buggy at the livery, mind checking on it when you walk by?"

"My horse is there too, I'll check them." Cordell left the porch and struck a fast stride headed down the street.

Fallon walked down to Congress Street. Making his way along the boardwalk, he was trying to decide what to say to Helen. Everything he thought of sounded lame, pathetic, or an excuse. He was having second thoughts about returning to Austin after seeing her again and remembering what she had once meant to him.

Lost in thought he was standing in front of the bakery before he knew it. He looked in through the window and saw Helen handing wrapped parcels of bread to customers. He took a deep breath, opened the door, and walked in. A tiny bell on the door tingled. Helen looked up and directly at him.

He waited behind two customers and then stepped up to the counter. Helen smiled politely, "Good morning, Fallon."

Fallon sought to fight off the shame he felt and struggled with his words. He wondered how he could be so eloquent in court and the court buffoon here. "I know you are working, but it is important that I talk to you. I will only take a minute of your time."

"Alright." Helen asked her fellow worker to cover for her for a moment.

Helen followed Fallon out to the boardwalk.

"Helen, I have to be gone for a few days."

"Are you going back to Austin now?" Her eyes reflected disappointment while at the same time her lifted chin was an effort to remain detached from the feeling.

"No, this is business with my brothers. I will

return to Tucson. I wish to see you again and try very hard to earn back your trust that I so foolishly lost." He paused holding his breath awaiting her reply.

She crossed her arms and fought back the urge to cry. "Why? You are going to return to your life in Austin. I am not interested in a romance by mail, especially since I know you won't write."

The accusation hit Fallon hard. She was right, there was no reason to trust him. He had to earn it back. "I won't be returning to Austin if you give me a second chance."

Helen's mouth opened to speak, her eyes suddenly flashed with excited hope. Then, the look faded as she forced it away. "What about your business and office in Austin?"

"Tucson is a city in growth, I would open an office here in town."

Helen bit her bottom lip. "You will return after your business is finished?"

"I promise I will."

In a soft voice she replied, "Please, do not make promises you do not intend to keep."

He had that coming and he knew it. "Never again. I swear I will come back to you."

Helen pushed a loose strand of brown hair back away from her face. "Alright. You come to see me and we will talk. If you fail to show up, please, never bother me again."

He put his hand gently on her arm. "I will be back." He turned and walked away feeling the burn of her comments that he knew were completely justified. He had treated her cruelly in his submersion into himself.

He arrived at the depot to find his brothers

waiting for him.

Adam handed him a ticket. "How did it go?"

Fallon shrugged. "When I get back we're going to talk."

"That's a start," Adam said.

Fallon mumbled, "Probably more than I deserve."

Fallon turned his attention to Cordell. "What did Hiram say?"

"At first he felt he had an obligation to tell Scott about the bullets. Although, I don't think he wanted to, he doesn't like Scott very much."

Fallon snorted, "That puts him in the majority."

"After I explained to him about Cain he agreed that we had a right to deal with Cain in our own way and what Scott didn't know wouldn't hurt him. He promised to keep it under his hat."

In the distance the whistle to the eastbound train sounded. The clerk in the ticket window called out, "Train for El Paso is coming in."

The four Mexican banditos rode north out of the Rio Sonora country. Crossing unseen into the Arizona Territory, they made their first stop in Black Water. It was rumored that two of Silvio Ortiz's gang members, who were also his cousins, had been shot to death in that hole in the desert.

Silvio's inquiries among his shirttail relatives and fellow Mexicans in the cantina brought back the name Cordell Monroe, described as a young Anglo, tall, with long blonde hair. He did not know the gringo, but those he spoke with indicated that Cordell Monroe was *un hombre malo* with a gun. Silvio scoffed at that. No man was better than he was with a gun. He carried two pistols and had left many for the vultures who were called bad men on both sides of the border.

No one knew where Monroe lived for certain. He was a wild cow catcher and sometimes cowboy. He had sold cows to an Anglo rancher and rode north. A man who had earned two dollars from Monroe for helping push the cows to the ranch said Monroe was from Tombstone, or maybe it was Tucson, he wasn't sure except the town started with a 'T' sound.

There were only two towns Silvio knew of that started with the Anglo 'T'. They would ride to Tombstone and if he was not there they would go to Tucson. It did not matter how far Cordell Monroe ran, they would follow. Silvio Ortiz had a reputation to uphold and if he didn't hunt down Monroe and kill him that reputation would suffer. Monroe would die for his arrogance in killing the cousins of Silvio Ortiz.

Silvio and the three with him skirted the western edge of the barren rock Dragoon Mountains. Their path wound through mesquite groves interspersed with yucca and open miles of sand hot enough to dry a corpse to leather inside two days. The desert sun beat down on the four mounted figures spread slightly apart from each other. They knew to move slow and easy in the heat. This was a time when they should be looking for shade to nap the heat of the afternoon away, but they were men on a mission and naps would need to wait.

The four rode heavily armed, rifles in their saddle scabbards and pistols on their hips. Belts of rifle and pistol cartridges encircled their waists. They had long since abandoned raids into Texas as the Rangers had proved too formidable and had made the practice of stealing from Texans far too costly. Arizona did not have the benefit of Rangers and no one had turned the Arizona Territory dangerous for them yet.

They had often crossed the border into Arizona to raid. It was simple, stealing cattle, robbing, and killing, then riding back to the safety of their own country. They were looked on with hatred and fear by both Anglos and north-of-the-border Mexicans alike, but Silvio appreciated the fear and fed off it.

They studied every white face they passed. Some eyed them right back, others turned their faces away. Settlements were scrutinized for a tall gringo with long yellow hair. There were more than a few longhaired gunhands and outlaws, but none young and yellow haired.

They were further north than any of them, save Silvio, had ever ventured. As they moved along the base of the mountains they could see off to their left a town rising out of the desert. Silvio told them it was Tombstone. They reined their horses over and rode toward the buildings.

A dirt street ran past the end of the town spilling out into the brush, rocks, and sand of the desert. They picked up the street riding past the prostitute cribs and cat houses running down the first side street they crossed. They rode slowly looking from side-to-side and peering intently into each window.

Miners dressed in rough work clothes glared at them as they moved along. Gamblers stood at the side of the street smoking cigars and watching them with interest. It was a town where armed men were not uncommon and hardly raised an eyebrow. Heavily armed Mexican riders were another matter.

Coming to another cross street, Silvio, who could read and speak English, read the signs telling him they were at the corner of Allen and 5th Street. To their right was a saloon with the word *Oriental* written on it. Without a word to those with him he reined his horse up to a hitchrail and dismounted.

Silvio's three companions followed him to the side of the street, but held their place when a rough voice called out to them. They turned their heads to look at the hard faced man walking toward them. They saw his badge and his gun, which he wore like a man skilled in its use.

Virgil Earp didn't care for the look of the four heavily armed men. It was clear to him these were not vaqueros, he knew banditos when he saw them. "Hold your ground right there," Virgil called out with authority.

Virgil stopped six feet from Silvio. "What do you want here?"

The three banditos still mounted spoke no English and only stared at him. They couldn't understand, but knew a tough man and a no-nonsense voice when they heard one. They watched him carefully.

Silvio frowned at him. He felt the need to hold up a tough appearance and not let this gringo order him around in front of his men. "We wish to eat," he replied with a surly tone.

"You won't find grub in there," Virgil jerked his head toward the Oriental saloon and gambling house."

Silvio glanced toward the saloon. "A drink then. We have ridden far and are thirsty."

Virgil matched Silvio's willful stance. "I don't care for heavily armed men riding into my town, and I care less for them in places like this one, getting liquored up."

Silvio squared around to face Virgil. It was important to show his defiance of the gringo lawman. He glared into Virgil's eyes.

Virgil casually lowered his hand to rest just above his holstered pistol and met the glare. He said nothing for several seconds then casually instructed, "You can eat down the street, but you aren't drinking in my town. Eat, then ride out."

Silvio's lips turned up in a defiant sneer. They were four to his one. "And if we choose to stay and drink?" His challenge was clear.

"Then, we'll bury you here." The voice came from behind him.

Silvio carefully turned his head to see two men in black suits facing him from the middle of the street. One carried a shotgun, the other a holstered pistol.

Wyatt's glacial eyes glared into Silvio. His brother Morgan stood beside him with the shotgun cradled in his left elbow eyeing the three still mounted.

"And if you need to make it eveners, you can count me in." Doc Holliday leaned against one of the Oriental's porch posts, lighting a cigar.

Silvio looked at the skinny, sickly man. His first impression was to laugh at him until he looked into the man's eyes and saw the killer underneath. His eyes flickered around to see men standing around watching.

Silvio continued to hold his pose, refusing to let down while at the same time knowing they would all die very quickly if he pushed it. He spoke to Virgil. "We are looking for a man who killed my two cousins. We were told he lived in Tombstone."

"Where did he kill them, Mexico or America?"

"Black Water, on the border."

"I know the place. Does this man have a name?" Virgil asked.

"A gringo . . ." He stopped when he saw the lawman in front of him stiffen at the derogatory name for his race. "An Anglo, Cordell Monroe."

"I might know him."

"Where is he?"

"He's not in this town, but I do know the men he killed down there were banditos." Virgil's glare intensified, "We don't take to Mexican outlaws coming up here on the hunt."

Silvio nodded slowly. "I see. You protect your own."

"He's not mine."

Silvio growled, "But, he is a *gringo*, that is enough."

"You just wore out your welcome in my town. You've got five seconds or plan on staying forever. All I want to see is four horse tails leaving town . . . now."

Silvio looked at the two men standing behind him and then to the sickly one leaning on the post. He turned slowly and stepped into the saddle. He looked the men over with a defiant sneer as he led his companions out of town.

In Spanish he spoke to them, "The gringo is not here. Then, he is in Tucson. We will go there."

Chapter 9

The two burly men moved slowly through the saloon. The brown coats of their cheap suits, stretched taut at the shoulders and buttons, matched the bowler hats tipped slightly to the sides of their heads. The bulges under their arms indicated shoulder holstered guns. Theirs was the back street realms of El Paso where criminals, gamblers, and prostitutes frequented.

The pair were recognized as thugs employed by either the Manning brothers, who sought to control the crime business of the city, or one of a number of petty tyrants. They enforced for loan sharks and collected on gambling debts not paid. Any man who had never borrowed from a shark, or welshed on a debt, paid them no attention. Those who owed watched with terrified eyes to see if they were the one targeted by the enforcers.

The men continued a slow walk through the place. It was obvious they knew their man was in here. He was likely snitched off by another indebted individual to save himself. Stopping, one of the men peered across the dimly lit room to a corner table where a man sat with a woman on his lap. Both were drinking liquor from the same glass and laughing. He elbowed his partner who looked where he indicated and nodded.

They made a beeline for the man who could not see them for the woman on his lap. The first thug grabbed the woman by the arm and yanked her off the man's lap. He gave her a push, yet not hard enough to knock her down. She began to protest, but stopped when she saw the target of the men was the man she had been with. She quickly slipped away into the crowd.

The second thug grabbed the man by the front of his shirt and arm as he jumped up. The shout never came from his open lips as the burly man slammed him face down on the table. The chair he had been sitting on bounced hard off the wall. The first thug grabbed the man's free arm and together they dragged the dazed man out of the saloon as blood trickled out of his nose and mouth.

The patrons of the bar had stopped their activities long enough to watch the show. It was over in a moment, the enforcers knew their business and made short work of collecting their prey. Activity resumed in the room with jokes and ridicule directed at any man fool enough to owe a loan shark or crime lord.

The thugs dragged the man into an alley behind the saloon. The fact it was mid-day didn't matter as the law of the city was of no consequence. The marshals, being too busy shooting each other or staying away from the places they were paid to stay away from, would not come on them.

They pushed the man up against the wall of the saloon holding him in place. Realization came to him as his head cleared. His eyes suddenly filled with terror. The enforcers stared in his face.

"How much do you have on you, Baker?" One of the thugs belligerently hissed in the man's face.

The man opened his mouth to speak, but could only emit squeaks in his fear.

"You borrowed from Mr. Cain with a promise to repay. Your deadline was yesterday. Five hundred dollars is owed."

Baker licked his bloody lips. "But I only borrowed two hundred."

The thug smiled, "Did you forget about the interest?"

The second thug reached into Baker's pocket and took his wallet. He opened it and counted out two hundred dollars. "This all you have?"

Baker nodded. "Take it. Tell Mr. Cain I'll get the rest."

"How? Rob a bank? You won't have three hundred dollars tonight and you know it."

The thug holding Baker against the wall glanced at his partner holding the money. "At least Mr. Cain will get his investment back."

"Yes, he will." Baker grasped at hope.

The thug holding him shook his head. "Here's a little gift from Mr. Cain." He slipped a short knife with a two inch blade out of his pocket and plunged it into Baker's abdomen.

Baker screamed out in pain as he slammed his hands over the wound and crumpled to the dirt.

"That won't kill you, but you won't be feeling

very good for a while. We'll be back for the rest of the money."

The two enforcers walked away leaving Baker writhing in pain on the ground.

The two enforcers sauntered in the back door of the Desert Rose. They stepped into a hallway where the madam of the house met them. The two men smiled at her. She did not return the smiles.

"Who did you take off?" the woman asked.

One of the thugs smirked, "Why should I tell you?"

The woman dug her fists into her waist and glowered at him. "Because, I asked you a question and I expect an answer."

"We don't work for you."

"I am second in charge here and you have to answer me."

The thug smiled and made a sweeping bow. "Yes, your majesty."

The second thug cast a tired scowl at his partner. "Knock it off, Rudy." He looked at the woman, "It was Baker."

"Oh, yes. A bad risk, I told Winston as much. Did you get anything out of him?"

"Two hundred."

The woman held out her hand. "I'll give it to him."

Rudy barked a mocking laugh. "Sure you will. I'll give it to him myself."

The woman's lips tightened in fury. "Don't forget your place," she seethed between her teeth.

Undisturbed by her bluster Rudy replied, "I take my orders from Mr. Cain, and him alone. I don't take orders from a whore herder. You ran the show while the boss was in Tucson cutting a deal with that Turner fellow, but he's back now."

Rudy pushed rudely past her with his partner following and continued down the hall to Cain's office. They knocked on the door and waited until a voice from the other side of the closed door told them to enter.

Cain sat behind his desk. His slicked back gray hair, still showing a few streaks of black, and a perfectly trimmed and waxed mustache framed his face and cold eyes. "Well?"

"We found Baker."

Cain's eyes reflected his impatience at having to drag the information out of them.

Rudy read the look and quickly got on with his report. "He only had two hundred of the five he owed." He laid the money on the desk.

Cain scowled at the man. "I sent you out to collect five hundred. I suppose you told him it was all right to stiff me."

"No sir. That's all he had on him. I gave him a belly ache and told him we'd be back for the rest."

"Give him two days and if he doesn't have it, kill him."

"Yes, sir. Anyone in particular you want us to go after next?"

Cain flipped a couple of papers around on his desk and then paused as he read one. "Johnson. He beat the house for two thousand at Draw. He had to have been cheating. Bring him in, I want to talk to him myself. Hold him in the stable and let me know when he's here."

"Yes, sir." The two men quickly exited the office closing the door behind them. In the hall Rudy whispered to the other. "He had to have been cheating to beat a stacked deck."

The other laughed. "The last time someone cheated here Cain shot him."

"Or took Cain's money by actually winning," Rudy chuckled.

They passed the madam in the hall. She glared her hatred at them. "I am going to tell Winston what you called me."

Rudy grinned, "So, what is it you do here exactly, *Angel?*"

The women spit out, "My name is *Angelique*, not Angel."

"So, what do you do here, *Angelique?*"

"You know full well what I do."

"Yeah, like I said, a whore herder. Am I wrong?"

"And you're a two-bit ape with the intelligence of a wooden banister. Winston can go shovel up another like you at the livery anytime he chooses." She spun on her heels and stormed down the hall, her dress swirling around her legs. She jerked open the door to Cain's office and stomped in.

Cain looked up at her. "Don't you understand the art of knocking?"

"I want you to fire that Rudy."

Cain grinned as he studied the woman. She wasn't bad looking for being in her forties. She dressed nice and smelled nice. The problem was she wanted too much control. It never paid to let anyone have too much control, especially an unscrupulous woman. "He called you names again?"

"Yes."

"Ignore him. Good enforcers that don't skim

are hard to come by. What else do you want?"

"How did the meeting with Turner go in Tucson?"

Cain leaned back in his chair and smiled. "Good. We are going to open a gambling house and brothel outside of town. The good people of Tucson would object to such an *unsavory* establishment in their fair city so we'll put it out a ways. The men will find it. I also had the good fortune of accidentally running into a couple of old friends." His smiled widened at the thought.

Angelique looked at Cain. She was in love with him, but it wasn't returned on his part. She was jealous whenever he showed interest in any of the girls. "An old girlfriend, I suppose?"

Cain held the smile. "Possibly."

She knew he was taunting her. With a huff and a swirl of her blue dress she stormed back out the door. She could hear Cain laughing behind her.

Cain sat thinking about how he had spotted Tessa coming out of a store. He couldn't believe his eyes. Tessa was a good looking woman and even in her older years she was unmistakable. It only stood to reason that where Tessa was, Beau was as well. He followed from a distance and saw her go into a house. He waited until after dark and paid his old friends a visit.

He laughed to himself when he thought back on it. He had simply walked right in. They were sitting in the kitchen drinking coffee. He was disappointed in Beau though, he had lost his edge. In the old days he could never have gotten up on him like that. What an old fool he had become. He had sat there with his mouth open like a dead fish. It was all too easy. A bit disappointing actually.

He shot Beau first, just in case. He had given Tessa a chance to leave with him, to live. All she did was stare like a stupid cow at Beau laying on the floor. When she started to scream he shut her up too.

The fire had been a last minute idea. A brilliant idea. Torch the house and blame it on the fire. He was long gone before the smoke even made it out the windows. He had to see it before getting back on the train the next day. He smiled at the thought. The house was a pile of black rubble and people were scurrying around it like ants. It was a beautiful sight.

He stood up and straightened his collar and tie. He was in a good mood. He left the office and wandered down the hall. Pushing aside the heavy curtain that hid the hallway from the patrons, he entered the main lobby. Several men sat waiting in red plush chairs, their feet on the dark thick carpet. This was a palace in a dung heap he thought as he surveyed the room.

Two of the house guards stood against opposite walls from each other. They were attentive and watching. A third was posted beside the entry door. He wandered into the first of the three gambling rooms and watched his dealers work the cards. They glanced at him even as their hands slipped cards in and out of the decks. He had hired well and paid them well.

He walked out of the room and up to the bar where the barkeep quickly set a glass on the bar and filled it from a special bottle of bourbon saved exclusively for Cain. Cain did not acknowledge the man as he took the glass and wandered into the second room where two faro tables were set up. He watched until he was satisfied that the cards were turning over for the house.

He stepped back out into the bar area and saw two of the young drink girls resting on a settee. Placing his empty glass on a table he walked up to them. They looked up at him nervously.

In a low voice he snarled, "You can't move drinks or get men drunk enough to spend their money by sitting here like a couple of frogs on a log. If you don't want to move drinks I can transfer you to Angelique and you can lay around all the time."

The girls jumped up without a word. A look of fear was etched on each of their faces as they hurried into the gambling rooms.

Cain watched them go. He'd fire them both except they were good looking girls and they did move a lot of drinks. It was a combination hard to come by in this town. Any woman could work in the brothel, but not all were young with fresh enough appearances to move men to drink. He didn't care about them personally, he only saw them as money makers. Pretty girls and too much liquor would cause a man to lay down every nickel he had on a card.

One of Cain's guards walked out of the third card room with a distraught looking man beside him. He stood watching the two as they drew closer to them. Cain knew the man would say he had lost more at the table then he had. He would be wanting him to cover his loss and would promise to pay it back. He had seen it over and again. He loved it.

Cain looked at the guard. "What do we have here, Gary?"

The guard gave Cain a slight smile knowing what was to follow. "Mr. Robbins here did not do so well at the table."

Cain turned a sympathetic eye to Robbins. "Didn't quite beat the dealer, Mr. Robbins?"

Robbins pulled a white handkerchief out of his pocket and wiped his sweating face. "No, sir. I am afraid I can't meet my last bet."

"Came up short, did you?"

Robbins nodded, "Yes, sir. I can pay it, I just don't have it on me right now."

Cain shook his head and sighed. "You know you should never bet what you don't have."

"I know," Robbins sighed. "But, I had a full house, a full house. I thought I had it."

"That is a pretty good hand. What happened?"

"The dealer drew a fourth ten. I couldn't believe it."

Cain snickered to himself, his dealers were good. "Bad luck alright. How much were you short?"

"Only a hundred dollars."

Cain chuckled, "Is that all? I'll tell you what I'll do, Mr. Robbins."

Robbins looked at Cain with hope.

"I'll stand you the loss if you promise to pay back the hundred, with a small bit of interest, within the week."

Robbins's face brightened. "Oh, yes sir, Mr. Cain, I'll have it for you. Thank you. Do you need me to sign anything?"

Cain waved a hand, "A gentleman's agreement."

"A gentleman's agreement it is then. Thank you."

"Why don't you have a drink on the house,"

Cain said with a smile. "To settle your nerves."

"Why, thank you. My nerves are a bit jumpy right now."

"Gary, escort Mr. Robbins to the bar and tell Brant to give him the house drink."

Gary nodded, "Yes sir." He walked with Robbins to the bar.

Brant frowned as he pulled a bottle from a corner under the bar and poured a shot glass full.

Robbins slugged the drink straight down. He turned and headed for the door with Gary at his side. Half way across the room he stopped and put his hand to his forehead. "All of a sudden I don't feel so good."

"Let me help you sit down," Gary offered.

"Yes, I think so."

Gary supported Robbins' arm as he walked with him to the back hallway behind the curtain. Stopping beside a chair against the wall Gary said, "You can sit here where no one need stare at you."

Robbins nodded, sat down on the chair and passed out. He fell heavily to the carpeted floor.

Cain pushed the curtain aside and walked in. He looked down at Robbins. "Check him."

Gary dug into Robbins's pockets finding nothing of value. He pulled out the man's wallet and checked it, it was empty. "I'm not finding anything, Mr. Cain."

Cain pulled Robbins's suit coat off and felt all over it. He suddenly stopped moving his hands and squeezed a spot. "Here it is." He pulled a jack knife from his pocket, opened the blade and carefully cut into the spot. Slipping his fingers into the slit he pulled out a sheaf of bills. He counted out five, one hundred dollars bills. He put the money in his pocket.

Gary watched Cain, then commented, "He was going to skip."

Cain nodded. "Take him out and drop him in the alley. Let Rudy know he owes me two hundred dollars and I want it collected day after tomorrow."

"Yes sir." Gary picked the man up under his arms and dragged him down the hall and out the back door.

Cain wandered back out to the floor. Evening was approaching and more men were making their way in. Angelique appeared from the back area and began engaging the men in conversation. He watched her for a bit and then walked into the third card room.

Three tables were set up for Draw and Stud poker. He watched one dealer in particular, a new man named Grubbs. He was clumsy. Grubbs had sworn he was a good dealer, could bottom deal with the best of them. He was giving the man a try. What he saw wasn't making him very happy.

Cain strolled back out to the lobby where Rudy approached him. Rudy moved in close and whispered, "We've got Johnson."

Without a word Cain followed his enforcer out of the room, down the back hallway, and out the door. Behind the House was a shed, inside it was a stable, but to the outside world it was merely a storage shed. Inside Cain kept two horses fed and watered, one always saddled in case he had to make a quick run for it. A habit held over from the old days.

The sun was setting leaving the interior dark save for the glare of a lighted lantern hanging from a rafter. Rudy's partner had Johnson sitting on the dirt floor with a gun on him. Cain walked up to them and stood over Johnson looking down on him.

Johnson looked back at him without fear. "Your trained monkeys said you wanted to talk to me."

"Yes, I do," Cain answered casually. "You seem to have cheated your way to two thousand dollars of my money."

Johnson chuckled. "Well, if that ain't the pot callin' the kettle black. Your boy in there handles cards like an old granny. Oh, yeah, he was cheating . . . badly."

Cain looked at Rudy, "Grubbs?"

Rudy nodded.

Cain returned his attention to Johnson. "So, you cheated the cheater?"

Johnson smiled, "Now, why would I tell you that?"

Cain scratched the side of his cleanly shaven jaw. "I don't like people cheating me."

Johnson smirked, "Don't like the competition, huh?"

"Something like that." Cain reached his hand inside his coat and brought it back out holding a pistol. Without hesitation he pointed it at Johnson's forehead and pulled the trigger.

Johnson slammed back against the stable wall and slid lifeless to the ground.

Cain looked at Rudy and his partner who were not affected by the execution. "I like this little Webley revolver. It gets the job done without making a mess." He gestured toward the body as he reholstered the gun. "Get rid of that. Then I want you to take Grubbs out and come back alone."

Chapter 10

The train was an hour out of Tucson before the conductor made his way down the narrow aisle checking tickets. As he passed each pair of seats the passengers handed him their tickets, he would punch the paper and hand the ticket back. He was not particularly friendly as he stuck strictly to business without unnecessary conversation.

The car was not full as there were several empty seats. Fallon sat in the aisle seat with Adam sitting beside him looking out the window. Cordell sat across the aisle from them in the window seat, the aisle seat between them was empty.

The conductor reached their seats. He took Fallon's and Adam's tickets as they handed them to him. He punched the tickets and handed them back. He then turned toward Cordell. He stood with a frown studying Cordell's trail worn clothes, long hair, and general rough appearance.

Cordell stared out the window ignoring the conductor knowing he was being scrutinized by the stiff railroad man.

"You had better have a ticket," the conductor said unpleasantly.

Cordell turned his head to see the conductor glowering at him. "Why wouldn't I have a ticket?"

"Because, you look like trouble to me. The kind of person who thinks he can ride for free. More of an outlaw than a passenger I'd say."

Cordell's eyes danced with mischief as he held a stoic expression. "I *am* an outlaw. Actually, let me rephrase that, I am a black sheep. That's the same thing in most people's books, huh?"

With an aggravated harrumph the conductor snapped, "You are also a smart mouthed young man."

Cordell smiled at him, "Yes, I am." He turned his head back to look out the window.

With a cough the conductor said, "Then I am correct, you have no ticket?"

Still facing the window Cordell answered, "I never said I didn't have a ticket."

"You did as much say so."

"You said that I had *better* have a ticket. You didn't ask for my ticket."

The conductor's face grew red with anger. He began to say something when Fallon broke in. "Excuse me, sir."

The conductor turned to face Fallon.

Fallon looked up at the man. "Sir, I am an attorney from Austin. More specifically, I am Mr. Monroe's attorney." He pointed at Cordell.

The conductor glanced at Cordell with a look of confusion.

"I agree with Mr. Monroe, you did not ask for his ticket. You stated that he had 'better have a ticket.' There is a difference. You may not be aware that Mr.

Monroe is the sole heir to a million dollar cattle empire in Texas, as well as being a major stockholder in *this* railroad. He may appear to be an unkempt saddle bum, derelict, and no account outlaw and gunfighter with poor personal hygiene and of low class; however that is merely his personal idiom."

The conductor stood with his mouth hanging open in shock. He slowly looked back at Cordell with a sick look on his face indicating he knew he had committed a major error in insulting an important man.

Fallon spoke across to Cordell, "Mr. Monroe, would you please show the good conductor your ticket?"

Without turning his face from the window Cordell held his ticket up in the air.

With a quick flurry of motion the conductor took the ticket, punched it, and placed it back in Cordell's waiting hand. "Thank you, Mr. Monroe. I apologize for the misunderstanding." He hurried along to the rest of the car.

When the conductor punched the last ticket and returned to the caboose Cordell turned from the window and looked across at Fallon. He was grinning as he waited for Fallon to look back.

Fallon finally sighed and turned his head to look at Cordell. "What?"

Cordell's grinned widened. "Mr. Fancy Pants told a lie."

"No I didn't. You *are* an unkempt saddle bum, derelict, and no account outlaw and gunfighter with poor personal hygiene and of low class."

"Admit it, you like me."

Fallon scowled at his young brother. "You're

a mess, Cordell. Why don't you get a haircut?"

Holding the grin Cordell answered, "It's my personal idiom."

"Shut up, Cordell." Fallon leaned back and tipped his hat down over his closed eyes.

It was nearing dark when the train pulled into the El Paso station. With a slow grinding of brakes the train came to a stop. Steam blew out from the locomotive's drivers and smoke from the stack. The conductor walked through the car announcing their arrival in El Paso.

The brothers followed the other passengers out of the car. They stood on the wooden platform surrounding the depot house and waited for the crowd to dissipate. Moving to the side of the depot out of earshot of others they looked around at the buildings where lights were beginning to glow behind the windows.

"Now, we have to find it,' Adam said as he looked around.

"We can ask the ticket agent," Cordell suggested. He looked at Fallon. "You look respectable, like a lawyer in a suit, you ask him."

Fallon snapped, "Oh, wonderful. I should waltz up there and ask him where the Desert Rose whorehouse is. Great."

"Sure. He'll probably think you're just looking for a good time. If it's a high roller place like Leroy said, then you look the part. I look like a derelict and a low class bum remember?"

Adam agreed. "He does have a point, Fallon. You could get the information faster than either of us."

"Why don't you ask him?" Fallon shot back at Adam. "You're in a suit."

Adam's face began to turn red as he stammered, "I would, but I don't think . . ."

"He's shy, remember?" Cordell cut Adam off.

Fallon gave a knife thin smile to both his brothers. "Fine." He walked toward the clerk's open window.

The clerk looked at him. "Can I help you?"

"Yes, can you tell me where to find the Desert Rose?"

"You mean Winston Cain's gambling house and bordello?" Accustomed to shouting over crowds and trains, the man's loud voice carried across the platform.

A pair of middle-aged women waiting on the platform snapped their heads around and glared at Fallon. They moved several more feet away from him.

Fallon glared at the clerk. "I'm not sure who owns it. I was only told it was a good place to play cards."

The clerk grinned. "So, I've heard. Going right for the entertainment are you?"

Fallon glanced toward the women who had their backs turned to him. "I'm only interested in the gaming tables," he said loud enough for the women to hear.

"Of course." The agent winked. "Well, head straight down that street there. Go past the big livery, turn right and you can't miss it. Big fancy building. Looks mighty out of place back there, the way it looks and all. The law leaves things alone back there so you don't have to worry about them coming around asking embarrassing questions."

"I'm sure they do. What's the closest good hotel?"

"A block down that way, the Pacific Hotel. Nice place, you can eat there too."

Fallon nodded at the man and walked back to where his brothers waited.

Cordell was bent over trying to control his hysterical laughter. Fallon glared at him. "I'm glad you enjoyed the show."

Cordell straightened and stifled a laugh. "The whole town enjoyed the show. I thought those ladies were going to have apoplexy when that clerk blurted out 'bordello.'"

"Then, I suppose you heard the directions as well?"

Cordell nodded.

"Let's check in at the hotel we can spend the night at and get something to eat."

Adam frowned clearly annoyed. "Spend the night? I thought we were going to go right over there, deal with him, and go back home."

Cordell stopped laughing and turned serious. He shook his head. "The place will be packed come tonight. We want to go there in the morning before the place gets busy. Catch Cain off guard."

Fallon nodded. "I have to agree, that is the best way to go about this. Let's go get the rooms and eat."

"Then, we should take a walk over to the Desert Rose and scout out the place," Cordell added.

Fallon agreed. "We can plan our strategy."

"What strategy?" Adam snapped. "Just go in and . . ." He stopped, looked around him and whispered, "shoot him."

"That's not how it works," Cordell tried to sound patient. "Cain's survived this long by being careful. Those places have guards and hired thugs. We'll have to go through them first before we can get to Cain."

Adam gaped at him, "You never said anything about having to shoot our way in to him."

Fallon eyed Cordell with suspicion. "You seem to know a lot about these kinds of places."

Cordell ignored him.

Adam was irritable, hungry, and tired. "You didn't say anything about that or having to stay overnight here. I thought we would just do it and go home."

Cordell hated Adam's naïve nature and childish pouting. He glared at Adam and growled, "How old are you, three? Scared to be away from home for one night? When you hunt a man down you have to think it out ahead of time. Cain isn't going to stand there and say, 'shoot me.'"

Fallon glanced at the two. "We need to eat and then we'll feel better and talk calmer."

"Yeah," Cordell snorted, "get cranky here some coffee or a milk bottle."

"I'm not cranky," Adam snapped.

"You're all wrought up again like back at the Congress Hall when Leroy first told us about this. You need to buck up and act like a grown man, for God's sakes."

Adam glared at him. Cordell met and matched the look.

Fallon started off toward the hotel. "I'm hungry, follow me or the devil take you."

Cordell and Adam broke their stares and

followed him.

As they walked along Cordell said low to Adam, "Sorry about that."

Adam was silent for several seconds before asking, "Do I act like a three year old?"

"Only when you're hungry and tired, or you hear something you don't like and don't want to do it. You get argumentative and stubborn, you refuse to hear something out. There's a lot of things you don't understand."

Adam sighed heavily. "I know. Laura has told me the same thing."

"Ouch, that's embarrassing."

"Tell me about it. Guess I need to work on that."

Cordell grinned, "Coffee, coffee fixes everything."

Adam chuckled, "That and a thick steak."

With the rooms paid for and a filling dinner under their belts the three felt better. They spoke low over cups of coffee discussing their next move. It was decided to follow Cordell's lead and make a visit to the Desert Rose to see how the place was laid out.

Leaving the restaurant they walked down the dark street. Lights shown through the windows of the businesses still open while others had blown out the lamps and closed for the night. The further from the business hub they walked, the seedier the environment became. Buildings showing lack of care, and men who only come out after dark to frequent the places respectable men shun, were predominate.

Arriving at the livery the train agent had described they stood on the street corner and studied the approach to the Desert Rose. It was a two story building with lights glaring out of the lower floor windows into the black street and the empty space around it. Dim lights shone through the curtains of half the upstairs windows that were arranged like a hotel. There was no chance of missing the building in the dark.

Horses and various vehicles ranging from expensive buggies to freight wagons lined both sides of the street. The livery beside them was large with stalls inside the barn and a corral where several horses stood with a back hoof up and sleeping. The sign over the double barn doors declared they sold and rented horses and tack.

They walked down the street until they stood in front of the Desert Rose. Men were walking in and out of the main door at an equal rate. They circled around to the rear; however, the night was a deep black and they were unable to make out much as no light shone out the rear of the building. An alley ran behind the building and there was a structure across from it that appeared to be a storage shed.

"Pretty dark back here, "Adam commented. "Can't see much."

"All the better to haul men out here and deal with them," Cordell replied.

"What do you mean?" Adam asked.

No sooner had Cordell said it when a door opened throwing a shaft of light across the sand. Two men dragged a struggling man out the door and threw him, he landed with a heavy thud several feet outside the shaft of light.

A voice shouted from the darkness, "You cheating coyotes."

The sound of a fist striking flesh resounded from the dark followed immediately by a cry of pain. The silhouettes of two men were outlined briefly in the light and then a door slammed shut returning the alley to pitch black. They could hear the man mumbling and cursing as he picked himself up off the ground and shuffled away.

"That," Cordell answered Adam's question.

They walked back around to the front of the building and stood in the dark across the street.

"How do you want to do this," Adam asked Cordell.

"We don't want to all go in together, that will be too obvious. We go in alone a few minutes apart from each other and look the place over good. In half an hour we'll meet back by that livery and compare notes."

"Okay," Adam agreed. "What exactly are we looking for?"

"How the bar and gambling rooms are arranged. Look for doors that lead away from the main areas. Count the guards and where they are."

"What about the upstairs?" Adam asked.

"That will be the brothel, we don't need to worry about that. Gambling, bar, and back offices will all be on the main floor. That's where we'll find Cain."

"Oh," Adam said. "Guess I don't know too much about gambling halls and brothels."

Cordell grinned, "Sure, you don't."

"I'm a married man, thank you very much," Adam spit back.

"Then, you go in first, married man."

"What am I supposed to say if someone asks

me what I want?"

"Tell them you want a blonde."

Adam ground his teeth and hissed, "Dang it, Cordell, stop."

"Just go up to the bar and order a drink, then look around while you're standing there. If one of the girls approaches you tell her you have a social disease."

"*Dang it*, Cordell."

"Just go do it."

Adam growled and walked away toward the door.

Fallon glanced at Cordell. "You know things like that embarrass him. Just because you're a man of the world."

"Not as much as you think. Your turn, fancy pants."

"One of these days Cordell I'm going to knock your head off."

"You mean you'll *try* and knock my head off."

"There won't be any *try* about it."

"How about if you *try* to get your butt in there?"

Fallon gave him a dirty look and headed for the door.

Cordell waited another five minutes then walked across the street.

Cordell walked in the door and cast a quick glance around the lobby. A guard stood just inside the door eyeing him as he looked around. The room was ornate. Polished small tables in between plush chairs. Patterned carpet on the floor. In front of him was a staircase going up to the second floor with carpeted steps. Men were walking up the steps with the girls.

To the right of the stairs was a heavy drape covering a doorway. He guessed that to be the office area.

To his left was a long highly polished bar with a mirror running the length behind it. A large painting of a naked woman was above the mirror. A cluster of men stood against the bar as the barkeep was kept busy pouring drinks. The sounds of shuffling cards and wooden chips sliding across tables emanated from the side rooms. The low din of voices and clinking glass melded in with the gaming.

Two more guards were standing on either side of the lobby, and another two wandered in and out of the gaming rooms. Drink girls in low cut dresses worked through the crowd encouraging men to drink and letting them know when chairs at the gaming tables had opened up. He began a slow walk perusing the room.

He spotted Adam at the bar. His face was crimson with embarrassment as he desperately tried to avoid one of the prostitutes who had moved up beside him attempting to engage him in conversation. Cordell shook his head, Adam was a babe in the woods. He then saw Fallon walking around with a drink in his hand as if interested in all the aspects of the place.

A woman in a dark red gown buttoned to the throat with a choker of pearls around her neck moved gracefully among the men. She stopped frequently and spoke to them. The woman spotted Cordell and gave him an appraising once over. Breaking into a practiced smile she strolled up to him.

Cordell smiled at her, "Evening, ma'am."

"Good evening. Are you interested in the upstairs or downstairs?"

"Both. It's a mighty nice place you have here. Unfortunately, I can't stay for either." He leaned in closer to her, "I've come to retrieve my wayward brother."

"Why? Is he too old to be let out alone?" She gave him a coy wink, "Or *too* young?"

"He's *too* married to be let out alone." He pointed at Adam as if he had just found him. "There he is. He's a sucker for the girls and his wife is going to kill him if I don't get him back without her knowing he was here."

She glanced at Adam. "You mean the red faced one whose about to have a seizure? Doesn't seem a lady's man, more like a terrified schoolboy."

Cordell cursed to himself, Adam was going to tip Cain or someone off. "He looks like that when he's had a few. He doesn't hold his liquor well."

She then gave Cordell a suggestive leer. "Well, we certainly wouldn't want to be the cause of marital discord, but why don't you come back some time when you don't have to play nursemaid?"

"I fully intend to come back, thank you, ma'am." Cordell nodded to her and walked casually across the room stopping in front of the girl and Adam. He could see Adam was flustered beyond words.

Cordell smiled at the girl, "Excuse me, ma'am." He then fixed an angry eye on Adam. "Here you are! Laura is worried sick about you. I thought we had this talk before, you need to stay out of these places. Now, don't argue, you're coming home with me." Before Adam could reply Cordell took him by the arm and dragged him across the lobby.

Men were watching and laughing as they

approached the door. Fallon saw them and made his way toward the door.

Once outside Adam growled at Cordell, "Dragging me out like that was embarrassing."

"Watching you act like that sure was. You were so red I thought your head was going to explode like a tick. You were drawing attention from the wrong people acting like that."

Adam huffed and growled until he took a settling breath and let it out. "Thanks. I was way over my head. She latched right on to me and I didn't know how to get rid of her. She was so persistent."

"That's what they do."

"I didn't get to do much looking around."

"That's okay, I saw all I needed to."

Fallon met Adam and Cordell in the street where they had stopped. He looked at Adam, "Are you all right?"

Adam nodded.

Fallon jerked his head toward the livery, "Let's talk over there."

They walked down to the livery, stopping beside the corral.

"I've got the layout of the place," Cordell said.

"I got to talking to one of the guards," Fallon began. "He said they have the law paid off to stay away. No matter what happens, they stay away."

Cordell grinned, "That's good. Then shooting won't draw any attention."

"Unless someone there sets the law on us," Fallon remarked.

"That could happen if they control it, but not before we get good and gone."

"We'll have to make it fast."

"How many guards did you see?" Cordell asked.

"Five," Fallon answered.

"Yeah, I saw five, but there could be more in the back."

"I think I saw Cain." Fallon said. "Tall, pushing sixty, gray hair, handlebar mustache. Dressed expensive and talking intimately with a woman in a red dress in a back corner."

"That would be his madam, we met."

Fallon raised an eyebrow. "Your idea or hers?"

Cordell grinned, "She gave me a personal invitation to come back."

Adam was listening, taking in all the information he had missed while fending off the girl.

Fallon shook his head and turned his attention to Adam. "What did you learn?"

Adam looked embarrassed. "I didn't learn anything."

Cordell broke in. "One of the girls took to him and he was engaged in lively negotiations."

"What?" Fallon snapped.

Adam clenched his jaw and hissed, "*Cordell.*"

"Don't worry, I won't tell Laura."

Fallon glared at his little brother. "Cordell, I swear. Stop."

"It's not my fault we can't take a good looking fellow like Adam into a cathouse for a little scouting work." He looked at Adam's angry expression. "I'm joking with you, ease up or you're going to get yourself killed in there tomorrow."

Adam took a settling breath. "Sorry. I've never done anything like this before."

"It's about time you did something like this, you've been sheltered for too long."

"I don't think I've been sheltered," Adam said defensively.

"Have you ever left Tucson? Have you worked anywhere except for Red? You were raised by Ma and then taken care of by Laura. That's sheltered."

"What am I doing that's so wrong?"

"First off, you're tighter'n a catgut fiddle string. When you're too nervous you miss things and can't think straight. That's when you take a bullet in the gut. Second, you're too timid. You need to toughen up and set your mind to what's going to happen in the morning."

"I don't have your experience, Cordell. I've never killed a man."

"You will tomorrow. We'll have to shoot our way through those guards to get to Cain."

Adam gave Cordell a nervous look. "Why?"

"Because the guards will cover for him," Fallon put in.

"If we need to shoot the guards to get at Cain, we do it," Cordell added.

Adam licked his dry lips. "So, we should figure on gunplay before we reach Cain?"

"I always figure on gunplay, that's why I'm still alive."

Adam took a deep breath. "What's the plan?"

Cordell looked back at the Desert Rose. "We go in tomorrow morning and demand to see Cain."

"What do we say?" Adam asked.

"We say we are Beau Whitlock's boys. That should open the ball right then and there."

Chapter 11

The brothers finished an early breakfast and started their walk to the Desert Rose. The morning was already hot with the rising sun promising a day of intense heat. Adam and Fallon wore their heat absorbing black suit coats. They were uncomfortable, evidenced by the sweat running down their faces, but they wanted the guns on their hips covered. Cordell's buckskin jacket was lightweight and reflected heat while serving the purpose of covering his Colt.

Cordell's mind was calculating all they might encounter and how to eliminate each problem to reach Cain. He glanced at Adam to see him looking nervous. Fallon seemed cool enough, but he was a lawyer and accustomed to pressure, yet he had to admit there was a toughness to Fallon under the lawyer front.

They reached the livery and stopped to study the Desert Rose. There were no horses or vehicles in the street. The customers were the stay up late, sleep late type; however, Cordell had told his brothers to expect Cain and his staff of thugs to be in.

Cordell pulled his Colt, flipped open the loading gate and rolled the cylinder until the empty sixth chamber was under it. He slipped a cartridge into the empty spot. He closed the gate and reholstered the gun. "Fill your empty chamber," he said to his brothers. "You might need that extra shot."

Adam and Fallon both did as instructed.

The aged owner of the livery watched them from inside the barn. He had been in the country all his life and knew a shooting was headed for the Desert Rose. He had heard enough bad about Winston Cain and the place to not be surprised. Those boys were set to kill someone in there, likely Cain.

The brothers continued on until they stood in front of the house, now quiet and devoid of the activity of the previous night. Cordell spoke without looking at his brothers. "When the thugs pull their guns start shooting. Don't hesitate, don't draw a breath first thinking about it or it may well be your last. Pull your guns and start shooting because they sure will."

"Are you sure that's how it will go?" Adam asked.

Cordell turned a hard eye on Adam. "Are you up to this?"

"I guess so."

Cordell snarled, "There is no *guess so*. You *guess so* and you're going to die in there. If you're not up to it stay out here and out of the way."

Adam stared into his younger brother's fierce eyes. He wished he had Cordell's nerve. He was a brave man, but a gunfight was frightening. He suddenly became angry with his fear, drew in a deep breath and let his self-frustration out with it. "I'm with you. Let's go."

Cain had been called into his office early to deal with one of the girls who had withheld money. He was irritable at having been bothered by something Angelique should have dealt with herself. He wasn't sure if he was more aggravated with the girl or the madam. He would deal with them one at a time.

He stood looking down on a terrified young woman seated in a heavy straight back chair. Behind her stood Angelique and off to the side was Rudy with his arms crossed over his chest. It had been reported to Angelique, from one of the other girls hoping to curry favor, that the girl had kept back some money a customer had given her. The girls were required to turn all money over to Angelique and she had not.

Cain's hair was slicked and oiled, his mustache freshly waxed and twisted into points sharp enough to punch a hole in leather. He studied the girl with cruel and merciless eyes as she squirmed in fear. She had been up the entire night and exhaustion showed in her eyes as her black eye makeup dribbled down her face where her tears had streaked it.

"You think we are fools?" Cain asked her.

The girl shook her head.

"We can account for every penny that passes through this place. We hear things you don't and we heard you were given ten dollars extra from a customer last night. What are you supposed to do when you get extra money?"

The girl squeaked in a low voice, "Give it to Miss Angelique."

"Did you?"

The girl squeezed her eyes shut forcing tears to roll down her cheeks and shook her head.

Without warning Cain slapped the girl hard across the face knocking her out of the chair. She rolled into a ball on the floor weeping in fear and pain.

Angelique stared down at her with an expression of cold contempt. "There are more where she came from."

Cain bent over and grabbed the girl's hair in a hard fist and jerked her head back. "I hope it was worth it." He threw her head back down.

Standing up straight he looked at Rudy. "Get rid of her."

The sudden crash of breaking wood followed by a loud crash resounded from the lobby. Cain scowled at his closed office door, and then at Angelique. "Go see what that's all about," he snapped angrily.

Angelique left the office and headed down the hall.

She swept the hall curtain aside and hurried into the lobby to see two of the house guards confronting three men. The front door hung lopsided from the upper hinge, the only one that had not been torn off when Cordell slammed his boot into the locked door. She recognized Cordell locking a furious glare on him.

Cordell grinned at her. "You invited me back. The door was stuck so I gave it a little nudge. Seems I nudged a little too hard though."

"What do you think you're doing!" she screamed at him. "You can't kick in a door to a closed business."

"We want to see Winston Cain," Cordell said calmly.

She gave him an incredulous look mixed with rage. "*What?*"

"Winston Cain," Cordell repeated. "You know, the pile of horse manure that runs this place."

"Mr. Cain doesn't just *see* people, especially people who kick in his door."

Cordell's mild expression slowly turned cold and hard. In a low, deadly voice he said, "The son-of-a-bitch will see us."

Angelique's mouth dropped open in disbelief.

"Get him out here . . . *now!*" Cordell's sudden demand made Angelique involuntarily jump.

The two guards calmly held their place waiting for orders. Two additional guards entered the room taking up positions flanking the brothers.

Cain pushed aside the curtain and stepped out looking over the group. He took in the poised guards and the broken door. He sauntered across the lobby. "Did I hear someone call me a son-of-a-bitch?" As he drew closer he studied the brothers with a growing look of consternation in his eyes. They looked familiar.

"That would be me," Cordell said in a challenging tone.

Cain smiled without humor. "I killed the last man who called me that."

Cordell snorted, "Shot him in the back did you, or was it the head?"

Cain held a steady eye on Cordell. An uneasy

feeling began to creep up his spine. The kid looked like Beau Whitlock at a younger age. "What do you want?"

"You."

"And who are you?"

"Beau and Tessa Whitlock's boys."

The names froze Cain to the spot. His eyes widened as fear and panic welled up to consume him. He flicked his eyes back and forth to see the two extra guards working their way in closer. There were four now and two more somewhere. He began to see a way out. He gathered his wits and calmed himself. "Why should those names mean anything to me?"

Cordell grinned with malice, "You're not getting away with it."

Cain saw his guards closing in and knew he had the pat hand. His cocky confidence returned. He smiled, "Looks like I did."

Cain turned to head back to the curtained hallway, then looked back and laughed. "I gave Tessa the chance to leave with me, but she declined." With a sneer Cain flipped his hand in the air, "Boys, get rid of these miscreants." He headed for the curtained doorway with Angelique following him.

The two guards in front of the brothers pulled guns from their shoulder holsters. Cordell's hand slapped down on his Colt and brought it up driving a bullet through the thug to his right, and just as quickly shot the one standing next to him. The two men dropped to the floor.

Cain and Angelique sprinted for the curtain and disappeared behind it.

Fallon shot the guard coming in from the left side.

Adam shot the one on the right and then ran after Cain.

A guard on the stairway fired a shot that broke a lamp on a table. Cordell and Fallon both fired at him at the same time. The man fell face first and slid down the carpeted stairs. Cordell raced after Adam.

Fallon pointed his gun at the barkeep who put his hands in the air indicating he was not in the fight. Fallon lowered his gun and ran for the curtain tearing it down from the ceiling as he yanked it aside.

Angelique had stopped in the hallway attempting to block any pursuit of Cain. Adam stopped in front of her. "Lady, get out of my way."

Angelique did not reply as she slipped her hand into the hidden pocket of her dress and brought it out.

Cordell charged down the hallway shouldering into Adam knocking him up against the right side of the hall. He stepped again shouldering hard into Angelique causing her to fly into the open office to the left where she slammed into the heavy chair the girl had been in and dropped to the floor unconscious. In the hall lay a double barreled derringer.

Cordell didn't break stride as he headed for the open door showing daylight at the end of the hall. Rudy stepped into the open doorway from the outside and fired a shot at Cordell that tore into the wall papered wall. Cordell fired two shots into the man's chest and thumbed back the hammer over his last cartridge.

He leaped over the man's body at the same time he heard a hard running horse going away from him. He landed in the dirt alley in time to see Cain escaping on a horse riding at a full gallop. He fired the last cartridge at him in what he knew was a futile attempt to hit him. The shot missed.

Adam and Fallon ran out behind Cordell. "What happened?" Adam shouted excitedly.

Cordell cursed. "He had a saddled horse in that shed. He's on the run."

"We need to get after him,' Fallon snapped.

Cordell was quickly ejecting the spent brass from the Colt and reloading. Holstering the Colt he ran across the alley and opened the shed door to see the open doorway in the rear and another horse inside. Adam and Fallon were behind him. He took a quick look and found a saddle and bridle.

"Go back to that livery and get horses," Cordell instructed. "I'll saddle this one. Go!"

Fallon and Adam ran for the livery as Cordell bridled and saddled the horse in the shed. He then began to study the tracks left by Cain's horse as he waited for his brothers to return.

The girl, who was only moments away from being murdered, stared at Angelique's unconscious body. She tentatively poked her head out the office door and peered up and down the hallway. She snuck out to the lobby and saw two of the guards rolling and moaning on the floor. One on the stairs and two others lay on the floor not moving. She looked at the barkeep who had his hat on and was headed for the shattered door.

"I'm getting out of here," he said to the girl. "If you were smart, you'd get."

The girl burst out the open doorway and ran down the street toward the train station. She had money hidden in her clothes and California called to her.

Cordell led the horse as he followed Cain's trail memorizing the prints left by the horse. He knew they would have to track him. The direction of Cain's escape was east and there was nothing that way but prairie.

It took twenty minutes for Adam and Fallon to rent the horses and tack and return to Cordell. They found him down the alley leading his horse and looking at the ground. They rode up to him.

"What are doing?" Fallon asked irritably.

"Memorizing Cain's horse's tracks."

"Why?"

Irritated at losing Cain and Fallon's tone he scowled at him. "We're going to need to track him. Every track is like a signature, remember that from Pa's teaching?"

"Of course I do."

"Then, why are you asking me? You been in the city so long you forget everything you were taught?'

Fallon clenched his jaws, but didn't reply.

Cordell swung into the saddle, "Let's get on his trail before the law shows up."

"I thought they didn't come here," Adam remarked.

"I'm not interested in sticking around to find out. We've lost enough time." He kicked his horse into a lope following the way he had seen Cain disappear.

Cordell was mindful of the people he encountered making his way out of town. He had no intention of riding wildly through the streets endangering people. They'd find Cain no matter how much lead he had.

Cain's tracks were lost in the tangle of wagon and horse tracks on the street. Nearing the edge of town Cordell pulled up next to a man with a woman and child in a wagon beside a general store. "Did you see a man fly by here on a bay horse? He was dressed slick."

The man scowled, "I sure did. The darn fool blasted past here, almost run over my little girl. I shouted at him, but he kept right on going."

"Which way?"

The man pointed to the flat country out to the east. "Last I saw his dust it was that way."

"Thanks." Cordell reined over to the store.

"What are you doing?" Fallon snapped. "He's getting away."

Cordell stepped out of the saddle. "There's nothing out there but sagebrush, sand and rock. We're going to have to chase him and we won't make it without water.

"So what are you doing?"

Cordell answered without looking at Fallon. "Buying canteens. Then, we're going to fill 'em at the town pump, and ride that man down."

Chapter 12

Cain brought the hard running horse down to a walk once all aspects of the city were far behind him. All that surrounded him now was miles of open country covered in sand, sage, and mesquite. The bay was digging hard for air as white lather dripped from the edges of the bit and his body shone with sweat in the bright sun. Cain knew killing the horse wouldn't serve his purposes. There was little sense in keeping a saddled horse only to run it to death two miles out of town.

He peered across the horizon to the east as the sun rose higher in the sky. It was already hot and he was out in the middle of some of the most inhospitable country in the west. He was quickly coming to realize the flaws in his escape plan. He had a saddled horse with a bedroll tied to the cantle. A Colt .45 with extra ammunition was in the saddlebags along with some slabs of dried beef. What he had forgotten was far more critical, water and a hat.

He turned in the saddle and studied his backtrail. El Paso had disappeared and the open land behind him held no rising dust cloud or indication that he was being pursued. He knew intimately the country east of San Antonio, the Indian Territory, and Arkansas. All he knew about this was the trail he had ridden to El Paso several years before, and that was a sketchy memory at best.

He cursed himself for a fool. He had lost his razor sharp edge and savvy wallowing in the midst of his easy lifestyle. He had gotten soft and stupid, evidenced by the fact he walked right into that mess in the house lobby. Now, he was out here wondering which way to go.

Turning back and forth in the saddle he scanned the country around him. Sand, rocks, and sage to all sides. To the south was Mexico, but no decent gambler would give you good odds of an American surviving in Mexico right now or avoiding a Mexican prison. Aside from that, his pursuers could follow him into Mexico. He needed to stay on this side of the border.

His mind wandered back to the Desert Rose. He had no idea Whitlock had sons. He should have sought out that information before taking the course of action he did. He only saw the opportunity to enact his revenge on the thief and the woman who jilted him for the man who had become his enemy. He had no regrets for killing them, he only regretted his mistake of carelessly putting himself in a position to be discovered.

How had he been discovered anyway? Obviously the fire failed to destroy the bodies. The blonde haired kid had made the comment about shooting them in the head. They had found out. Another mistake. How had they traced it to him though? That was a mystery he may never know the answer to. In the end, all that mattered was they had and he needed to get away.

He searched the country behind him. Nothing. He had expected pursuit . . . unless his men had killed them. A glimmer of hope and relief rose up in him. If they were dead he could go right back. Then, he remembered the blonde kid's eyes.

The image of a young Beau Whitlock hovered in his memory. The kid looked just like him and he threw a gun every bit as fast as Whitlock. He had seen enough to know the kid had beat the first two guards. With all the shooting that had gone on behind him anything could be the outcome. He worried on it for several minutes. The other two didn't look all that formidable, but that kid did. Would Beau Whitlock have survived that encounter? He knew he would have and if that kid was half of what Beau was, he did.

He needed to know for sure if they were after him. He needed to stop and see, but if they were that would only serve to let them catch up. He had a lead and he needed to keep it. On the other hand there was no reason to torture himself out here if he didn't need to run. He had a choice to make, keep going or wait and see.

The country around him offered nothing high enough to see back a couple of miles. The ragged bare mountain chain rose to his right, but they were a long way off. The safest bet was to keep going until he found a place high enough to climb up and look back. He wished now he had a hat and water and he wasn't wearing a tightly tailored suit unfit for riding. He had forgotten a change of clothes as well.

To the east was nothing. To the south he would eventually intersect the mountains or at least some land high enough to climb and look back. Bits of memory were coming back to him. He had come up that way from San Antonio. There was a smattering of miner shacks along the way and what passed as a two-bit settlement. If memory served him the settlement was not all that far. He wracked his mind for the location. It didn't matter, he'd either be going on to San Antonio or back to El Paso.

Reining the horse over he put the sun to his left shoulder and headed toward the bare peaks of the mountains in the distance. He would find the first high spot and study his backtrail which was clear enough to follow if those boys of Whitlock's could track. The kid could, he had seen it in his eyes, he was savvy and tough. If they were after him he'd keeping heading south and figure out what to do from there.

Once the brothers had cleared the town and the maze of tracks, Cordell cast back and forth in a wide arch trying to pick up Cain's trail. He knew what the shoe prints of Cain's horse looked like and his would likely be the only fresh trail dug deep in the sand by a fast moving horse.

They lost another hour searching until Cordell shouted out that he had the trail. Adam and Fallon rode up next to him to look.

Cordell pointed out the clear churned up sand. "He's still at a gallop, but if he keeps it up that horse will drop dead."

"We can hope that happens," Adam said, his

tone reflecting a crestfallen tone.

"Don't count on it. Cain's an old time outlaw, he won't want to be on foot."

They took to the trail at a lope trying to make up some of the lost time. Cordell kept one eye on the trail and one on the lay of the land. When the horses began to labor for breath they dropped them down to a walk.

"Any chance he'll lay an ambush for us?" Fallon asked.

Cordell frowned. "It's possible, but he'd need a rifle to do it. Country's too open for a pistol, we'd see him."

"What's to say he doesn't have a rifle?"

"Nothing," Cordell answered. "We'll keep our eyes open. That's all we can do."

They followed on until Cain's churned up trail became simply a line of hoof tracks. "He's walking now," Cordell commented.

Staying on the tracks that were still aiming east they kept an eye out all around. The trail made an abrupt turn to the south. Cordell pulled his horse up and narrowed his eyes against the sun-bright sand as he studied the country to the south.

"He's going into Mexico," Fallon commented.

"I doubt it," Cordell answered. "Mexico's unfriendly to Americans right now, I'm sure Cain knows that. If he wants to get away that's the wrong place to go."

"But, he's headed south," Fallon argued.

"The border runs north to south right here, then swings east to west. He's going to head for the mountains where he can hide and there might be water. He'll either skirt or take to the mountains on the American side."

"You seem to know this country," Adam said.

"I've rode it a time or two," Cordell replied as he searched the horizon.

"Any ranches along this way?" Fallon asked.

"Not that I know of, but there are some miners living up against the mountains. We can get water from them."

Adam stood in the stirrups and scanned the miles of open country around him. "Any towns down this way?"

"About a hundred miles south is a rough little settlement. A couple hours south of it is Van Horn Wells, used to be a Butterfield stagestop there."

"That's it, huh?"

"That's it. A few years back the Rangers were chasing Victorio and his Apaches all over that country. So, there hasn't been a lot of settling through here."

Fallon asked, "Think Cain will head for that stage stop and take a stage out of here?"

"Butterfield doesn't use it anymore. It's just a shack now and a water hole."

Fallon looked around him. "I'm not sure what Cain thinks to accomplish by heading into this country. He probably doesn't know either."

Cordell looked at Fallon. "You're right, he doesn't know. He's running scared that's all. We'll stay on him until we tree him."

"That could take quite a while," Adam mumbled.

Cordell looked disgustedly at Adam. "More'n likely. If you're worried about Laura and the ranch you can head on back."

"No. I'm committed to this."

Cordell held the look. "Good." He glanced over at Fallon, "How about you?"

Fallon threw his brother a dirty look, "What about me?"

"You stickin' or heading back for the comforts of town?"

Fallon nudged his horse up beside Cordell's and glared directly into his face. "You're not the only one in this family with sand. I'll go you step-for-step, mile-for-mile and best you at anything."

Cordell never flinched as he met his brother's angry glare. An amused smile crossed his lips. "You might turn out alright after all."

The sun was dropping down the western side of the sky before Cain found a hill high enough to climb where he could see for miles down his backtrail. He urged the tired horse up the hill to the top and peered intensely to the north. He could see several miles of flat sand and low rolling hills speckled with sage and brush. The lowering sun eliminated the shimmering walls of heat that obliterated a long distance view. He held his hand over his eyes to shield the sun off and again cussed himself for not including a hat in his escape plan.

He searched the country for several minutes. Seeing nothing that looked like riders he began to relax thinking that his hired men might have killed the Whitlock boys after all. He could head back home.

His cracked lips and parched throat ached for water. There was plenty of water back at the Desert Rose. Then, he spotted movement. He squinted and studied the movement, it was well to the north. Then, it disappeared. He decided it was animals or just the sun playing tricks with his eyes.

His face and neck were burned and blistering. He had thrown away the ridiculous tie and collar and shed his expensive coat tying it on top of the bedroll. It wasn't until he was thoroughly cooked that it dawned on him to hang his coat over his head and neck in Arab fashion for protection.

He nudged the horse with his heels to descend the hill thinking that he would never go out in the sun again. He looked up to give the country one last scan to make sure the movement was nothing. The thing he had seen was back as it topped a distant rise. He pulled back on the reins stopping the horse. To his dismay the object separated into three individual objects that now resembled three riders and they were on his trail.

He cursed bitterly as he watched. The movement was definitely three riders. It didn't take much imagination to figure out who they were. He tried to think of his next move. His choices were Mexico, which was the worst choice. Finding a way to cut back to El Paso, bypassing the Whitlocks; however, would require wandering miles out into the open prairie leaving an easy trail for them to follow. That was a futile effort at best. His third choice was the most practical, to just go on to San Antonio. He could hide out in San Antonio, and then come back when the Whitlocks had lost him.

He reined the horse back to the south angling toward the bare rock mountains to his right and kept riding. He needed water and food. He had rejected eating the dried beef for fear of choking to death on it without water to wash it down. That little settlement would have food and water, he was sure it was only a few more miles.

Hours passed until the sun hung low over the western horizon. He had reached the base of the mountains, but not the settlement. The rocking of the horse had lulled him into exhausted sleep as his coat flopped around his painfully burned and blistered face. His tongue was swollen and he was feeling sick from the sun and dehydration. He needed water and shelter from the sun.

In the fading light he saw the settlement in the distance. He had finally made it. He forced the exhausted, thirst wracked horse to continue on. The bay dragged its hooves in the sand. He mentally cursed the animal's slowness as his mouth was incapable of forming words. He swayed side-to-side until the horse came to a stop up against the rails of a corral.

Cain forced his burned eyelids to open over his sand and wind reddened eyes to see a shack alongside the corral. His spirit sank, it wasn't the settlement, but there might be water. He slid off the horse being mindful to tie the animal to a corral rail lest it ran off. He stumbled around the shack until he found a door and pushed it open and fell on his face inside.

Throwing the coat off his head he got up on his hands and knees and looked around. There was a wooden bucket of water on the floor, he crawled to it and stuck his face in the heat warmed water. He sucked in water and let his tongue and lips soak in it. Lifting his head up he felt slightly better. Looking around it was evident someone lived in the shack.

There were clothes and food.

Taking another drink he sat on the floor feeling thoroughly dazed and exhausted. He needed to stay here until he recuperated, but wondered how long he could before the Whitlocks caught up to him. Looking out the window he saw the brilliant sunset. They wouldn't follow in the dark as it was too easy to lose the trail if they did. That gave him the night to rest.

His mind was working slowly as he tried to think out a plan to escape his pursuers. The dullness of his thought process was aggravating. He had gotten soft and he hated the feeling. In the past he had always been hard as a rock and nothing could weaken him. So he was sixty years old, what was that? He would use this rest period to get his edge back and escape the hounds.

The sound of a horse's hoof falls drifted through the open door. He wondered if they could have caught up this fast. It was impossible, he was miles ahead of them, but what if it was? As he thought it, he pulled his pistol from the shoulder holster and waited to see who came in the door.

A man wearing dirty, worn work clothes walked in the door and cast an angry glare on him. The man snarled, "What are you doing in my house?"

Cain was unable to speak past his swollen tongue. He looked up at the man from his place on the floor.

"I'm not running a charity for saddle tramps, get out!"

Cain knew he needed to stay in the shack. He needed the water, food, and shelter it offered in order to get back on his feet and stay ahead of his hunters.

It irritated him that the man was so inhospitable as to not only refuse to render aid, but to throw out a man in his condition.

The shack had all he needed to survive and self-preservation had always been Winston Cain's number one priority. He thought it amusing the things a man notices when he is close to delirium. The foul tempered man standing over him was wearing a wide brimmed hat. He needed a hat like that.

The miner glared down at the man on his floor, growing angrier by the second because he was not jumping up to get out as ordered. "I'll throw you out then," he snarled. He charged forward.

Cain lifted the pistol and shot him in the forehead. The man's head snapped back as his eyes rolled up to only whites. He fell straight down to the floor.

Cain struggled to his feet and holstered the pistol. He picked up the man's hat and put it on his head. He stepped over the dead man and out the door. He looked around and saw no one else.

Tied next to his bay was a saddled strawberry roan with a filled canteen slung over the horn. There was also a bucket of water outside the door. He wasn't sure where the water source was; however, this gave him enough water for his needs. Taking the canteen and picking up the bucket he went back inside.

Remembering his horse, Cain carried the bucket of water he had soaked his face in out the door. Unsaddling the bay he looked at the roan and had an idea. He took the miner's saddle off the roan and threw it behind the shack. He put his saddle on the roan and put the bucket of water down in front of the roan. The horse buried its muzzle in the bucket and quickly sucked it dry.

Leading the bay out a ways to the east he slipped the bridle off and slapped the reins hard across the horse's rump. The horse jumped and bolted away. Cain laughed to himself. The Whitlocks could follow that horse. He would ride south on the roan and cover his tracks. By the time they figure it out, if ever, he would be in San Antonio.

Returning to the shack he searched it over and found a can of peaches, canned meat, and a pot of cooked beans on the cold stove. Further checking revealed a cigar box containing knives, forks, spoons, and a can opener. He quickly opened the can of peaches and stuck a peach slice in his mouth and let the juice soak into the dry tissue. He sighed with relief.

He didn't want to keep looking at the dead man on the floor and didn't have the strength to drag him outside. He found a canvas tarp and threw it over the corpse. The feet and one arm stuck out, but enough was covered so he didn't have to have a corpse for a dinner companion.

He ate the remainder of the peaches. He spooned up the beans eating them cold from the pot along with the canned meat. Drinking most of the canteen's contents he refilled it from the bucket. Between the food and water he was feeling better. Laying down on the bed he fell asleep.

Chapter 13

Adam glanced at the setting sun and the brilliant streaks of orange and red swirled into the blue of the sky. It was a beautiful sunset, unfortunately it reminded him that they had not planned for a chase. They had no food or warm clothes for the night's chill. He said as much to his brothers.

Fallon mumbled, "We'll get by."

Cordell turned in the saddle and looked at Adam. He wanted to tell him to stop whining, but held his tongue. "Don't worry about it, Adam."

"I could sure use something to eat, it's been a long time since breakfast."

Cordell shook his head and continued riding. Cain's trail had led them closer to the mountains. He kept his eyes and ears open until he heard a familiar sound, the collected peeps and cooings of a quail covey. The quail turned his thinking to that night's camp. The birds would be searching for a safe place to roost for the night.

Pulling his horse to a stop he looked in the

direction the quail sounds had come from.

"What are you looking at?" Fallon asked.

"Supper," Cordell replied. "Listen."

"There," Cordell pointed at a covey of a couple dozen quail working their way into a cluster of mesquite and sage.

Stepping off his horse Cordell tied him to a mesquite bush. He looked at his brothers who remained mounted. "I could use your help," his voice held a hint of irritation.

Adam and Fallon dismounted and tied off their horses as Cordell pulled his knife and cut three multi twigged mesquite branches. He handed one to each of his brothers and explained. "We surround that thicket where the quail went in. They're roosting in and won't fly if we move in slow. Once we're on top of them they'll fly, but get slowed down in the branches. Just start swattin' 'em down as they fly by you."

Adam and Fallon nodded their understanding and followed Cordell's lead as he directed them how to surround the quail. Moving in slowly they could see the quail bunching together and fidgeting nervously. Suddenly, with an explosion of beating wings the entire covey burst into flight. The brothers swung at the escaping birds as fast as they could swing the branches.

In seconds the covey was fifty yards away and still flying. On the ground lay six birds, three of which Cordell had swatted down. He picked up the birds by their feet and handed two each to his brothers. "Supper," was all he said as he walked back to his horse.

Adam and Fallon caught up to him. "Are we

eating these raw?" Fallon carped at Cordell.

Cordell pulled the cinch knot loose and began unsaddling his horse. "You can do whatever you want with yours. I prefer mined cooked."

"How do you plan on making a fire?"

Cordell ignored Fallon as he placed his saddle on the ground beside the bush. He walked off and began breaking branches off a dead mesquite tree and dried tumble weed. He walked to a spot clear of sage and laid the branches for a fire. Reaching a hand into his jacket pocket he brought out a tin box. Opening it he removed a full box of Lucifer matches, struck one on his thumb and lit the branches. He put the matches back in the tin box and returned it to his pocket. He never spoke a word as his brothers watched him.

Cordell next cut two long inch thick green branches and trimmed them clean. He pulled the feathers off his two quail, cleaned them, impaled them on the sticks, and jammed the ends into the ground letting the raw birds hang over the flames. He added more wood to the fire. Picking up his saddle he set it beside the fire and sat back against it.

Adam looked embarrassed and quickly followed Cordell's example. Fallon scowled and reluctantly did as his brothers had done. Adam walked out and brought in an armful of dead mesquite branches. They sat down around the fire in silence.

Cordell was frustrated with what he perceived as weakness in his brothers. He wondered what had happened to them, they had the same father. He supposed they had merely chosen different paths from him. Paths that made them soft as far as he was concerned.

Night had fallen before Adam broke the awkward silence. "Good thing you had matches."

Cordell nodded without a reply. He started eating his first bird.

Adam sighed. "I've spent too many years walking to the cook shack or Laura having supper on the table for me. Guess, I've forgotten how to do a lot of things. Maybe I have been sheltered."

Cordell picked at the hot meat. "Pa always said to keep matches on you at all times. Between those and your brain there's no reason to go hungry."

Adam nodded. "I do remember him saying that. I'm starting to remember a lot of things he said. Being out here is bringing them back."

"I use what he taught me every day," Cordell replied. "My biggest regret is that when I left home I didn't come back enough to see the folks. I figured they'd be around a long time yet. Pa was my best friend."

Fallon stared into the flames in silence as he ate his birds. A look of agitation was on his face.

"You're a lot like Pa," Adam said.

"Is that bad?"

"No, not at all. You're just like him more than I am . . . I guess."

"We chose different paths, Adam. You got married at nineteen and settled right down. How long now?"

"Laura and I have been married three years. We stayed on the ranch from day one."

"You went to work for Red at what, seventeen?"

"Yeah, that's how I met Laura."

"That's okay. That's the path you have chosen."

Adam frowned. "I only wish I hadn't lost all the skills I learned and you retained."

Cordell shrugged, "This little adventure will bring it back."

Adam studied his younger brother for several minutes. They were only two years apart, but worlds were between them. Cordell was a survivor, tough and capable. He had a reputation as a troublemaker and a gunfighter, but he knew there was a lot more to his brother than that. He felt the need to catch up to him in a lot of ways.

"I remember what Pa taught," Fallon snapped defensively. "So, you had matches, so what? I'm wearing my suit, I don't usually go riding in a suit. If I was in my riding clothes I'd have matches too."

Cordell turned his eyes toward Fallon. "You remember everything Pa taught you?"

Fallon glared into the fire. "You aren't the only one who knows something."

"Then, get your eyes off that fire," Cordell rebuked.

Fallon's head snapped up as he glared at Cordell, "What?"

"If you remember everything then you remember Pa saying to never stare into a fire because it ruins your night vision."

"I'm not looking in the fire," Fallon argued back. He threw the last bird bone into the fire and skidded backward away from it. He stretched out on the sand with his head on his saddle.

"Whatever you say, Slick," Cordell responded.

"You don't know everything," Fallon

growled. "I've got an education and a law degree. You've got a box of matches, I'm not impressed."

"Your education and law degree didn't feed you tonight, did it?"

"I can shoot every bit as good as you, too. I nailed two of those thugs back at Cain's."

"You did that alright," Cordell agreed. "Nice shooting."

Fallon turned his head and looked at Cordell a bit surprised by his compliment. "So, don't think you're the only one."

Cordell studied Fallon. He could never quite figure him out. He stuck up for him against Scott, and that snooty conductor, but all other times he seemed to hate his guts. There had been issues between them all along in the past.

"What made you want to be a lawyer?" Cordell asked.

"I like the law."

"You broke it today when you shot those thugs."

"The law doesn't cover every contingency. Sometimes you have to deal with criminals in other ways."

"Maybe you should have been a lawman instead."

"There's more of a future in being a lawyer, but a gunfighter wouldn't understand that."

Cordell snorted, "Your *future* sure did a fine job with Ma and Pa, didn't it?"

Fallon clenched his jaws and rolled over on his side turning his back to his brother. "Go to the devil, Cordell."

Accustomed to rising early, Adam and Cordell stirred at first light. It had been a cool night with nothing to cover themselves with but their jackets and saddle blankets. Fallon sat up and rubbed his hands over his face. He threw a dirty look at Cordell as he stood up and began to saddle his horse.

Adam glanced at both of his brothers and sighed at the animosity he saw between them. He broke the mood with a laugh. "Cordell, you wouldn't happen to have some bacon and eggs in that jacket of yours would you?"

Cordell patted the buckskin jacket all around. "I thought I did, but I must have lost them."

Once saddled the brothers set off on Cain's trail. The tracks were beginning to fill with loose sand as the edges began breaking down. There was still enough of a trail left to follow even though the individual tracks were becoming obscured.

It was late-morning when they arrived at the shack along Cain's trail. "Looks like Cain pulled in here," Cordell commented.

"We should check with whoever lives here and find out if he's seen Cain," Adam suggested.

"He definitely came here. If anyone lives here he probably did see him."

Cordell stepped off his horse and walked to the door. He knocked hard on the plank door and waited. He looked up at Adam and shrugged. He pushed on the door and it opened slightly.

"Anyone in here?" Cordell called into the opening. He pushed the door the rest of the way open.

The first thing he saw was the canvas covered mound on the floor. A closer look and he could see worn work books and an arm sticking out, and a pool of congealed blood showing from the edges of the cover. He stepped back out and looked at his brothers. "There's a dead man in here."

Adam dismounted and walked to the door. Looking in past Cordell he saw the covered body. "Think Cain killed him?"

Cordell moved carefully to the body and lifted the canvas off the head of the corpse. "Shot in the forehead. I'd say it was Cain."

Cordell left the cabin closing the door behind him.

"Should we bury him?" Adam asked.

"We don't have time for that," Cordell answered.

"It would be the decent thing to do," Fallon remarked with a surely tone.

Cordell didn't look at Fallon. "Then, you bury him." He began to circle the shack looking for tracks.

Fallon called out, "Hey, smart boy, he went this way."

Cordell walked to where Fallon sat on his horse pointing at the tracks of an eastbound running horse. He gave the dug in tracks a close look and then scanned the country around him.

Adam walked up beside him. "Looks like he changed directions."

"That's what has me wondering."

Adam look at him confused, "What do you mean?"

"There's nothing to the east, but rugged wild country. If he wants to make a town south is the only direction."

"He could be circling around to go back to El

Paso," Fallon said still holding the surely tone.

"He could, but I doubt it. He's not sure if it's safe to go back, we could be waiting for him for all he knows."

"Maybe he knows we're following him and he figures to double back on us. Ever think of that?"

"If he knows we're following him and wants to make a sneaky move around us why leave a trail a blind man could follow. No, it doesn't add up."

Fallon stiffened with indignation. "You're just being contrary because it was my idea. I can track too and it's obvious he went this way."

Cordell looked up at Fallon with a calm expression. "Then, follow it."

"You're not coming?"

"I think it's a false trail, but you're the one with the God almighty education and law degree so you must be right. I'm only a gunfighter and a bum with an unimpressive box of matches. Follow it for all I care. If you're right and you come on him shoot him. If you find a bareback horse you can catch up to us."

Fallon snarled at Cordell, "I will." He jerked his horse's head around and put him into a lope following the eastward trail."

"I've never seen him this bad," Adam commented.

"He's got a burr under his saddle for me," Cordell answered. "We don't get along, never have."

Adam shook his head. "I guess. Why don't you think this is the right trail?"

"For the same reasons I just said. As soon as that horse stops running you'll see the tracks are sinking only a bit into the sand because there is no saddle or rider to make for deeper tracks."

"Why do you think there's no saddle or rider?"

Cordell pointed into the corral behind the shack to the saddle carelessly thrown on the ground. "Two men, one dead, one gone, no horses, although tracks indicate two horses were here, and a saddle thrown away. Why would Cain throw his saddle away? I doubt he plans on riding another seventy miles bareback. That means Cain is riding one saddled horse and . . ."

"And the other was sent off that way to throw us off the track," Adam finished the sentence."

Cordell grinned at him, "See, you're catching up already."

Adam smiled. "I swear I'm going to get my skills back up to snuff."

"Come on," Cordell said. "We need to find where Cain left out of here and see if the tracks are his old horse or if he took the dead man's. I want to see those tracks."

Adam followed Cordell as he slowly circled the shack and corral.

Completing the circle Adam commented, "There are no other tracks leading out of here."

"Cain brushed them out."

"That proves he knows we're on his trail. A false trail and brushed out tracks, he's smarter than we thought."

"He's an old time outlaw, he's no fool. He got caught flatfooted that's all and he has to get his bearings again. Once he does he's going to be one smart old he-coon."

"Looks like he already has his bearings."

Cordell nodded. "It does appear so. I'm sure he still intends to head south to that settlement."

"What's beyond it?"

Cordell glanced at Adam, "San Antonio."

"If he gets to San Antonio we'll never find him."

"That's his plan."

"Then, we'd better get him first."

Cordell smiled at Adam, "Now, you're sounding like a Monroe."

"Or a Whitlock," Adam grinned back at him.

Cordell chuckled. He began walking a sweeping search for evidence of the trail.

"Why don't we go right to that settlement and cut him off?" Adam asked.

"Because, I might be wrong and he'll cut off someplace else. We have to stay on his trail to make sure we end up where he ends up."

"Just as long as it's not San Antonio," Adam said with a frown.

"That would be bad. The man who lived here must have had a water supply why don't you try and find it while I unravel this."

Adam went off as Cordell continued his search concentrating on the south side of the shack. He began to pick up on a side-to-side sweeping pattern in the sand that was inconsistent with the ground around it. He walked bent over examining the sweeping strokes. Fifty yards out from the shack he stood up straight looking north and south. The sweeping strokes became an obvious path going south.

Adam walked up to him with their canteens full. He handed Cordell's to him. "He had a hole dug down in a dry wash to the waterline and the hole was full of water."

"Good. There was a bucket by the shack for the horses." Cordell took a long drink from his canteen.

"Already took care of that, they're drinking. What have you found?"

Cordell tipped his chin to the north than south. "What do you see?"

Adam studied the sand for several minutes before a light of revelation lit in his eyes. "There's a straight line of back and forth brush marks."

"That's it. He's getting crafty. Let's go."

"What about Fallon?"

"Once he finds that bareback horse we'll see him."

"He's going to be in a foul mood."

Cordell snorted, "Now, that would certainly be unusual, Mr. Law Degree in a bad mood. Come on."

Chapter 14

Cain was still laughing to himself two hours after leaving the shack. He was certain the hunters would be thrown off by his tricks. It had worked on lawmen in the past. It had taken time he didn't have to keep going back and brushing out his tracks for over a hundred yards, but the time he spent would gain him his escape in the end. He had several hours lead on them to begin with and once they went off chasing the other horse he would gain that much more.

The blisters and burns on his face and neck were painful, but he now had a hat and water and that made all the difference in how good he felt about his chances. He had obviously misjudged the location of the tiny settlement. He wrote the miscalculation off to it being years since he came through it the one time. Shrugging to himself he knew he would reach it eventually. Then on to San Antonio and disappear for a while.

He knew Angelique would hope him dead so she could take over the house. Never trust a calculating woman that didn't possess a single moral fiber in her being. He couldn't help but grin when he thought of the shocked look on her painted face when he walked back in and put her in her place. She and Rudy were sure to be at each other's throats. The thought of those two butting heads came to him as funny. He didn't care, as long as they kept making money for him until he got back.

Cain's mind wandered back to the San Antonio days. There were still people he knew there who would give him shelter and assistance. Beau Whitlock had betrayed him there by stealing Tessa from him. There was also the issue of his stealing the bank robbery money, but it was finding him married to Tessa that threw him into the fit that brought the guns out. Rube had tried to back his play, but he was never a patch on Beau when it came to shooting.

He sulked as he recalled that Tessa had never responded to his promises to make her a happy and wealthy woman. It certainly wasn't because she abhorred outlaws, because Whitlock was as bad as they came. To this day he wondered what the difference between them was in her eyes.

He had run after the gunfight with Beau, not because he was a coward though. He had justified this course of action many times over until he came to deny that he ever had run. In turn, he set the blame for all his difficulties squarely on Beau and Tessa, but none of it mattered any longer, he had wreaked his vengeance on them both.

The confrontation in the Desert Rose was unexpected. He had walked out of his office to see what the commotion was all about. He had thought it was some disgruntled fool who had lost at the tables or that idiot barkeep dropping a box. Then, he looked into Beau Whitlock's eyes. For a moment he thought Beau had come back as a ghost, but it was worse than a ghost. It was the flesh and blood recreation of the man he hated, and the kid epitomized his father to a fault.

The old anger welled up whenever he thought of Beau Whitlock. He had fixed him though, he had fixed them both. He pushed aside the voice inside his head that reminded him that once again he was running from Beau Whitlock.

Thinking of Beau made him wonder, would Beau have fallen for the ruse he laid out back at the shack? He knew Beau would never have been fooled. How well had he trained that boy of his? Would he fall for it? The other two would, he could see they weren't on the same level as the kid, but would the kid? The thought worried him and suddenly his lead didn't seem so great.

The flat country was melding into the mountains with higher hills pushing up out of the sage. Reining the horse toward the highest hill he could see, he rode toward it. Reaching the base of the hill he pushed the horse to the top and looked out over the expanse of arid country. The land that appeared flat from the surface, when looked on from above, showed washes, dips, arroyos, and all manner of places that could hide any number of men.

Huge white clouds drifted through the brilliant blue sky casting shadows over the land as they crossed between the sun and earth. The mix of light and dark on the land made it difficult to spot something as small as riders in the vastness of the arid prairie. He scanned the country thoroughly for dust clouds or objects that could be mounted men. With a satisfied sigh of relief he saw nothing of the kind.

Maybe the kid wasn't as smart as he gave him credit for or maybe he simply had a better lead than he thought. He reined the horse around and rode down off the hill and continued south. San Antonio as getting closer all the time.

Cordell and Adam rode along the sweep marks in the sand. Then, as if coming out of the ground, was the trail of a single shod horse. Adam grinned at Cordell.

Cordell pointed at a thick leaf covered branch lying several yards off the trail. "There's what he used."

Adam looked at the branch and nodded. "Clever."

"It's an old trick, but a good one."

"You learned it from Pa?"

Cordell smiled at the memory. "It was one of the times him and I went out hunting for a few days. While we out in the desert looking for deer he was teaching me all about tracking and how to hide a trail. He showed me tricks he used to use to escape Apaches."

Adam stared off into the desert. "I should have spent more time with him." His tone was melancholy.

"Why didn't you?"

"I don't know. I Guess I had other things going on that at the time seemed more important. Now, I know what was important and I've lost those opportunities forever."

Cordell studied his brother's doleful face.

"I've noticed you start off saying something with the words 'I guess' a lot. Aren't you sure of what you're saying or thinking?"

Adam was silent for several seconds. "I do use those words a lot don't I? Guess . . ." he shook his head. "I don't seem to have the ability to say straight out what I mean. I'm never sure of my own thoughts or . . ." he faded off.

"Or the courage of your convictions?"

"Maybe. I've never really been tested, and . . ."

"And what?"

"Dang it, you make me nervous, Cordell." Adam said with emotion. "You are younger than me and have done so much more and experienced so much more than I have. You have been tested over and again and proven your mettle. I herd cows, and have never been put to the test."

"You're being tested now, and you're doing a good job of proving your mettle. When this is over you won't ever say 'I guess' again," Cordell assured him.

"Thanks. I still wish I had spent more time with Pa."

"After Fallon went off to school and you were working on Red's ranch it was just Pa and I. We talked and rode out a lot. He didn't really care to be locked into that store living a tame city life. I believe he wanted to pass his knowledge on to someone and I was a sponge soaking it all in. I asked and he showed me."

"You were the smart one, Cordell."

The two rode in silence for several minutes skirting the base of the sheer rock mountains to their right. Adam broke the silence. "You were right about the other trail being a ruse. Too bad Fallon didn't listen."

Cordell snorted, "He's too high and mighty with his fancy education to listen to the likes of me."

Adam looked at his brother. "Fallon doesn't hate you."

"Could have fooled me."

"He stuck up for you twice since we've been together."

"I wonder why? Seems it would soil his finely educated self to do so, then again aren't lawyers noted liars?" He cast a glance at Adam.

"Fallon's not a liar, Cordell."

Cordell was silent for a moment, then said, "No, he's not. But he is a puzzle."

"You know, I don't think Fallon wanted to go to law school."

Cordell looked at Adam, "What makes you say that?"

"Just a hunch. He was talking marriage to Helen and had a job at Uncle Elwood's bank. He seemed happy and then he headed off to law school in Waco leaving everything. I only saw him a few times in the years after that and when I did, he was not a happy man."

"Huh. I always thought it was his idea."

"I'm not so sure it was."

"Whose was it then?"

Adam shrugged. "The folks maybe."

"Why does he hate me so much then?"

Adam looked Cordell squarely in the face. "I think it's because he was forced into something he didn't want and you are footloose, doing what you please, and it was with Pa's approval."

"Meaning?"

"He envies you."

Cordell barked a laugh thick with sarcasm. "Envies me? I doubt that."

"Don't doubt it, in a lot of ways I envy you too."

"That's the reason I make you nervous?"

"Don't get me wrong, I love Laura and I've got a good place at the ranch, but I missed a lot that you didn't. You learned a lot from Pa and spent time with him. Now that he's gone I see how much I missed. Your life is filled with adventure and mine is staid. You're lucky, Cordell."

Cordell shrugged, "I figure a man makes his own luck."

"By making the right choices."

Cordell chuckled, "I don't think Clay Scott or Virgil Earp would agree with that."

"I mean in the choices you made with Pa."

Cordell sighed. "I didn't come back much after I left and I sorely regret that."

The angry buzz of a hornet zipped past Adam's ear. He threw his hand up over his ear and yelped. "What the heck was that, a hornet?"

The report from a rifle sounded from behind them as another hornet zipped in between them followed by a second rifle report. Cordell turned quickly to see a man galloping toward them with a rifle at his shoulder. Another report sounded. "Hornet, nothing, we're being shot at."

The two kicked their horses into a gallop away from the shooter.

"What's his problem?" Adam shouted.

"Why don't you go ask him," Cordell shouted back.

Cordell swung his horse in an arch toward an outcrop of rocks that led up to the barren mountain side. Shots continued to sound from behind them. Pulling his horse to a sliding stop behind the rocks, he jumped out of the saddle as a bullet ricocheted with a deadly whine off the rocks. Adam jumped off behind him.

Cordell peeked out from around the rock to see the man still coming on. Another bullet smacked into the rock and whined away. It was a long shot for a .45 but Cordell wanted to let the shooter know it wasn't all his way. He fired a shot at the rider as did Adam.

The rider jerked his horse over to the rocks and bailed off. He fired another shot at them then ducked in behind the rocks.

Cordell cursed under his breath. "We don't have time for this. Cain's getting farther ahead while we play siege the castle with this idiot."

Cordell shouted out to the man. "Why are you shooting at us?"

"Why?" the man shouted back. "You yellow bellied cowards killed my partner back at the shack."

"That wasn't us."

"And you're a liar. I followed your tracks from the shack."

"He was dead when we stopped there."

"Liar." The man fired two more shots that hit the rocks around them.

Cordell scowled toward Adam. "We could be doing this all day."

Adam peeked over the rocks. "Let me try."

Adam shouted out, "We know the man who killed your partner. He murdered our parents in Tucson and we've come to get him. We jumped him in El Paso and he took off this way. When we got to the shack your partner was already dead. He killed him, not us."

"Hogwash," the man shouted back.

Adam looked at Cordell and shrugged. "Now what?"

Cordell shouted out, "Do you plan on staying there shooting at us for the rest of your life?"

"Only for the rest of your lives," came the angry reply.

Cordell began to study the rocks. He asked Adam as he looked up, "What, he's about fifty, sixty yards from us?"

"About that. What are you thinking?"

"I'm thinking I can slip up through that gap in the rocks, work my way towards and above him until I can get the drop on him."

Adam looked at the route his brother referred to. "You might be able to at that. You plan on killing him?"

"Only if he won't listen to reason. How many cartridges do you have?"

Adam checked his belt. "Five in the gun and a dozen on the belt."

"That ain't much. Okay, don't waste 'em. Fire one at him every half minute, enough to keep his head down."

Cordell made his move toward the upward route. "Now."

Adam fired a shot that smacked the rock three feet from where the man was hiding. He continued to pace his shots while keeping an eye on Cordell's progress. The shooter in the rocks returned fire.

Cordell couldn't see the man, but had the rocks he was in pinpointed. He wormed his way through the crease on the rocks keeping cover between him and the shooter as much as possible. Each time Adam fired he made a big move closer. After a few minutes he was above and slightly behind the shooter. The man was probably seventy years old or at least looked it. He was so intent on watching Adam that he never looked up or around.

Adam fired again and the man ducked down trying to look around the rocks. When he shouldered his rifle to shoot back. Cordell threw a fist sized rock that hit the man hard on the shoulder. The force and surprise of the impact knocked him over onto his side.

The man looked up to see Cordell pointing his Colt at him. He lay still looking back at Cordell.

"Get up you darn fool," Cordell ordered. "Leave the rifle and walk out in the open."

The man held his hands out and struggled to his feet.

"He's coming out," Cordell shouted back to Adam.

Adam walked out from his hiding place, gun in hand, and made his way toward the man who was now standing in the open with his hands in the air.

Cordell climbed down from his place in the rocks picking up the dropped rifle when he reached it. He could see the old man had no other gun on him.

The man's eyes shifted nervously from Cordell to Adam and back again. In spite of his position and nervousness he was holding a defiant expression. "Go ahead, shoot me too you lily livered cowards."

"Shut up," Cordell snapped at him. "We didn't kill your partner."

"Liar."

Adam stepped up and yelled directly in the man's face. "Winston Cain killed him you hard-headed old coot. You deaf or just plain stupid?"

The man eyed Adam and then shifted his gaze to Cordell who still held his Colt on him. A look of uncertainty was on his face. "I got back this morning, found him, and followed your tracks from the shack."

"You follow everyone's tracks and shoot at them?" Adam yelled in anger.

The man stammered and then said softly. "I thought."

"You thought?" Cordell said. "You thought we did it, so you come after us shooting? Before finding out who we were because you, *thought*?"

The old man continued to stand with his arms raised looking confused.

Cordell holstered his Colt. "Put your stupid hands down, I'm downwind from you and the stink's making my eyes water."

The man cautiously lowered his hands. "What are you going to do with me?"

"I ought to shoot you on general principles," Cordell answered. "We're after a man, the man who killed your partner. You've slowed us down and given him a better lead."

"If he's the one what killed my partner I want to ride with you."

Cordell snorted, "Not a chance. This is our hunt and I sure don't want some fool, who shoots at everyone he sees, along for the ride."

The man turned angry, "You can't stop me from hunting him too."

"Help yourself, just not with us."

"How you plan to stop me?"

"First off, you have no idea who he is," Cordell began. "Second off, I'm taking your rifle with me. I don't feel like being shot at again. I'll drop it off a mile down the way. You're going to sit your tail on that rock right there and not move for one hour."

"And what if I don't?"

"I'll take your horse and leave you on foot."

"That's horse stealing."

"I'll turn him loose, you won't know where though."

The man's face twisted in anger, but realized he had no other choice. "Fine," he growled.

Cordell stepped forward and put his face directly in the old man's dirty, whiskered face. "If I see you on our trail I'll shoot you. Understand?"

The man nodded. He walked over to the closest rock and sat down. His horse was standing in the rocks watching them. He glanced over at the horse and then back to Cordell and Adam. "I never cared that much for him anyway.

Adam gave him an incredulous look. "Then, why were so bent on shooting us for him?"

The man shrugged, "Seemed like the proper thing to do."

Cordell barked a sudden laugh. "What are you doing out here anyway, mining silver?"

"Maybe."

"Then, you need to stick to that and stop trying to get your old fossilized self killed."

The man fidgeted on the rock. "If I give you my word not to follow can I take my horse and leave?"

Cordell jacked the remaining cartridges out of the rifle. "I'll leave your rifle where we pick up our horses. Remember what I said about following us."

"Yeah. I've better things to do than get myself killed over that jackass."

Cordell and Adam walked back to their horses leaving the man sitting on the rock watching them go. Cordell leaned the rifle against a rock and stepped into the saddle.

Adam mounted his horse and glanced back at the man still sitting on the rock. "Can you believe that? He didn't even like the man!"

Cordell laughed, "These old sage rats can be a peculiar lot." He kicked his horse into a lope back to Cain's trail.

Chapter 15

Cordell and Adam returned to combined short loping spurts and walking the horses to try and close the gap between them and Cain. With water being scarce forcing thirsty, dehydrated horses beyond their endurance was risky. They rode until the last hour of daylight. They found a water seepage that would likely be dried up in a few more weeks and stopped for the night.

Cordell looked the area over and then dismounted. "Adam, you want to water the horses while I pot a couple of these zillion jackrabbits."

Adam nodded as he stepped out of the saddle and led the horses to the seep. The horses eagerly dove their muzzles into the water. He watched his brother walk out into the sage and wondered how Cordell never seem to tire. He was used to working long hard days on the ranch, yet he was bone weary and exhausted.

When the horses lifted their heads he led them away from the water and tied them to a clump of mesquite where they immediately began ripping off the leaves and eating them. He stripped the saddles off and dropped them where they would make their camp.

He walked out and cut branches to cook the rabbits on at the same time collecting an armload of dry mesquite and sage to set up for a fire. He sat down and watched Cordell shoot three rabbits, one a time, one shot each.

Cordell walked back to where Adam waited. He held up three rabbits, "They're scrawny and tough, but its food."

"I see you got three, expecting company?" Adam grinned.

"Big brother should be catching up before too long, figured he might be hungry."

"I'm going to fill the canteens, I was waiting for the water to settle after the horses stirred it up. You are the official holder of the matches so you can get the fire started and all." He collected the canteens from the saddles and walked to the seep.

With the fire set and the rabbits cleaned and spitted they sat back and watched the sun sink into brilliant colors as it slid lower into the horizon.

"Think we made up any time?" Adam asked.

"Hard to say. It depends on what Cain is thinking. He might still be in a hurry or he might have slowed down because he thinks he tricked us off his trail. If he's determined to reach San Antonio no matter what, he'll be in a hurry."

"He might not be thinking San Antonio. What if he plans to circle back to El Paso? I can't see him deserting his business."

Cordell nodded. "That is a possibility. That's why I want to stay on his trail in case he suddenly switches back. San Antonio is only a theory of mine, it's not cast in stone."

"Yeah, it wouldn't do to be standing around in that settlement waiting for Cain to show up only to have him halfway back to El Paso."

"That's my thinking."

Adam stared out into the deepening darkness. "What do you think Pa was like when he was our age? It's hard to picture him a wild outlaw and gunfighter."

"He couldn't have been too ruthless or Ma never would have married him." Cordell grinned, "He was probably like me."

"Black sheep of the family?" Adam smiled.

Cordell laughed lightly. "No doubt."

"I remember how tough Pa was on the ranch, but once we moved to Tucson he seemed like any other aging, easy going store owner."

"He was always good to Ma and us, that's all I care about. I do know that some of the things I learned from him came from someone other than a storekeeper."

The hoof falls of a slowly moving horse approaching the camp came out of the dark. Cordell called out. "There's a seep off to the right, why don't you water that horse, he sounds about ready to drop. There's supper on for you, too."

The sound of creaking saddle leather and a man's boots landing on the ground came from outside the glow of the fire. The boots and hoofs moved away toward the seep. Cordell and Adam listened to the horse sucking water. When it stopped the footfalls came back toward them.

Fallon pulled the saddle cinch and dropped

the saddle to the ground letting the horse wander off to join the other two in the mesquite bush. He stepped into the fire glow and sat down heavily without a word.

Cordell handed Fallon his canteen. He took it and drank continuously for several seconds. He then handed the canteen back to Cordell and whispered, "Thanks."

"Give that rabbit a few more minutes and half of it should be burned enough to eat," Cordell said casually.

Fallon sat in brooding silence watching the rabbit closest to him sizzle over the fire. The side facing the flames was black, the upper part red. He rolled the stick over so the black was on top. He tore off the legs and ate them.

"Long day," Cordell commented.

Fallon glanced up at him. "Yeah."

Silence fell over the camp until Fallon could no longer stand it. "Okay, say it. I know you want to," he growled.

"There's nothing to say," Cordell answered.

"Don't you want to gloat on how you were right and I was wrong?"

"You found that out for yourself. Why should I want to gloat? You're the only one who's making it a contest between us."

Fallon scowled. "I found a bareback horse on the trail. I rode back but you two were gone. I found three sets of tracks going this way. So, I followed them. I came on some old miner riding north on the tracks. I asked if he had seen two men. All he did was jerk his head this way and keep riding."

Adam broke in. "He was the partner of the

man Cain killed in that shack. He came shooting at us thinking we had killed him. We got the drop on him and sent him back home."

"Why didn't you kill him?" Fallon asked.

"He didn't need killing," Cordell answered. "He just needed it explained to him."

Fallon shrugged.

They sat in silence for several more minutes before Fallon asked if they had seen anything of Cain.

"He's still ahead of us," Cordell answered. "We need to be cautious in case he decides to set up an ambush."

"What makes you so sure he even knows we're following him?" Fallon asked.

"At first I wasn't sure he knew or not. He could have thought we were killed back at the house. Even the horse you followed could have been merely turned loose when he took the dead man's horse. It was the hundred yards of brushed out trail that cinched it for me."

"What brushed out trail?"

"The one the three sets of horse tracks were on. That was a brushed out trail. Cain wouldn't go through all that work if he wasn't thinking we were on his trail."

"That doesn't prove anything," Fallon argued. "He could have done it only as a precaution."

Cordell was quickly becoming exasperated with Fallon's argumentative attitude about everything. "He knows now."

"Why?"

"Because if I were him I would know by now and act accordingly."

"By setting up an ambush," Fallon

commented sarcastically. "You think like an outlaw, that's not surprising."

Cordell ground his teeth together and snarled, "I learned it from Pa."

Fallon huffed a mocking laugh, "One outlaw teaching another."

Adam saw the fight brewing and broke in. "Okay, we're all tired with frazzled nerves. We didn't expect this to turn into a chase across the desert, but it has."

"I told you it might not go quick and easy," Cordell replied.

"You were right," Adam agreed. "We should have listened to you and expected it."

Fallon glared at Cordell. "Excuse us for not having all your outlaw experience."

"You had the same opportunity to learn from Pa, but you decided to go off to be a high tone lawyer instead. So, put the blame on yourself, big shot!"

Fallon's eyes blazed with rage. "I wasn't *daddy's* little pet boy like you. As if I wanted to be a stinking outlaw like he was anyway."

Cordell sprang to his feet, leaped across the fire landing a solid punch to Fallon's face. Fallon fell backward as Cordell jumped toward him only to be met with Fallon's boots in his stomach. Fallon jumped up and the two exchanged punches.

Adam drove his body in between the two. He shoved Fallon hard in the chest sending him backward and grabbed Cordell by the front of his shirt. "Stop!" he shouted. "What is *wrong* with you two?"

Cordell and Fallon glared at each other as they dug deep for settling breaths.

"I'm sick of your high and mighty ways," Cordell shouted at Fallon.

"And I'm just plain sick of you," Fallon returned.

"And I'm fed up with both of you," Adam snapped. "You act like a couple of five year olds. The idea of this whole thing is to find Cain and kill him, not each other. We didn't expect this, but we're in it and I intend to run that man to ground. You can kill each other afterwards if you hate each other that much."

Cordell snapped, "I'm not an outlaw." He turned, walked back around the fire and sat down. He took a drink from his canteen and ripped a chunk off the rabbit chewing it angrily.

Adam pushed Fallon away from the fire into the darkness. He put his face inches from Fallon's, "What is your problem with him? You have been an absolute jackass ever since you got to Tucson."

Fallon glared at Adam. "I'm sick of the baby boy."

"No you're not. You're jealous of him and you know it."

"*What?*"

"You heard me. I know it as well as you do. Think about it, and stop acting like a spoiled brat." Adam turned and walked back to the fire leaving Fallon standing in place.

Fallon walked away into the darkness. He found his horse and tied him solidly beside the other two. He looked back at the fire willing himself to rejoin his brothers, but he couldn't bring himself to do it. He sat down with his back against a rock and dropped his face into his hands.

Cain climbed up on a high pile of rock to look around. He was uneasy about the Whitlocks, not certain that his tricks had fooled them. He would keep riding in the dark except he knew the danger of that. Should his horse step in a hole and break its leg or fall off a ledge he'd have no chance of staying ahead of them.

He took in the star filled sky and listened to the coyotes yipping wildly across the sage. Turning his attention to the country around him he scanned slowly right to left. A wink of light caught his eye down the way he had come. He strained his eyes focusing on the wink. It was a campfire, he had seen enough distant fires to know.

It was hard to tell the distance; however, the fact it was visible said it couldn't be all that far away. It could be anyone, but he knew it wasn't. He cursed viciously. It was that kid.

He started down off the rock when a thought struck him. Maybe it *was* Beau? Had he actually killed him? He shook his head, now he was thinking crazy, the heat and stress were getting to him.

He climbed back down to the flat ground. Sitting on a rock he considered his location. He had entered into the gap between the mountains. If memory served him right, that settlement was not that much further. Then again, his memory about the place had failed him all along. Standing up from the rock seat he lay down on his bedroll and rolled up in his blankets.

Before sleep came he thought back on his experience with Beau Whitlock. Beau had been a dangerous man, one of the few that ever made him nervous; however, in his mind, Beau had one serious flaw. Beau's problem, that ultimately proved his downfall, was the streak of good that ran through him. Had Beau been a relentless man and followed him after the shooting in San Antonio, and finished him off, he would still be alive.

Cain snorted with a mocking sneer. It was that streak of weakness that did him in. Made him sit like a fool while he shot him. In the end he wasn't so dangerous after all. The only problem, as it was turning out, was that his sons *were* relentless.

It was noon when Cain rode into the little settlement. It hadn't changed much since he had last come through. A few buildings which included a little store and a saloon. Horses were tied to rails their heads down and sleeping in the heat. A few Mexicans sat in the thin shade of the buildings and a scattering of Anglos with the look of outlaws lazed about. All were watching him with the idle interest of the thoroughly bored.

He spotted a tank of water near a central water pump and reined the exhausted horse toward it. The horse picked up the pace and plunged his muzzle into the water. The action scared a rattler out of its cool spot at the back edge of the tank. Cain watched the snake move slowly away then looked down into the hot water with dirt and green scum swirling all through it. He decided he wasn't thirsty enough to drink it.

When the horse lifted its head Cain reined him back to the saloon. Dismounting he tied the horse to the rail, dug the Colt .45 out of the saddlebag and stuck it in his waistband. He had the Webley shoulder holstered. It was a pretty little thing with its pearl grips, and looked impressive in the house, but if he found himself in a gunfight, he wanted the Colt.

An Indian sitting against the saloon wall stared into his face. A sign on the wall beside the door read, "No Indians."

Cain gave the Indian a disgusted look, "Sign says 'No Indians,' what are you doing here?"

The Indian continued to stare at him without a hint of expression. "Can't read," he said.

"Worthless and stupid. That's why you vermin ought to be exterminated." Cain entered the propped open doorway of the saloon.

He gave the single room a quick survey placing four men at the tables and two more along with the barkeep at the bar. The barkeep leaned on his elbows lazily watching him, a matchstick clamped between his teeth at the corner of his mouth. He turned his head and spit a stream of tobacco juice toward the floor behind the bar ending in the slight ding of a spittoon. He then resumed his former position.

Cain stepped up to the bar across from the barkeep who maintained his lazy pose. The barkeep removed the match from his mouth. His speech was as slow as he appeared. "You look like your face caught on fire and someone . . . ," he turned his head and spit, then finished the sentence, "threw dirt on it and put it out with a hay rake."

Cain did not respond to the comment. "Give me a beer, and try not to spit in the glass."

The barkeep grinned sardonically, "Yes, your lordship." He reached his hand down under the bar and brought out a bottle of beer. "Sorry, your

Lordship, no glass."

Cain twisted the wire off the cork and popped it off. He drank it straight down, it was warm, but wet and quenched his thirst. He put the empty bottle down. "Give me another."

"They're a dollar each."

Cain glared at him, "Give me the beer."

A second bottle was placed on the bar but the barkeep held on to it. "Two dollars on the bar."

Cain pulled his wallet from his hip pocket and slid two dollars out and dropped them on the bar. Replacing the wallet he snatched the bottle out of the man's hand, opened it and drank slower.

He looked behind the bar to a small mirror propped up on a shelf holding whiskey bottles. He was shocked at his appearance. His face was burned red and black, dirt covered the crusted flesh where the blisters had broken and oozed down his face. The oil had melted out of his hair leaving it hanging out in a greasy tangle from under the hat. As with his hair the wax from his mustache had melted leaving the long hairs hanging limply around his mouth.

At the end of the bar was a plate with sliced bread and a second with pieces of cooked meat. Flies buzzed around the food and the small sign indicating the plates represented lunch for paying customers. Cain picked up the beer and walked over to the plates. He swung his hand through the flies and piled meat on a slice of bread and capped it with a second. He bit off a big bite, chewed fast, and swallowed it with a swig of beer.

Two of the men sitting at the table closest to him began to laugh. One snorted and said to Cain, "Boy, if you don't look like something a coyote killed and drug around for a week."

Cain glanced at him as he wolfed down the sandwich. He made a second.

"Hey, don't eat it all," the barkeep called out to him.

Cain glared at him, "Scared to cheat the flies?" He took a bite of the second sandwich.

The man at the table spoke again. "I take it you don't get out in the sun much, seeing's how you look sorta melted and all. The last time I saw something that scary I'd gotten into some bad tequila and saw all kinds of crazy things."

Cain studied the talker's dirty face and scraggly beard. "If I had a dog that looked like you I'd shave his butt and teach him to walk backwards."

The man's eyes narrowed in anger and then he suddenly burst out laughing. "You're pretty skookum for a burned up old pilgrim."

Cain swallowed the last bite of sandwich washing it down with the last of the beer. "I was riding the outlaw trail while you were still hanging on your mother's drapes."

"Must have been a long time ago. Did they have horses yet or did you ride one of them there dino-sours?"

Cain held his eyes on the man. A plan was forming in his head. He could use this idiot to get the Whitlocks off his trail.

The second man had his eyes on the Webley. "That's a mighty pretty little gun you got there under your arm."

Cain shifted his eyes to the second man. "I like it."

"Interested in selling it?"

"Got two-hundred dollars?"

The man grinned, "That's a lot for a gun. What if someone was to flat take it?"

Cain gave the man a deadly grin that reflected no humor. "Now, what would a dead man need with a gun?"

Both men laughed. "You're a tough old bird," the first one said.

Cain stepped up to their table, pulled back a chair and sat down. "Can you shoot a gun as well as you shoot your mouth?"

The first man smirked, "We've buried a few."

"Interested in making a hundred each?"

Both men's eyes flared open as they leaned into the table. "Doing what?"

"I've got three men on my trail. They will end up here sometime today I'm sure."

"And you want us to kill them for you."

"Very good. You catch on quick."

"If you're such a tough outlaw why don't you kill 'em yourself?"

"You want the money, or not?"

"Relax, just asking."

"Don't ask, just say yes or no."

The man grinned, "Yes. Let's see the money."

Cain pulled out his wallet, removed two fifty dollar bills, laid them on the table and put the wallet back in his pocket.

The man snickered, "I ain't been but to fifth grade but even I can see that's not a hundred apiece."

"You get the other half when the job is done. I want to make sure you don't take a walk with my money and not do the job."

"So, how do we get the rest?"

"Ever hear of the Desert Rose in El Paso?"

"Yeah, but it's a little too rich for my blood."

"You go there and get the rest. Ask for Cain."

"And you'll be there with the other hundred?"

Cain nodded. "Make a clean sweep of it and there might be a bonus."

The first man glanced at his partner. They nodded at each other.

Each of the men took a fifty and pocketed it. "You've got a deal," the first man said.

The second man asked, "What do they look like?"

"All in their early twenties. One has long blonde hair. Two were wearing suits. Shouldn't be too hard to spot, it's not like people are busting the doors down to get in here."

"We don't want to make a long ride to El Paso and then have you want proof we did it," the first man said. "What do you want for proof?"

"Bring me three sets of ears and the blonde one's scalp."

The man chuckled, "You must be part Apache."

"No, just thorough." Cain stood up and walked to the bar where the barkeep was back to leaning on his elbows.

"What time does the stage come in?" Cain asked him.

The barkeep laughed. "There ain't no stage comes through here."

Cain scowled, "No stage service here at all?"

"Nope. About ten, twelve miles south is the wells. Butterfield has a stage stop there." He stopped talking, turned his head and spit into the spittoon. He looked back to see Cain disappearing out the open door. He finished his sentence in a low voice to himself, "But, it ain't run through there in years." He shrugged and leaned back on his elbows.

Chapter 16

The brothers rode out the morning in silence. Cordell and Fallon both wore the marks from the previous night's fight. Fallon had a bruised cheekbone and split lip, Cordell's nose was swollen. Cordell rode in the lead while Fallon's horse was to the right and slightly behind Adam.

Adam pondered the problem between his brothers. Fallon had gone off to law school at nineteen. Cordell was already getting into trouble and Ma was worried about him, but Pa spent a lot of time with him. In light of what he now knew maybe Pa was trying to straighten him out. He also recalled Fallon's anger over Cordell's behavior during those years and questioned why Pa let him get by with so much.

Fallon had come home periodically from school, but when he graduated and took up an office in Austin he didn't return. What he did recall on Fallon's last visit home was walking into the house and hearing angry voices coming from the kitchen. It was Pa, Cordell, and Fallon. Their mother was in the sitting room very distraught. Cordell had stormed past him, out of the front door, and rode away. Five minutes later Fallon left by the backdoor and got on the stage. That was three years ago. It was six months before he saw Cordell again, and this was the first time Fallon had come back to Tucson since then.

Friction between Cordell and Fallon, with their father in the middle, had built to a breaking point and shattered the family on that day. This is the first time his brothers had been face-to-face in three years. The division and animosity between them had remained over those years, especially with Fallon toward Cordell. Now, this situation had widened that gap when it should have brought them closer.

His observations of Fallon's constant barrage of derogatory comments and hostility toward Cordell led him to the shocking realization that Fallon was jealous of Cordell. He obviously resented what Cordell knew and he did not. His angry rebuke to Fallon last night about his being jealous had popped out without meaning to, yet as soon as he said it he knew he was right. Fallon, eldest brother, educated attorney, with plenty of money, was jealous of his younger brother who only had the clothes on his back and a horse and saddle. Why?

It was three o'clock when they rode into the scattering of small rough buildings that passed for a settlement. Cordell's head moved from side-to-side as he took in the wind and sand battered structures and the positions of the men around them.

Cordell pointed to a little store. "Adam, you want to pick us up some grub?"

Adam looked at the little store that was no bigger than a tack room. "Sure."

"Pick up a couple boxes of .45's while you're at it. I'm going to check out this saloon up here and see if anyone's seen Cain."

Adam reined his horse over to the store and dismounted.

Cordell eyed the saloon in front of him. Two unkempt men leaned on the wall watching them ride in. He locked eyes on one of the loungers as a challenge to their unwelcome attention. Both men casually turned and ambled back into the open door of the saloon.

Cordell and Fallon pulled up to the water tank and let the horses drink. Although their horses stood side-by-side neither man looked at or acknowledged the other. Both horses lifted their muzzles out of the water at the same time.

Cordell reined his horse back and moved toward the saloon. Dismounting down from the saloon he spun a rein around the hitchrail and slipped the loop off the hammer of his Colt. He walked to the saloon.

Fallon stopped beside Cordell's horse and dismounted.

Glancing at an Indian sitting against the wall and then at the "No Indians" sign beside the door Cordell walked in and looked the place over. The barkeep was lazily carrying a wooden box filled with beer bottles from a back room. He dropped the box on the bar.

The two men Cordell had spotted out front were sitting at a table trying not to be obvious about watching him. Warning bells went off in Cordell's head, there was something about those two that warranted concern.

Fallon walked up to the bar. He pointed at the box of beer bottles, "Give me two of those."

The barkeep removed two bottles and put them on the bar. "That's two dollars."

Fallon gave the man a dirty look. "You ought to wear a mask when you say that."

"It ain't cheap getting beer out here, take it or leave it."

Fallon tossed two dollars on the bar and took the bottles as the barkeep lifted the box and set it on the floor behind the bar. Fallon tore the wire off the top of one and popped the cork.

Cordell stepped up beside Fallon. Fallon handed the second bottle to his brother. Their eyes met without a word. Cordell knew it was a silent peace offering. He nodded his thanks and accepted the bottle.

As Cordell removed the stopper from the bottle he asked the barkeep, "You see a fancy dressed dude come through here today?"

The barkeep shifted the match in his mouth with his tongue. "I see a lot of people come through here."

Cordell drank down half the bottle without taking his eyes off the barkeep. Setting the bottle on the bar he said, "Yeah, this is like the capital city, people just everywhere. Sure can't expect a busy man like you to see every one of them."

The barkeep sneered at the sarcastic comment.

Cordell went on, "He's wearing a gray suit, probably looks trashed by now. Gray hair, twisted mustache, about sixty years old."

The barkeep stared silently at him.

The two men from the table got up and slowly meandered out the door. Cordell watched them from the corner of his eye. They were up to something. He finished the beer and gave the barkeep a mocking smile. "You told me plenty."

Fallon turned from the bar and began walking toward the door. Cordell gave a last glance around the room and headed out three steps behind his brother. As Fallon reached the doorway Cordell caught the movement of a man's shadow lying across the ground in front of the door.

Jerking the Colt out of his holster he ran forward, planted his hand in the middle of Fallon's back and shoved hard just as he stepped out the door. Fallon flew forward at the same time a pistol shot popped.

Fallon slammed hard, face first into the street, blowing a cloud of dust into the air. Cordell stuck his Colt twelve inches from the stomach of the man to the right of the door and fired. The man crumpled up double and fell to his knees. In a flash of movement he swung the Colt to his left across his body as a bullet blew a chunk out of the door jamb beside his head showering his cheek with splinters. His first shot took the man in the mid-section, his second through the heart. The man fell dead in the dirt.

Fallon's initial reaction was anger at being hit and knocked down in the dirt. His second immediate reaction was surprise at the swiftness of the gunfight. A few shots, a few seconds, and two men were down in the dirt. One rolling on the ground gripping his stomach and moaning, the other spread eagle in the dirt, his unblinking eyes staring up. Cordell, Colt in hand, was looking intently around.

Adam came on the run from the store carrying a stuffed cloth sack. His eyes were wide as he took in the scene of the fight and Fallon picking himself off the ground. An Indian sat on the ground his back against the saloon wall looking undisturbed by the fight that had taken place only a few feet from him.

Adam caught up to Fallon and helped him up. "Are you alright?"

Fallon nodded as they both watched Cordell who calmly rammed the spent brass from the Colt and reloaded.

Cordell kicked the leg of the man he had shot twice. Satisfied that he was dead he turned to the second man who was curled up on the ground gripping his belly with bloody fingers and whimpering. Taking a few steps over to the wounded man he looked down on him.

The would-be assassin stared up at him with frightened and pain wracked eyes.

Cordell used his boot toe to push the man over on his back. "That dude hire you to kill us?"

The man only stared up at him as the curious began drifting toward the scene.

Cordell kicked the man in the side causing the man to scream out. "I asked you a question." Cordell's tone was cold and deliberate.

"Yeah, the dude," the man moaned.

"Where did he go from here?"

"I don't know."

Cordell kicked him again.

The man gasped for a breath. "I don't know. He told us to look him up in El Paso, that's all I know."

"I hope he paid you good."

The man dug for a settling breath as he groaned. His eyes held on Cordell's face. "You ain't going to leave me like this are you?"

"That's what you intended to do with us, isn't it?"

The man didn't answer for several seconds then whispered, "I need a doctor."

"I doubt there's one in this town and I'm sure not packing you to San Antonio."

"You're a cold hearted dog."

"Yeah, I know. I don't have much sympathy for a backshooter."

Cordell began to walk away when he heard the Indian say, "He went to the wells."

Cordell turned to look at him. "Van Horn wells?"

The Indian nodded.

"Thanks." Cordell tossed him a silver dollar. "Get yourself something to eat."

The Indian caught the coin and gripped it in his hand.

Cordell turned to look at his brothers. He walked up to them and looked up and down Fallon's dust covered clothes and face. "Sorry to shove you like that. You're not hurt are you?"

Fallon shook his head. "I didn't see that coming."

"I did. I know where Cain is going."

"Where's Van Horn wells?" Fallon asked.

"About three hours south of here. Used to be a Butterfield stage stop there."

Fallon's expression showed alarm. "He'll get a stage out of there and be gone."

Cordell shook his head. "Butterfield pulled out of it years ago. All the lines are going north out of San Antonio now."

Adam looked confused. "You mentioned that earlier. So, what does he hope to accomplish by going there?"

"He probably thinks the stage still runs through."

"Is there still a stage station there?"

"There was last time I came through the wells about a year back. Kind of rundown, but a man can find shelter in in."

"Then, he might hold up in it waiting for the stage to come," Adam said with a hint of hope in his tone.

"Until he figures out there's no stage coming." Cordell looked at the cloth sack in Adams' hands. "Get what we need?"

"Enough."

"Get the .45's?"

"Yes."

"Let's go," Cordell said as he walked toward his horse.

Adam gestured toward the men Cordell had shot. "What about them?"

"What about them?" Cordell kept walking.

"Shouldn't we do something with them?"

"I did. I kept them from killing us."

Fallon followed Cordell to his horse. Adam looked at the dead man sprawled out and the wounded one still curled up in a ball. He felt funny leaving them like that, but what could he do anyway? He glanced at Cordell and then turned and walked to where he had left his horse by the store.

The three rode out of the settlement headed south toward the ridges of barren hills. They rode in silence following Cordell who knew the way to Van Horn wells. Adam turned in the saddle and in the distance saw several men dragging the dead man out into the desert. He wondered what would become of the wounded one. It was a hard country with hard rules. If a man intended to survive it he had to understand that. It said a lot about why Cordell was the way he was.

The sun had sunk almost to the western horizon as they approached a line of hills. Cordell pulled up. "The wells are on the other side of this ridge. We need to get a look before riding into it."

Cordell reined his horse toward a low saddle in the ridge and began to climb. He stopped before reaching the crest, dismounted and tied his horse to a dead mesquite bush. Adam and Fallon followed suit.

They walked to the crest of the saddle, hunkered down low, and looked to the flat country before them. Cordell pointed out the location of the wells a half mile to the south. "The wells are actually only a wide seep. The Apache use it, and then the army. The stage line ran into here because of the water, the only water for miles in any direction."

In the area indicated was a building with a corral behind it. Even from where they stood the old stage station and corral were obviously run down and abandoned. Standing tied to the outside of the corral was a saddled roan.

"Is that him?" Adam asked.

"I'd be willing to bet on it," Cordell replied.

"How should we do this?"

Cordell looked up at the sky, studied the low

plain of the sun, and then back to the distant building. "I don't want to close in on him now and take a chance on his slipping away when night falls. I'm for spending the night on the back side of these hills where he can't see us and then surrounding the shack at first light. That way if he should get the jump on us we have all day to run him down." He looked at each of his brothers for confirmation.

Adam thought for a moment and then agreed to the plan. Fallon nodded his approval.

"I want to keep an eye on the place until dark," Cordell said.

Adam nodded. "I'll get a camp set up."

"Keep the horses saddled for now in case Cain takes off," Cordell told him. "And no fire until after dark. I don't want him seeing the smoke."

Cordell sat down alone in the saddle of the hill and watched the country before him. Deer wandered through the sage while hawks and vultures drifted on the wind currents overhead. He thought about the shooting at the saloon and was grateful for having been on his toes with the two men. Fallon would have certainly walked into that first bullet. They might not like each other, but he wasn't about to let his brother step into an ambush.

The sun was setting when a movement at the building caught Cordell's attention. A man walked out of the building and stood looking around. He became concerned when the man untied the roan, but then relaxed when he saw him walk the horse to the water. The man continued to look around him while the horse drank. When the horse had finished he led the animal into the corral and stripped the saddle and bridle off then went back into the building.

Cordell sighed with relief. It had looked like Cain was going to ride on, and with it being almost dark that would have proven to be a problem. As it was, he felt confident Cain would still be there at dawn. He stood up and walked back down the hill to where his brothers waited.

"We can go ahead and unsaddle the horses. Cain just stripped his horse and put him in the corral. He's settling in for the night."

As darkness enveloped the land the evening star appeared big and bright in the sky. It was soon followed by an ever increasing number of stars. Adam built up a small fire for light as they didn't have anything to cook over it.

"What kind of food did you get at that store?" Cordell asked Adam.

Adam laughed lightly. "Pickin's were slim. I got slabs of dried beef and hard tack." He pulled out a slab of the dried meat and held it over the fire examining it. "I think it's beef anyway."

"Doesn't matter, it's food," Cordell responded. He held out his hand and Adam handed him the sack. Cordell took out a piece of meat and a hard cracker. He handed the sack to Fallon who took it from him with a nod of thanks.

They sat back against their saddles and ate.

"Why don't you pass out those .45 cartridges," Cordell told Adam.

Adam pulled one of the paper boxes out of the sack. He opened it and dumped a dozen cartridges into his hand and passed them to Cordell who took some and handed the box to Fallon. Cordell filled the few empty loops on his gunbelt and put the rest in his pocket.

The brothers sat in silence for several minutes until Fallon broke it. He was staring at the ground when he said, "Thanks for getting me out of the way of that ambush, Cordell."

Cordell looked over at Fallon watching the small flames reflect off his face. He could see his brother was deeply troubled. "No problem. Just because you hate my guts doesn't mean I'm going to let you get killed. You're still my brother after all."

Fallon winced like he had been slapped. He was silent for another minute then said, "I don't hate you, Cordell."

"Could have fooled me."

Fallon finally looked directly at Cordell. "I've been a lousy brother to you."

Cordell was momentarily too shocked to answer. Adam stared at Fallon with interest at what he would say next.

"We're different, that's all," Cordell said in a low voice.

"We shouldn't be. I should have been your big brother and helped you when you were getting into trouble as a kid. Instead I was too busy thinking about myself."

"That's water under the bridge," Cordell replied.

"Maybe, but its muddy water that needs to be cleared up."

Cordell only looked at Fallon waiting for what he had to say.

"You really took charge of this whole affair," Fallon began. "You pulled us together to go after Cain. You gave us a heads up as to what would happen with the guards, which more than likely saved our lives. Then, when Cain got away you tracked him. You have known what to do every step of the way. Then, you read that ambush and got me out of the way and shot both of our attackers. You're good at what you do Cordell, none better."

Cordell was stunned at Fallon's comments. "I'm used to being around men like those two, that's all. I could tell they were watching us, and then got suspicious when they followed us in and then walked out."

"How did you know they were right outside the door?"

"One of them let his shadow fall across the doorway. I knew they were on each side of the door and there could only be one reason for that."

"To shoot us when we walked out."

Cordell nodded, "Yeah."

"See, that's what I mean, you know these things." Fallon paused for a second then concluded, "I wish I did."

"What I know isn't much more than survival." Cordell reasoned. "What you know is worth a lot more, Fallon. You have an education and you're an attorney. That's pretty impressive, even though I've said some nasty things in regards to that."

Fallon scowled into the night. "I hate being an attorney."

Cordell and Adam both looked at him with surprised expressions.

"What?" Cordell asked.

"I hate it. I hate dealing every day with liars and manipulators. I never wanted it."

"Why did you go to law school then?"

"It wasn't my choice."

"Whose was it?"

Fallon shook his head, "Never mind. I shouldn't have said that."

"No," Cordell said. "Tell me. I'm your brother, talk to me."

Fallon released a heavy sigh. "Ma and Pa wanted it. They wanted their eldest son to amount to something. Ma wanted me to go to law school and become a lawyer. Pa made the arrangements and paid the tuition. I didn't want to disappoint them, they had their hearts set on me being somebody. So, I went."

"I didn't know," Cordell said softly. "I thought it was what you wanted."

Fallon shook his head. He looked back at Cordell. "I wanted what you got. I wanted to ride out with Pa and hunt and track. To ask him all the questions for all I wanted to know, but all he could do was talk about me making something of myself. Now that I know what his past was I understand why it was so important to both of them."

"Except, you had no say about it," Cordell said.

"No. I did what was expected of me. Then, I saw Pa doing with you all that I wanted to do with him. He let you get into trouble and defended you while I was expected to *make something of myself*. I came to resent you, and hated Ma and Pa for forcing me into something I never wanted, while you were allowed to be whatever you wanted, even a troublemaker and it was all right."

Adam asked, "What happened that last night when you two and Pa had the fight in the kitchen? That was the last time I saw you Fallon until three days ago."

"It was over me," Cordell said. "Fallon was angry with Pa for defending me when what I needed was to have my head knocked off. Pa argued for me. I stormed off mad at Fallon for saying what he did." He looked at Fallon. "For what it's worth, you were right."

Fallon nodded at the comment. "Pa and I really got into it then. I told him I hated him for forcing me into being a lawyer and being a father to Cordell and not to me." Fallon sighed, "I can still see the look of shock on his face. I left and never went back.

"With time I grew more bitter and blamed Cordell for my separation from the family. I knew that it was my fault, but I had shifted the blame to him."

Fallon paused. The small light from the fire shown on his face. A sniff escaped him and then he said, "There were so many times I wanted to go back, to apologize to Pa, to take it back, but I was too ashamed to face him after what I had said." His bottom lip began to quiver as his voice choked with emotion. "Then, I got the letter." Fallon buried his face in his hands and sobbed, "Now, I never can." He wept.

Cordell moved over next to Fallon and put his arm across his back. "I'm sorry for all that."

Fallon lifted his face out of his hands and sniffed. "I'm sorry, too."

"Is that why you stuck up for me to Scott and then the conductor?"

Fallon nodded. "You're my brother. No one has a right to treat you like that. Then, I turned out to be the worst one of all."

"I can understand why you felt like you did."

"No, it's a poor excuse. It was something Adam said to me that other night that made me start thinking."

"What was that?"

"He said I was jealous of you. That's why I was being so nasty to you."

"Jealous of me? The black sheep of the family?"

"You're not the black sheep, and I'll fight any man who says you are. But, yes, I was jealous because you know all the things I wish I did. I felt I had been cheated by Pa, and you got what I wanted. If that makes any sense."

"Actually, it does." Cordell removed his hand from Fallon's back and held it out toward him. "I think it's time we bury the hatchet, what do you say?"

"Way past time." Fallon gripped his brother's hand in a firm handshake.

Adam watched them and smiled.

Cordell asked, "So, with Helen, she kind of ended up lost in all that?"

Fallon nodded. "I went to see her whenever I was back and wrote to her while I was at school. Then when Pa and I had the fight and I left, I dug such a hole of anger and self-pity that I forgot about Helen. Now, I'm trying to make amends, but I don't think she wants me anymore."

"You know, I bet if you told her exactly what you just told us she would understand. The truth will take you a lot farther than holding it back from her."

"You think so?"

"There's only one way to find out."

"Helen's a fine woman," Adam added in.

"Tell her the truth."

"Okay, I will. When we get back."

They sat in silence for several minutes. The tension between them was gone, replaced with a feeling of friendship.

Cordell asked, "Why don't you move back to Tucson and open an office."

"I do want to come back to Tucson, but not to be a lawyer."

"What would you want to do then?"

"I had tossed around the idea of being a lawman before going to school."

"Then, be one. With your education and legal background you'd make a top notch lawman."

"You know," Adam began. "Pima County is going to have a sheriff's election this fall. You are well respected around Tucson. You'd be perfect. There's plenty of time to start campaigning, Red has a lot of connections in the county, and I'd sure stump for you."

Fallon looked across the fire at Adam. "I'll have to think about that."

Cordell grinned, "I'd stump for you too, but I might have an opposite effect on your success."

Fallon laughed lightly, "Maybe."

Cordell turned serious. "Why don't you head on back and let me and Adam deal with Cain."

Fallon frowned at him. "Why?"

"Because, if you're looking to be a lawman killing Cain . . ."

"Is exactly what I should be doing," Fallon finished the sentence. "I have no intention of letting Cain get away with murdering Ma and Pa. I can't ever apologize for what I said and did to them, but I can sure make their murderer pay with his own blood."

Cordell looked Fallon in the eyes, "Alright then. The three of us will get 'er done."

Chapter 17

Cordell climbed up to the top of the saddle in the hill to look down on the old Butterfield building. The sun was breaking over the east casting out enough light to see the stage stop. Their horses were saddled and they were ready to ride on the building and finish Cain off.

Sitting down Cordell shaded his eyes with his hands and studied the stage stop. Something was wrong. There was a horse in the corral, but it was a buckskin, not a roan. "What the . . ., he whispered. He began to curse as he jumped up and ran back to where his brothers waited.

"What's wrong?" Fallon asked.

"There's a buckskin in the corral."

Fallon frowned, "I thought I saw a roan out there yesterday."

"You did." Cordell jumped into the saddle. "Something's wrong."

Adam and Fallon mounted and followed Cordell as he carefully approached the stage building from the corral side. They spread out as they drew in closer. The buckskin looked up at them and walked to the rails where he let out a whinny to the other horses.

Cordell kicked his horse into a gallop covering the remaining distance in a few quick jumps. He slid the horse to a stop in front of the door of the building. He leaped out of the saddle, drew the Colt, and charged at the door. Driving his shoulder against the flimsy door it burst open. He jumped in and pointed the pistol at a man bolting up from his bedroll on the floor. It wasn't Cain.

The man threw his hands in the air with a startled expression. "Whoa, easy there," he called out excitedly.

Adam and Fallon walked in behind him and looked around the dilapidated room. Cordell held the gun on the man. "Where is the man who was in here last night?"

"He's gone."

Adam's head snapped around. "What do you mean he's gone?"

"You going to shoot me?"

"No. We were going to shoot the man who was here," Cordell answered.

"What happened to him?" Fallon asked calmly.

"Can I put my hands down and put on my boots? I talk better with my boots on."

Cordell holstered the gun. "Hurry up, we don't have all day."

The man sat back down and quickly slipped his spurred, high heeled boots on. His gunbelt with a revolver in the holster lay beside his bedroll. He made no attempt to pick it up. He stood back up.

"You a cowboy?" Adam asked pointing at his boots.

"Yes. I'm just passing through. This is a good place to spend the night."

"What happened to the other man?" Fallon asked again.

"Well, there was another fellow here when I showed up last night. We got to talking and he said he was waiting for the stage. I told him the stage ain't run through here in years. He got real upset about that, said he needed to get to San Antone.

"I told him he should head up to Pecos then 'cause the Texas and Pacific just ran track through there and he could catch a train to Fort Worth and then another down to San Antone. He asked how he could get there and I told him to follow the old stage road to the northeast and he'd get there in two days."

Cordell scowled and cursed.

Adam looked at Cordell, "Do you know that country?"

"I know the crossing at the Pecos River where the town is. I was on a cattle drive through there once, but I've never rode it from here."

"Follow the trace of the stage road out of here," the cowboy volunteered. "There's water at Ellis Water Hole and again at Apache Springs, but she's drier'n a temperance social between there and the Pecos."

"How long ago did he leave?" Fallon asked.

"I heard him light out about three hours ago."

Cordell nodded at the cowboy, "Thanks. Sorry I jumped you like that."

The man grinned, "Well, you scared about ten years off my life, but I reckon I'll survive."

The brothers filed out of the room with the cowboy behind them. He pointed at a gap in the hills to the east. "Trail runs through there, then kinda shifts to the north a bit."

The three nodded in unison.

"We need to water the horses," Cordell said, "and fill our canteens. Looks like the chase isn't over yet."

They led the horses down to the water.

Cordell glanced at Fallon. "See, I'm not always so smart. We should have jumped him last night when we had him."

"How were we supposed to know that cowboy would show up?"

"Bird in the hand, isn't that what they say?"

"He's only got three hours on us. We'll run him down."

"Even if he makes it to Pecos ahead of us I doubt the train runs through all that often," Adam said. "We'll catch him on the trail or kill him in the street if we have to."

Cordell and Fallon both glanced at Adam with surprise at the tenacity and firm resolution in his voice.

Cain had pushed the exhausted roan from the moment he left the Butterfield shack that morning. He wasn't sure if those clowns back at the saloon stopped the Whitlocks or not. They didn't appear to be any brighter than necessary and chances were they were the ones gunned down. Should that be the case the hunters would be on his trail again, providing they had any idea which way he had gone.

He never left anything to chance. He never

assumed the outcome of anything, especially where his life was involved. He had seen tough men die as quick as weak. Back at the Desert Rose he hoped his men could stop the Whitlocks, but when he saw the first two go down he didn't bank on it so he took off. As it turned out it was a good thing he did.

His suspicions about the stage stopping at the wells began when he saw the dilapidated building and corral. There were no spare horses, no hostler, no coach tacks, and the trail was overgrown with sage and grass. It was obvious the stage didn't stop here, at one time yes, but no longer.

He had no choice but to spend the night in the shack and try to figure out where to go next. He was forced to face the fact that San Antonio was too far to make by horseback if the Whitlocks were still hot on his heels. For all he knew they were right over the hill waiting to pounce.

Having the cowboy show up was fortuitous. Heading for Pecos had never occurred to him, then again, he had only heard of it in stories and had no idea where it even was. He had hoped for a stage headed east, but the train was even better. Fort Worth was as good a place to escape to as any. From there he could go to San Antonio or back to El Paso when he felt it was safe. Two days more and he'd be gone from this end of the state.

The horse stumbled jerking Cain in the saddle and out of his thoughts. He had to let the horse stop and rest or end up on foot. The cowboy had said a day through the hills and then another day across a flat waterless stretch to Pecos. If the horse dropped dead he would never survive that stretch.

There was supposed to be a waterhole around

here somewhere, the cowboy had called it the Ellis water hole. Scanning the area around him he watched several bees flying in a straight line. He dismounted and led the horse in the direction the bees had flown. Several more passed by him as he walked. He finally spotted the water.

Filling his canteen before the horse stuck his muzzle into it Cain capped the canteen while the horse drank. He kept up his relentless search around him. He hoped the Whitlocks were lying dead or at least left scratching their heads wondering where he had spirited off to. Yet, he would keep going as if they were right behind him.

The horse lifted his dripping muzzle out of the water and stared straight ahead at nothing in particular. The roan released an exhausted breath and closed his eyes. It was against his better judgment to stop, but a dead horse wasn't what he wanted either. Leading the horse to the shady side of some brush he sat down and let the horse rest.

It had been a brutal run of days. His face and neck were healing, yet painful. He was hungry and weary to the bone. Another day and he could eat and sleep all he wanted, but he had to make that one more day, it wasn't here yet. He had let himself get soft. He tried to justify it by reminding himself that he was sixty years old, but that was no excuse for losing his razor edge.

Lifting his head off his chest Cain realized he had fallen asleep. With a surge of panic he looked around and then to the sun. The fireball scorching the land had moved only slightly so he had not slept all that long. Standing up he searched the country around him. Seeing nothing that seemed a threat, he pulled the sleeping horse's head up and mounted.

The old trail led through the hills, eventually shifting toward the north as the cowboy had said it would. Cain swayed in the saddle weakened by fatigue and hunger. Several times he caught himself falling asleep and nearly sliding off the horse. He climbed to a high spot every couple of hours to check his backtrail. Much of the trail was hidden around the turns it took behind the hills and through low places. He didn't see anyone; however, that didn't mean no one was back there. He pushed on.

The day was drawing to a close when he reached the end of the hills. Out in front of him running in all directions were miles of flat, dry country. The tallest thing out there was grass. He groaned aloud at the sight before him. It would be necessary to cross that before he reached the river and the train that represented his safe escape.

He needed food and sleep. There was supposed to be one last spring around here the cowboy said. It was before you broke out onto that flat stretch of hell fire, the last water before the Pecos. The roan pulled toward his left and he let the horse go hoping he could smell the water. He fell asleep in the saddle until he realized the horse had stopped. Looking ahead he saw the water. His grip on the reins had prevented the horse from lowering his head to drink. Dismounting he let the horse walk to the water and drink while he collapsed in a sitting position on the ground.

There were deer tracks leading to and from the spring. He needed to eat, but held back on the idea of shooting game in case the Whitlocks were within hearing distance. The thought of getting up to hunt seemed like too much effort. His dulled mind rejected the idea. In the end his hunger won out and framed a compromise with his mind. He decided to sit and wait for an animal to come in for evening water and take the chance of being heard and shoot it.

The roan stood several feet from the spring sound asleep. He forced himself to rise and make his way to the horse where he pulled the Colt out of a saddlebag. He returned to his former spot, plopped back down and watched the trails leading into the spring. As he waited his head bobbed up and down on his chest between sleeping and waking.

The sudden sound of an animal bleating in terrified desperation jarred him fully awake. Uncertain of what he had heard he looked up and listened for the sound to come again. Seconds later it drifted to him again. Forcing himself to stand he walked toward the sound. He stopped and stood listening again. The guttural growling of dogs came to him from down the trail.

Staggering around a bend in the trail he spotted several coyotes tearing into a doe deer stretched out in the sand. He grinned, lady luck was with him. He approached the snarling coyotes whose attention was on the kill. He picked up several rocks, closed the distance on the predators and began pitching the rocks at them. Once the coyotes realized they were under attack they growled at him in temporary defiance, but then ran off a short ways and watched.

Cain stood over the dead deer. Pulling a jack knife from his pocket, he cut several chunks of meat from the deer's hindquarter. Leaving the rest he walked away carrying the meat in his hands. The coyotes quickly converged back onto their kill.

Catching up his horse Cain stripped the saddle off the roan and tied the trailing reins around a loose rock. The horse could drag the rock and graze on the short grass around it. Moving into the shelter of the rocks, he built a fire and cooked the meat in thin strips.

As each piece of meat cooked he ravenously devoured it. All the while he sat and ate he listened into the growing darkness for any sound that indicated danger. He heard nothing that represented a threat. Finishing the last piece of meat, he toppled over on his side and fell fast asleep.

The brothers sat around a small fire and discussed their situation. They had spent the day riding on Cain's trail. Cordell took the time to explain to his brothers what he was looking at and for as they moved along. The tension that had enveloped them since Tucson, and grew heavier as the hunt for Cain dragged out, was gone.

They had run out of daylight halfway between Ellis waterhole and the end of the hills that the cowboy said held the last water before the Pecos River. Leaning back on their saddles they gnawed on the dried beef and hardtack swallowing it down with brackish water.

Adam studied the piece of hard meat in his hand. "I'll bet they're sitting up at the table right now eating hot steaks and potatoes. Not that I'm complaining." He threw a guilty glance at Cordell.

"Complain," Cordell answered. "I could go for that right about now."

Fallon grinned at Cordell, "I thought you

liked living on simple rations?"

Cordell laughed under his breath. "I can live on them, doesn't mean I prefer it."

They were all exhausted and worn down physically and mentally. Their initial confrontation with Cain had not gone as anticipated. He wasn't supposed to lead them on a week long trek over rough country. Still, that is where they found themselves. Maybe their bodies and minds were worn down, but not their resolve to find Cain.

"I smell like a sweaty horse blanket," Fallon grimaced as he took a sniff of his thoroughly soiled white dress shirt. Good thing I have another suit and shirt in Austin. This one's about had it."

"Mine too," Adam said. "Only thing is it's the only one I own."

"I should have made sure we had trail rolls before we left," Cordell commented.

"How could you know?" Adam replied. "I sure don't ride the ranch in this outfit. I was thinking appropriate attire for the train, not what's appropriate for the trail. This whole thing has been a first for me."

Fallon asked from across the fire. "Think we closed the gap on him today? His trail was plain enough he wasn't trying to hide it at all."

"He's probably worn down and doesn't care anymore," Adam put in.

"Or, he thinks he's clear of us and doesn't need to worry about it," Cordell said. "But, I think you're right. He just wants to keep moving."

Fallon swallowed a dry bite of hardtack and choked as he washed it down. "His horse was leaving some deep scuff marks in the sand. It must be worn out."

"It is,' Cordell agreed. "The tracks were clean for the first couple of miles and then started to drag. The few hours a night when the horse isn't carrying him isn't enough to rebuild its endurance. He's flagging. Notice anything else unusual about his trail?"

Adam and Fallon thought for a second and then both shook their heads.

"There's no manure along the way. You ever follow a horse all day and never come across at least two or three piles?"

"No. That horse isn't eating," Adam said.

"Exactly. Cain's not allowing the horse to rest enough or eat. It's going to drop dead before long."

Fallon nodded. "Leaving him on foot."

At first light they continued on. The trail left by Cain's half dead horse was still evident in the sand although in places the sand was shifting down into the depressions. Huge white thunderhead clouds billowed in the sky drawing a sharp contrast against the stark blue of the sky. Shadows lay over the hills and sand where the clouds crossed between the sun and earth.

It was mid-morning when they reached the last hill and looked out over the flat brown plain ahead of them. The land did not bode well for exhausted horses.

"Now, that is ugly," Fallon commented.

"Not exactly green and inviting is it?" Cordell replied.

Adam scanned the land that rolled away through a sheet of shimmering heat waves. "It'll kill these horses."

Cordell dismounted. "Good chance it will.

Cain's tracks wander off the trail here I want to see where they go." He led his horse as he followed the horse's tracks away from the trail.

Adam and Fallon dismounted and followed him.

Cordell pointed ahead. "There's the spring the cowboy told us about." He let his horse walk ahead to the water and drink while he searched around.

Adam and Fallon brought their horses to the spring and let them drink. They watched Cordell as he coursed back and forth around the spring.

"He stayed here last night. He had a fire. Tracks everywhere."

His brothers walked up beside him and looked around. Fallon pointed out to the east. "Looks like he headed out into that paradise."

Cordell looked at the single horse trail leading away from the spring and onto the flats. "If it's a day across that would make it thirty miles anyway."

"I don't feel good about heading out there with the horses in this condition," Adam adamantly stated. "I might not know man hunting, but I know stock. We go out there right now and these horses will die."

Cordell nodded. "I agree. "We need to spend the day here, let the horses graze and water all they want, and then we head out after dark when it's cool."

"Navigate by the stars?" Adam asked.

"Put the North Star on your left shoulder and ride east."

"That's a good idea, ride while it's cool, and give these horses a break today," Fallon concurred. He glanced up at the sky, "Except, we might have cloud cover over the stars."

"That won't slow us down."

Fallon glanced at Cordell, "You have a built-in compass in your head?"

"No." Cordell dug into his pocket. "In my pocket." He produced a small compass and showed it to his brothers.

Fallon burst out laughing. "Next you're going to pull magic fairy dust out of that pocket and whisk us across this stretch of hell."

Cordell grinned, "Used up the last of my fairy dust two weeks ago, sorry."

Adam looked at the compass in his brother's hand. "You wouldn't happen to have a steak and a cold beer in there would you?"

"Fresh out."

Fallon caught up his horse. "Let's strip the gear off these horses and get them on the grass and catch a little sleep ourselves. It's going to be a long night."

"But, we should make Pecos by morning," Cordell said. "If Cain doesn't get a train out he's run out of rope because there is nothing else out here."

Fallon pulled the saddle from his horse. "We just have to make sure he doesn't get that train."

Chapter 18

Silvio and his three companions rode into Tucson from the southeast. They skirted the main business area on their way to the livery where Silvio's Uncle Manolito worked. Wagons and riders were moving in and out of town along the roads as they approached from the roadless desert.

The four riders swung around to the side of the livery keeping the big barn between them and the town so as not to be readily seen. They all dismounted watching cautiously around them. Silvio walked into the open double doors of the barn. He stood in the alley between the stalls looking around when the livery owner, Karl Faust called out to him.

Silvio turned to watch the man walk toward him. "Need to leave your horse?" the owner asked in a strong German accent.

Silvio shook his head. "I am looking for Manolito Herrera, he is my uncle. Myself and my cousins have come to visit him."

The owner glanced over Silvio noting the guns, cartridge belts, and rough appearance of the man. He was obviously a south of the border Mexican and not a resident of the American side. "Yes, Mano is around somewhere, saw him up in the loft a bit ago. Let me see if I can find him."

Silvio smiled, "*Gracias.*"

Faust walked toward the back of the barn and called out for Manolito.

Manolito answered from the hay loft.

"You have visitors."

Hay sifted down through the cracks between the boards of the loft floor as Manolito made his way to the ladder. Manolito climbed down the ladder and met the man. "Yes, Mr. Faust?"

"Your nephew is here to see you." He pointed toward Silvio.

Manolito Herrera narrowed his eyes as he looked at Silvio. "I will see him and then return to work."

"That is alright, take your time." Faust walked away.

Manolito walked up to Silvio, stopped, and looked him over. "You are a long ways from the Rio Sonora. I am surprised you have escaped the wrath of Don Fernando. You have stolen too many of his cows."

Silvio smiled, "As did you."

Manolito grinned, "But, I was smart. I got out of Sonora before his vaqueros hung me."

"Are you leading the life of an honest man now, Uncle?" Silvio gave his uncle a mock sympathetic look.

"I sleep in peace at night. I do not fear the rope or the guns of angry Dons or Anglo ranchers. Yes, an honest man can sleep at night. How well do you sleep at night, Silvio?"

"Like a baby."

Manolito snorted and laughed. "Why do you seek me out?"

"A gringo killed your nephews, Jorge and Nacio down in Black Water. We have been looking for him. We are told he lived in Tucson."

Manolito took the news with subdued anger. "I knew Jorge and Nacio as children. They were mischievous, but I liked them. Who killed them?"

"Cordell Monroe. Do you know him?"

Manolito nodded. "I do. He is a bad man with a gun."

"Reputations are often made of nothing more than whiskey and air."

"Not this one. I have spoken with him and he is a dangerous man, although very young. Still, if he killed my nephews that must be dealt with."

Silvio nodded his agreement. "Yes, it must. Where can we find him?"

Manolito pointed to a horse in an end stall. "That is his horse. He left him here five days ago. He paid for two days and said he would be back, but he is yet to return. I understand the parents of the three Monroe brothers died in a fire last week. Cordell left his horse here, as did his brother with his buggy and horse, neither has been back."

"Then they have gone off someplace that they could not ride to."

"That is likely."

Silvio stared at the ground as he paused in thought for a full minute. He then looked back at Manolito. "Unless he is dead he will return for his horse, no?"

"It would seem so."

"We will watch for him."

"Who do you have with you?" Manolito asked as he looked out the open doors.

"Miguel, Paco, and Ernesto."

"Yes, I know them. You can see this place from my house. You can stay there and watch for Cordell Monroe to return."

"That is generous of you."

"We are family and this must be rectified."

"That is why we have come so far, uncle."

Manolito led him out the back doors of the barn and pointed to his house a hundred yards away. "I have work to do, go now, but do not get into trouble in town."

Silvio nodded his agreement, turned and walked around the barn to where his companions waited. "We can stay at Uncle Manolito's house. He knows Monroe, he left his horse here five days ago and should be back soon. We will watch for him."

"Is there a cantina," Paco asked. "I am hungry, and would also like to quench my thirst."

Silvio stepped into the saddle. "We will find one."

They rode along the back streets without finding a cantina. Swinging around the end of town they rode down Congress Street drawing a great deal of attention to themselves. Spotting the Congress Hall saloon they reined their horses to the side of the street and dismounted.

Leroy Jackson was leaning against a porch pole in front of the business adjoining the saloon rolling a cigarette when Silvio and his group reined in and dismounted. He recognized the men for what they were. He licked the cigarette paper, put the cigarette in his mouth and lit it all the while keeping his eyes on the Mexicans.

They had stepped up on the boardwalk when Clay Scott approached them. "Where are you going?" he asked Silvio.

Silvio glanced at the badge on Scott's shirt and then into his stern eyes. "For a drink and a bit of food."

"You're a little heavily armed for our town. Where are you from?"

"Sonora," Silvia answered. "We must travel armed as the Apache are still active in Mexico and then there are the banditos to contend with as well."

Scott eyed the four men with suspicion. He wasn't familiar with Mexican banditos, but these men seem to fit the bill. They had broken no laws and they were as free as anyone to go in the saloon as long as they didn't cause trouble."

Scott eyed them with a scowl. "Just don't cause any trouble."

"We have no intention of causing trouble," Silvio smiled.

Scott looked them over one last time and then began to walk off when Silvio stopped him.

"We are looking for a man maybe you know him."

Scott looked back at him. "Who is it?"

"Cordell Monroe."

Scott scowled, his temper instantly rising. He had been hearing too much about Cordell Monroe lately as his daughter seemed to be smitten with the saddle bum and his wife was all too encouraging on the subject. He wasn't surprised these men were looking for Monroe. They were probably friends of his. Still, if they were friends they would have said 'friend' not 'a man.'

"I know him."

"Do you know where we can find him?"

A thought crept into Scott's mind. He wondered if these men had come for Monroe not as friends, but as hunters. If they killed Monroe that would end his daughter's infatuation with him. He wished he knew where the kid was, he wouldn't mind if these men killed him. The thought made him inwardly smile.

"I have no idea where he is. He seems to have left town, but I'm sure he'll be back soon enough."

Silvio nodded. "We have family in town and will stay with them until Cordell returns."

Scott glanced quickly around. "You want Monroe to renew old friendships, or something else?"

Silvio feigned incomprehension. "What else could there be?"

Scott glared at the bandito while speaking in a low voice, "I don't like Cordell Monroe and if he met with an accident it wouldn't hurt my feelings too much."

Silvio held Scott's eyes as a grin slowly crept over his lips. "Accidents have a nasty way of claiming a man's life."

"We can only hope."

Silvio smiled and nodded slightly to the marshal. He turned and stepped across the boardwalk and into the saloon with his companions following.

Scott watched them go through the door and then turned away with a satisfied smile. He looked down the boardwalk and met the eyes of the cattle buyer as he leaned against a post smoking a cigarette. He dismissed the idea that the man had overheard the low spoken conversation. Besides, it was no mystery he didn't like Cordell Monroe. Saying so to his friends was hardly grounds to make the man suspicious that he had set the men to killing Cordell.

Leroy had good hearing and had indeed overheard the conversation. He knew these men were hunting Cordell, and Scott was not only going to let them, he was encouraging it. He casually walked away toward the little adobe house he lived in. He would keep an eye out for Cordell's return and let him know the Mexicans were in town. It was time he buckled a gun back on, the kid might need some help.

Chapter 19

Cain had no idea how far out on the flats he had come, everything around him was the same dimension with no landmarks to gauge his progress. The roan moved slower by the hour dragging its cracked hooves through the sand. Cain had hoped the gathering of heavy white clouds would send some rain, but they only teased his heat fevered mind and swollen eyes that they contained a bit of relief.

He used the sun to guide his direction east. He hadn't lost all his wildland skills, he could still navigate providing his mind didn't turn on him and make him go off chasing visions. As he searched his back trail and all around him he only saw a shimmering wall of heat that blocked his long distance sight. Since leaving the so-called stage stop he had seen nothing of the Whitlocks. Maybe the clowns had pulled it off after all.

Sleep overtook him at some point. He woke and lifted his head wondering why he was standing still. He stared down at the curve of the roan's neck. The horse stood dead still its head hung down until its muzzle was only inches from the sand. Angrily he kicked hard into the weakened horse's flanks and belly which accomplished nothing.

Slipping off the horse Cain stumbled backwards but caught himself before he fell. Looking over the horse he saw a shallow breathing, pathetic creature with sucked-in, gaunt flanks. It's head was down, eyes closed, and hind legs forward under its belly. Rage overtook him as he cursed and screamed threats from a raspy throat. The horse did not respond.

In a fit of frazzled nerves from a heat sapped mind, Cain blew into a rage of temper. Kicking the horse repeatedly in the legs and punching its body with weakened fists Cain pummeled the animal. The horse held its position, too drained of strength to flinch or respond. Suddenly the animals legs folded and the roan dropped down on its belly. Laying with its head up and eyes closed it absorbed the man's beating.

Cain finally collapsed into the sand, his energy exhausted. He lay spread eagle looking up at the clouds floating through the sky. It felt good to simply lay down, to go to sleep. He had no idea how long he lain there before his sense of survival took over. Was he going to just lay there and let the Whitlock boys ride up and shoot him?

He fought to his feet and stood swaying until his head cleared enough to catch his balance. It was obvious the horse was done in. Cain yanked the canteen off the saddlehorn and dug the Colt out of the saddlebag. Orienting himself on the flat land he began walking east.

How far he walked and how many times he fell and got up Cain had no idea. His only thought was somewhere ahead was a train that would take him to safety. The sun was casting his shadow in front of him when he drained the last trickle of hot water from the canteen. Carrying a useless item only served to make his walk harder. He dropped the canteen and kept moving.

He stumbled on dragging his feet through the sand. The faint sound of hammering drifted to him. At first he thought it was his heart pounding blood into his brain. His head felt like it wanted to explode from pressure and pain. That had to be the source of the noise as it didn't stop, in fact it only grew louder as he moved along. He thought he saw buildings in the distance and feared his mind had gone leaving him to see imaginary visions. Continuing on until no heat waves blocked his view he stopped and tried to focus his eyes. He was still seeing buildings ahead.

The further he walked the bigger they grew and the louder the hammering. Then, he was close enough to see the spread of the town and it was no imaginary vision. The sound he had been hearing was the hammers of carpenters as they built a new town on the west side of the river.

The line of trees and brush marking the river's course was now evident to him. He made his way toward the slow moving, green tinted water until he reached the bank. Dropping down on his knees he dove his head into the water and let the wet soak in. Lifting his head out he took deep breaths as the water drained off his oily hair. He stuck his face in the water again and sucked in mouthfuls. It tasted bad, but it was water.

Feeling a bit of relief he sat on the bank for some time and stared off toward the buildings. There were a set of old weather worn buildings across the river from him. A wagon bridge crossed the river to where new constructions were going up fast on the west side of the river where he sat. Beyond the bridge was a trestle spanning the river with railroad tracks on top of it and running as far as he could see east and west. He smiled through his cracked lips. He had made it.

With an effort of will he rose to his feet and staggered slowly toward the tracks and the new constructions. Two carpenters watched him from the roof of a building as he approached. They took in his appearance without surprise, they had seen it before, a man lost in the desert finding his way to the river.

Cain reached the building holding the carpenters. It was only a skeleton with its shiny, clean framing lumber glowing in the sun. He looked up at the carpenters. "Is this the Pecos crossing?" he rasped.

"Pecos Station we call it now, but yeah, you found it."

Cain smiled with a loose neck nod. "Where is the depot?"

The man pointed north toward the tracks. "Brick building yonder."

Cain looked off in the direction indicated and saw a long brick building alongside the tracks. He forced his legs to move and continued on toward it.

The carpenters watched him shuffle away. One remarked to the other, "He's looks like the wrath of God."

The other shook his head. "Coming out of that country out there, it's more like he escaped the wrath of the devil."

Cain reached the depot and stepped up to the open ticket window. The agent was across the room.

He turned toward the window, the first thing the agent noticed was the shoulder holstered pistol and the Colt stuck in the man's waistband. He wasn't concerned as all men went about armed in this country. As he stepped to the open window the agent looked at him with shock and alarm at his appearance. "Are you alright?" he asked.

"Yes. I'm wonderful, never felt better. I'm having tea with the Queen of England, is she in? Do I look presentable?"

The agent frowned. "You don't have to get so smart I was only concerned."

Cain scowled and bit back his next terse remark. He needed this man to answer his questions and making him mad wouldn't help. "When is the next train to Fort Worth?"

"Whenever it comes back this way from dropping off its load to the west."

"What does that mean?" Cain snapped.

The agent was now irritated. "It means the train's first priority is to bring building supplies to this town, and rail and ties to the ongoing track construction to the west. They're laying track on through to El Paso, but she's got a ways to go yet.

"There's a rail car on it and when she's dropped the load and heads back this way she stops and picks up whatever passengers want to go to Fort Worth. In time there will be a regular schedule, but for now it's whenever she comes in and out."

"Has it gone west recently?"

"Yesterday. Probably be back through here tomorrow. If you buy a ticket now you can get on whenever she gets here."

Cain grumbled as he dug his wallet out of his

hip pocket. "Stupid way to run a railroad."

"From the looks of you you're not in a position to be picky, but if you want schedules and exact times head back east and stay there."

Cain threw a bill on the counter and scowled at the man.

The agent made out the ticket and slid it across the counter along with the change from the bill. He said nothing more to Cain only looking at him with disapproval.

Cain grabbed up the money and ticket and walked away. He would have to watch for the train, but he needed food, clean clothes, and a room with a bed. Standing at the end of the building he looked the growing town over. Behind him was the river and the old town across it.

He spotted a store, and further past it a sign that indicated baths were available. He headed for the store. Going in the store he looked around until he found assorted stacks of clothes. Rifling through the clothes he found a shirt, pants, socks, and drawers that would fit him. Paying for them he headed toward the bath sign.

An hour later he emerged from the bath house clean and in new clothes. He had thrown the remainder of the suit and other clothes away. He felt better, but hunger still gnawed at him competing with sleep for dominance. The man running the bathhouse told him where to find a room and a hot meal. He headed for the hot meal first. Clean and in new clothes he drew less attention than he had earlier. Things were looking up and he felt more positive about his future.

The brothers were saddled with canteens filled a half hour before dark. The horses had grazed, watered, and rested through the day. The men had taken turns sleeping while trading off on guard duty. With night drawing down men and horses were ready to cross the long flat stretch to the Pecos.

Darkness fell quickly with the final glimmer of sunset. The Evening Star was the first to appear, then the stars closest to earth broke out, and eventually the furthest away began to twinkle filling the endless sky with stars. The Big Dipper took shape, then the little dipper with the end of its handle being the North Star.

The men mounted. Cordell took a bearing on the North Star. He struck a match and checked his compass to verify their intended direction. He nudged his horse forward and directly east on top of Cain's trail. The air remained heated from the day, but was cooling. Heavy white clouds had drifted overhead the entire day, but lacked moisture. A cool breeze began to blow as the silhouettes of the hills disappeared behind them.

A sliver of a moon hung directly in front of them in the night sky. It offered little light as the total blackness swallowed the riders. They could barely make out the brother beside them in the black void. The desert held no features and left them feeling like ghosts drifting in nothing of substance. If not for the stars they could have rode off into any direction and not known the difference or where they were.

Cordell rode casually trusting to the North Star above his left shoulder. Adam and Fallon kept one eye on the star and the other on Cordell. The clouds occasionally covered over the stars as upper winds blew them along. As the clouds cleared the men were quick to check for the star and make sure it was still pasted on their left shoulder.

Far to the north heat lightening began to flicker thin tendrils of silent fire toward the earth. They watched the far off show as the lightening intensified, rolling horizontally from a central point flaring out east and west. As one spectacular light show dimmed another immediately took its place.

The clouds disappeared as they rushed toward the northern storm that eventually diminished and then ended. The sky above them turned perfectly clear. Adam and Fallon breathed a sigh of relief when they saw they were still on track with the handle of the Little Dipper.

They rode on without speaking as it seemed improper to disturb the perfect silence. Save for the creak of saddle leather and the hoof falls of the horses the night was silent as a grave. In this manner they passed the hours.

Dawn was casting a dim glow when they came on the roan horse. The men stopped and checked the animal that had now risen to its feet, yet was too exhausted to move on from where Cain had abandoned it.

"That's the roan Cain had in the Butterfield corral," Cordell told his brothers.

"Wonder why he left it?" Fallon asked.

"It probably stopped and refused to move," Adam answered him.

Adam dismounted and looked the horse over. "He looks pretty used up." Adam slipped the headstall off the horse's head and slid the bit out of its mouth. He tossed the bridle aside and then pulled the cinch knot and shoved the saddle to the ground. The horse let out a relieved sigh.

Each of the brothers poured a portion of water from their canteens into Adam's hat. Adam held the felt hat under the roan's nose and quivering lower lip. The horse sniffed at the water and then quickly sucked in the contents of the hat.

"Should we take him with us?" Fallon asked.

Adam put his hat back on and shook his head, "I don't want to force him to move. He's pretty worn out, best let him go at his own pace." Adam mounted his horse. "He'll eventually recover his strength and make it to the river."

They moved on leaving the roan standing in place.

Two hours later it was full daylight. The morning was quickly heating up as the wind turned hot. Pecos was not yet in sight as they stopped to give the horses a rest.

Adam looked behind them. "Will you look at that?"

Cordell and Fallon turned to see what Adam was talking about. In the distance moving slow was the roan following on their trail."

Cordell grinned approvingly. "Looks like he's going to make it."

They waited until the roan caught up to them. He stopped several yards away from them and stood still. They moved on. The horse followed.

Another hour and they were able to make out the trees and brush lining the course of the Pecos River. Upstream they could see the new lumber framed buildings of Pecos.

Chapter 20

They rode their horses directly to the river while they studied the rising constructions upstream. The horses stepped into the water and began to drink. Cordell gestured toward the old buildings on the east side of the river. "That's the part I remember. It was a stopover and supply point for the drives. Goodnight and Chisum, a lot of them, came through here. Ranchers still drive through here."

"With the railroad here now it will become a destination for shipping cattle," Adam added.

Cordell scanned over the new constructions. "That it will. It appears they're moving over to this side of the river though. Got a new bridge and a railroad trestle I see."

Fallon stood in the stirrups and looked at the new part. "I think that's a depot behind us to the north there."

Cordell and Adam turned to look in the direction Fallon had indicated. "Probably be a good place to check first and see if anyone's seen Cain," Adam said.

Cordell agreed. "If Cain's looking for a train that's the first place he'd go."

The horses lifted their muzzles out of the water. The men gathered up their loose reins and turned the horses back out of the water at the same time the roan waded out belly deep in the river and drank.

Cordell lifted his chin toward the roan. "He's a tough one in spite of Cain's best efforts to kill him."

They rode out of the river bed and on toward the depot.

The carpenters watched the three as they rode past the building where they were perched on the roof. One carpenter said to the other, "They come out of that hellhole. Wonder if they're trailing that fella what come by here yesterday looking like raw dog meat."

The second workman studied the backs of the riders. "Tough looking lot. I wouldn't want them hunting me."

The first man chuckled, "This could be interesting."

The three rode up to the side of the long brick depot and dismounted. Tying the horses to a rail they walked around to the track side of the building. Adam and Fallon studied up and down the tracks while Cordell went to the agents open window.

"Morning," Cordell greeting the man cheerfully.

"Morning," the agent returned. "Looking for the train?"

"In a way, but mostly we're looking for a man. He might have swung by here since he's thinking of jumping a train east. Fellow about sixty, gray hair, probably looks pretty beat up from the desert."

The agent snorted, "Sounds like the man that stopped by here yesterday. Nasty, rude, and altogether disagreeable. Looked like he'd been killed and buried, then dug his way back out."

Cordell grinned, "That's likely him. Know where he might have wandered off to?"

With a shake of his head the agent answered, "He bought a ticket, and was right snotty about it too. Went on his way from there."

"What time is his train for?"

The agent chuckled, "Whenever it gets here. Right now the train's main purpose is to run supplies to the end of line. When she comes back she stops here and picks up anyone who wants a ride to Fort Worth. I told this fella you're talking about to check back and forth until he gets his ride."

Cordell considered what the agent was telling him. "You told him to keep checking back?"

"I told him to watch the tracks and depot. I don't want that coyote in my window again."

"That's understandable. Any idea when the train might be back this way?"

"I'm guessing tomorrow by noon, from what I've seen before, but don't bet the ranch on that though." The agent poked his head out the window and saw Adam and Fallon standing in the shade alongside the building. "Those men with you?"

"Yeah, they're my brothers."

"I know it ain't none of my business, but would you be hunting that man?"

"We would. He murdered some folks back in Tucson, and they're not his first."

"That surely don't surprise me after meeting

him, no sir, not one bit."

"Thanks for the information," Cordell smiled at the man. "We're going to be having a look around. We'll check back, if you see him again let us know."

"I'll do that. Sounds like a man what needs to eat some lead."

"Oh, he's going to eat plenty." Cordell turned away and walked back to where his brothers stood.

"Cain bought a ticket for the next train that the agent thinks will pull in here heading east tomorrow morning."

"Did he say anything about Cain?" Adam asked.

"Yeah. He said Cain was snotty, rude, and a coyote."

Adam laughed, "Is that all?"

"He said he was 'altogether disagreeable' too."

"Sounds like our boy."

"I could go for something to eat," Fallon said.

"I know a place on the other side of the river that used to serve up a fair steak and beans. It's not fancy, but the cowboys all go in there," Cordell volunteered.

Fallon chuckled. "Well, that certainly is a capitol recommendation."

Cordell gave him a mock scowl, "I realize it's not dining with the upper crust of Austin, but it'll fill your belly . . . fancy pants."

"I'm not fancy pants anymore." Fallon swept a hand down his ruined suit pants. "Now, I look as much a scoundrel as you."

"Next you'll be wanting to take my black sheep of the family mantle."

"Maybe I'll borrow it first and see if I like it."

"Where's this place?" Adam asked Cordell. "I'll go eat while you two discuss fashion."

Cordell looked at Fallon while jabbing a thumb toward Adam, "I'm with him. We'll discuss the mantle later."

The agent stepped out the door. "I overheard you fellas. There's a good restaurant down the street there. Eat there all the time. Save you a trip across the river."

"Thanks," Fallon waved at him. He then looked at Cordell, "It's not cowboy beans can you handle it?"

Cordell scuffed his boot toe in the dirt. "Well, okay, if it makes you happy. I'm not putting on a suit to eat there though."

Adam was already heading for his horse. "Guess we'd better go with him," Cordell grinned.

"After you, little brother of the black sheep mantle."

Mounting their horses they rode down the dirt street until they found the restaurant situated next to a small hotel that was being added on to. The place was new with windows that let in light. A few men were sitting at the tables.

Fallon leaned down in the saddle and peered in the windows. "Looks alright, but the question is, do the cowboys eat here?"

Cordell stepped out of the saddle and spun the reins around a rail. "Probably just a bunch of flannel mouthed lawyers and bottom dealers." He looked up at Fallon, "I've heard they're one and the same."

Fallon nodded. "They are . . . most of them anyway. I know of one that isn't." He stepped out of the saddle and tied his horse off to the rail.

The three walked into the restaurant and sat down at a table. Cordell took in the small room with a quick glance. Six men were in the room all local types. A woman in her thirties, looking tired, walked up to their table and smiled. She set three hand printed cards on the table. "This is what we have," she said.

Fallon smiled at her. "Saves having to explain each time, makes your life a little easier."

The woman held the smile. "I got the idea from a restaurant I was in once out in Fort Worth. Looks a little nicer than writing it on a board on the wall."

"What do you recommend?" Fallon asked.

"It's all good. You can't go wrong with anything on there."

Fallon smiled a beaming smile at her and pointed to the list, "I'll have that."

The woman looked to Adam and Cordell. They each selected a meal.

The woman walked away and returned with three cups and a trail drive size coffee pot. She filled the cups and walked back to the kitchen.

Cordell leaned in closer to Fallon. "I know you were trying to charm that woman, but you'd appear a lot more charming if you didn't look like you just crossed two-hundred miles of bad country."

"So, what are you saying?" Fallon asked. "That I don't look charming?"

"You look like two-hundred miles of desert with a touch of hell's brimstone thrown in."

"You should know all about that."

"I know I look like the wrath of God," Cordell gave Fallon a taunting grin, "but I'm not trying to be charming either, am I?"

"Shut up, Cordell."

Cordell laughed as he leaned back in his chair and looked around the room.

The woman returned with their meals and set them on the table.

They thanked her and made comments as to how good the food looked.

Cordell stopped her as she was turning to leave. "Excuse me ma'am. Have you seen a stranger in town today or maybe yesterday? Looks out of place here. Man about sixty, gray hair, thin face, looks kind of slimy like a lawyer or bottom dealer?" He cast a quick glance at Fallon when he said it.

"We don't get a lot of folks passing through right now that ain't hooked up to some cow outfit or on the dodge. That will all change when the railroad finishes though." She paused in thought for a moment. "Come to think of it, there was a man like that in here for supper last night. He was shining like a new penny. New clothes, freshly scrubbed with wet gray hair. My sister waited on him, she helps me for the supper crowd. She said he wasn't very nice."

"That sounds like him."

She gave Cordell an appraising look. "You look like a gunhand. You hunting him?"

Cordell gave her a slight smile, "You folks catch on fast here."

"What did he do?"

"He murdered two men and a woman."

"Kin?"

"Two of them were."

"Are you fellows staying in town?"

"Until we can flush the rat out of whatever

hole he's in."

"If you stay at the hotel next door I'll send a message over if I see him."

"That would be good. Unless we catch him first."

She gave Cordell a smile and a wink. "Then, I'll hear the shooting and won't bother." She walked away from the table.

Fallon looked across the table at Cordell. "Women really are attracted to that long haired scoundrel look aren't they?"

Cordell grinned at him. "Can't help it if I'm naturally appealing to the ladies."

Adam concentrated on eating, not wanting to be part of this particular conversation. He was still reeling from his embarrassment with the woman in the Desert Rose.

They finished their meals and left the price on the table along with a bit extra. They waved at the woman as they walked out. She watched them go, especially focusing on Cordell. "If only I was ten years younger," she whispered.

They looked up and down the street. The wind picked up a cloud of dust blowing it between the buildings. Men were busy building and moving lumber from place to place. The little town was busy with obvious intentions of being a city one day.

"I think we should start a systematic search of the town and figure out where Cain is holed up," Adam suggested.

"He's likely at that hotel," Fallon said pointing at the building next to them.

"Cain might sleep there, but I doubt he'll be there during the day," Cordell replied.

"Why not," Adam asked. "Seems like a good place to hold up waiting for the train."

"It's also a good place to be trapped in," Cordell answered. "You have to remember he doesn't know if we are still on him or if he's lost us. He's not going to take any chances in case we are."

"Yeah that makes sense."

"Saloons would be the next best place to look," Fallon said.

Cordell agreed. "Let's make a search through the town like Adam suggested and if we don't see him then we go in the saloons. I'm sure there's more than one."

They mounted up and began riding down the main street. Their heads turned and their eyes searched every place along the way. They peered in the windows of businesses as they passed and became familiar with the lay out of the town. An hour later they had covered the place without success.

Cordell reined his horse up to the front of a saloon and stepped out of the saddle. "I'm going to check in here." He walked in the open door.

Standing inside the room Cordell looked it over and searched for Cain's face among the customers. He walked slowly through as the men at the bar and tables watched him.

As Cordell passed a fat man leaning an elbow on the bar he heard a kissing sound and a voice saying, "Come over here sweetheart, I love blondes."

Several men sniggered at the remark.

Cordell casually glanced toward the fat man and realized he was the one who had made the remark and it was directed at him. The fat man was grinning at him in a taunting manner.

Cordell stopped and looked in the man's face. He had fat jowls and little eyes surrounded by puffy fat cheeks. His dark pig-like eyes reflected a smug demeanor that said he was the barroom bully. "You say something to me?" Cordell asked with an icy edge to the words.

The fat man's grin widened. "I like your long blonde hair. Your ma must have wanted a girl. Did she set you up in dresses and bloomers to go to school?" He laughed, clearly pleased with his own imagined humor.

Several of the men in the room laughed with him. The rest recognized the young man for what he was and waited to see what would happen.

Cordell locked eyes with the fat man. "Bet your ma wanted a child and ended up with a hog instead. She have to feed you at the trough with the other hogs?"

The bully's grin dropped off his face. "No one talks to me like that." He shifted his bulk off the bar.

Cordell smirked at him. "I just did – hog."

With a clumsy step forward the fat man balled up his fists and snarled. "I'll show you, you long haired runt."

There was a quick wisp of metal against leather and then a deadly metallic click. The fat man stopped dead in his tracks looking down the bore of Cordell's Colt. He swallowed and flicked his little eyes back and forth.

"I don't like you," Cordell said calmly. "I don't like fat hogs talking about my ma either."

Lifting his hands palms up in front of him the man took a step back against the bar. "Take it easy mister, I was only funnin' with you."

"I don't like that kind of funnin'"

Fallon stepped up next to Cordell. He had been behind his brother all the while and heard the remarks the fat bully had made. "Thinking about plugging this hog for supper little brother?"

"Thinking about it."

"I don't think we need all that fat back though. Why don't you let this one go and we'll find the one we come to bag."

The room was still with every man listening and watching. Those that had laughed were trying to make themselves especially small.

Cordell lowered the hammer on his Colt. "This here's your lucky day, hog." Cordell turned and headed for the door of the saloon.

Fallon looked at the fat man whose face had gone pale and glistened with fear induced sweat. He shook his head and jabbed his thumb toward Cordell. "Gunfighters, what are you going to do with them? They have such short tempers. My little brother already killed his man today. One a day is the limit I keep telling him, don't be greedy." He laughed as he turned and walked out after Cordell.

The fat man mopped a beefy hand across his face as he turned back to the bar and asked for a drink. He ignored the laughter of the men in the room.

Adam was waiting in the street when his brothers walked out. He looked at Cordell's angry expression and then to Fallon. "What happened in there?"

"Some fat man called Cordell a girl and made fun of him," Fallon answered. "I stopped little brother from shooting him."

"You must be one persuasive attorney. I don't think I could have talked him out of something like that."

Fallon grinned at Adam then turned to Cordell. "Told you you need to get a haircut."

Cordell glared at Fallon's chaffing grin until he began to grin at the humor of it. "If I did I'd lose my charm with the ladies." He pulled his horse's reins loose and mounted.

They rode back to the depot to check with the agent to see if he had seen Cain again. He hadn't. They rode east along the street and crossed over to the old town side of the river. Most of the businesses had closed and moved across the river leaving a good number of empty buildings among the few still open for trade. Some of those closed still contained property destined for moving and had locks on the doors.

"One of these abandoned buildings would be a good place for Cain to hide," Cordell said.

"I don't know," Fallon disagreed. "He appears to be the kind who likes a little comfort."

"He's put up with a lot of discomfort staying ahead of us these last few days. If it means hiding from us I believe he could stand a little more."

Fallon agreed, "I'm sure it won't hurt to have a look around."

They rode on through and around the scattering of buildings. Several of the empty buildings looked like good places to hide out. They walked in and out of the few that were not padlocked shut without finding Cain.

Standing outside the last empty building they

checked Adam said, "Cain would need to get on the train at the depot. He couldn't get on it here unless he wants to jump on while it's going."

"He has a point," Fallon agreed. "Cain will have to get on at the depot when the train is stopped. This is too far from it."

Cordell nodded. "It's getting into afternoon now. We might find him at the hotel tonight. Let's head on back and pick out a place to watch the depot from."

While still standing on the ground the long, hoarse blast of a steam whistle drifted up from somewhere to the west.

"I thought it wasn't supposed to come through until tomorrow?" Adam remarked.

"Cordell swung quickly into the saddle. "We need to be at that depot *now*," he shouted as he kicked his horse into a gallop aimed at the bridge over the river.

Adam and Fallon fell in directly behind him as the plume of smoke coming from the Texas and Pacific locomotive could be seen down the tracks to the west.

Chapter 21

Smoke from the locomotive could be clearly seen drawing closer to the depot as the brothers raced down the dirt road headed for the brick building. The hooves of their horses pounded down on the dry dirt kicking up a cloud of dust around them. All eyes were searching for Cain making his way to the train.

With the depot in sight and the front of the locomotive coming into view Cain burst through a saloon door and quickly shot a look up and down the street. The train was early, he cursed the ticket agent for a fool. Fortunately he had nothing he needed to go back to his room to retrieve. He began to run for the depot.

Cordell was in the lead about to rein his horse toward the track side of the depot when Cain ran out of the side street and into the cross street at the rear of the depot. Cain looked down the street directly at Cordell. He froze in place for a second, then spun and darted back across the street into the town where had come from.

Cordell shouted, "There he goes." He jerked

his horse toward the place Cain had disappeared between the buildings. Fallon and Adam were close behind him.

They caught a glimpse of Cain as he sprinted down a back street and then cut left between the hotel and a new construction on the far side of it. The brothers split up as they searched the streets for Cain. They knew he had to make that train and would wind his way back to it before it pulled out. He only had minutes to get there.

The train blew a long whistle blast as it ground to a halt in front of the depot. Cain ran in pure desperation, he had to be on that train. He cursed his bad luck at having the Whitlocks find him when he was so close to escape. He had seen nothing of them while staying on the move between the saloons and his room at the hotel. He had not wanted to stay in any one place too long as a precaution, yet he felt he had lost them.

His breath came ragged and painful as he dug for air in the heat and dust. Then, in a flash of horror he heard the whistle blow two short blasts and the drivers start to move. The train was leaving already. Seeing a horse tied to a porch post he ripped the reins loose and swung into the saddle. He kicked the horse into an instant gallop headed for the river bridge. He would outrun them and jump on the train once it crossed the trestle as it would still be moving slow at that point.

Cordell rode back out to the street that crossed the river. He spotted Cain on the stolen horse with a good two hundred yard jump on him. The train was pulling out of the depot and Cordell knew what Cain was going to do. He kicked his horse into a pounding gallop trying to close the gap between him and Cain.

Cain reached the bridge ahead of the train. He gave the train a quick look over to see five empty flat cars, a lone passenger car behind them, and then the caboose. He looked back to see a cloud of dust and a rider bearing down on him. A hundred yards behind the rider were two more.

The train crossed the trestle. The caboose cleared it and Cain yanked the horse to a stop and jumped out of the saddle. He ran up to the side of the slowly passing flat cars anxiously watching the passenger car draw ever closer. He cast a quick glance at the rider bearing down on him and cursed. It was the kid, Beau reincarnated.

The front platform of the passenger car pulled alongside of him. Cain latched onto the black iron railing of the car's platform letting the movement of the train pull him off the ground at the same moment the rider tried to run him down. To his delight the kid missed as he pulled himself up and landed his feet on the lowest step of the car. He felt a surge of triumph as he climbed up the steps and to the platform. Wheezing and gasping for air he opened the car door and stepped into the narrow aisle at the head of the rows of seats.

Cordell screamed out in frustration as Cain jumped up on the car a second before he ran him down. He jerked the horse to a sliding stop and flung himself out of the saddle all in one move. As the passenger car slid past him he ran for it and grabbed the iron railing at the rear of the car. He yanked himself up on the platform.

Throwing open the back door Cordell burst in

and saw Cain standing in the aisle at the far end of the car staring at him, terror and uncertainty covered his face. Cordell ran down the aisle and collided with Cain. Wrapping his arms around Cain, he let his momentum hurl them back out the open door. With a twist Cordell launched both of them off the platform.

The two entwined men slammed hard into the sun baked ground and rolled. The force of the landing broke them apart. Cordell lay momentarily stunned from the fall. Cain stopped rolling twenty feet from hm.

Shaking his head Cain sat up and looked quickly around until he spotted the kid. He reached for the Colt in his waistband only to find it had fallen out on the impact. He grabbed the Webley out of the shoulder holster as the kid turned over to face him. He pointed and fired, hitting him in the arm.

A flash of pain and a spurt of blood suddenly soaked Cordell's left arm. He was laying on his holstered gun and had to roll over to get at it. As he rolled Cain fired at him again, but missed.

Cordell had his eyes on Cain as he got to his Colt and cleared the holster. A burst of gunfire erupted around him. He saw the impact of the bullets as they struck Cain one after another. Cain fell back, but with a growl of rage rose back up and fired the little revolver aiming above and past him. Cordell thumbed back the hammer and shot Cain, thumbed the hammer and shot him again. Cain fell back to the ground and didn't move.

The clatter of the train wheels on the track diminished as the train continued on its way east. Several men were crowded on the rear platform watching. As was the conductor hanging off the side of the caboose platform trying to figure out what had happened in his absence from the passenger car.

Fallon and Adam dismounted and ran up to where Cordell still lay on his left side holding the Colt in his right. They looked down at him as he looked up at them.

"We got him," Cordell said softly.

"We did that," Adam replied. "Looks like he got you too," Adam pointed at his brother's bloody sleeve.

Cordell sat up and pushed the blood heavy sleeve up his arm. The bullet had carved a deep furrow across his forearm.

"You're lucky it didn't bust your arm," Adam said as he tied his handkerchief around the wound. "We'll get you patched up better, but that will help for now."

Cordell nodded his thanks. "I thought he had me there at the end. I wasn't going to get on him before he nailed me."

"Fallon shot him first," Adam said. "He was a horse length ahead of me. I did get a couple into him though."

Cordell grinned his approval at Adam and then jerked his head toward Fallon. "Not bad for a big city lawyer."

Fallon held an assisting hand down to Cordell. "Just because you're a scoundrel doesn't mean I'm going to let you get killed."

Cordell laughed lightly as he holstered the Colt and took his brother's offered hand. Fallon pulled him to his feet. Cordell winced in pain. "I hit that ground pretty hard. Cain landed on top of me. I'm feeling it."

Together they walked up to Cain's body. He was dead with multiple gunshot wounds. "Hard man to kill," Cordell commented.

"You said he was tough," Adam replied.

Fallon turned to Cordell. "That was quite a circus stunt jumping on the train like that."

Cordell snorted, "Heck, if that old man could do it I figured I could. Truth be told, I never thought about it. I just knew I wasn't going to let him get away."

"How did you get him out of the car?"

"I slammed into him and we just kept going out the door. I threw my weight into him and off we went."

Three mounted cowboys approached them from the old town. "What's this all about?" one asked.

Cordell looked up at the man. "It's about riding down a killer."

"Who'd he kill?"

"Our ma and pa, and then another man."

"Where abouts?"

"Our folks were in Tucson."

"Long way to hunt down a man."

"Wouldn't you?"

The cowboy nodded, "I would." He pointed at Cordell's arm, "Looks like you got winged."

"I'll live."

The cowboy grinned and jerked his head back toward the buildings. "We saw the race and was taking bets on what the fuss was all about. Then, ya'll went to shootin'. All in all it was pretty entertainin'."

"They have an undertaker in this town?" Adam asked the cowboy.

"Beats me. We've a herd down the river and just rode in for supplies. If it was me, I'd leave him for the buzzards."

"Well, I don't think folks around here would care to have him rotting right out here in the open."

"Might be so."

The three cowboys turned their horses and rode back toward the buildings.

Cordell pointed out to the east. "I see a washout up there, let's throw him in it and kick some dirt over him."

"Works for me," Fallon replied. "He sure doesn't deserve a decent grave."

Cordell walked off and collected his and Cain's horses, leading them up to the body. Adam and Fallon lifted Cain's corpse and draped it over the saddle of the stolen horse. Cordell led the horses while his brothers led theirs. The low spot was a trench that at some time in the past had washed out during a heavy rain and emptied into the river. Pushing Cain's body off the horse it landed with a heavy thud in the trench. They collapsed the sides of the trench down on him.

Mounting their horses they headed back for the west side of the river. Adam took over the stolen horse and led him. They rode in slow silence each in his own thoughts regarding the series of events over the past week. A lot had happened.

Cordell moved his horse up beside Fallon's. Fallon turned his head and the two held each other's eyes for a moment before Cordell extended his right hand to Fallon. "Thanks."

Fallon took his hand. "I'm glad things are good between you and me now."

Cordell nodded, "Likewise."

They crossed over the bridge with the hooves of the four horses echoing loudly on the wooden planks. Several men were standing on the west side of the river watching them approach.

"We might have trouble with these folks," Cordell said. "No one is going to take us for killing Cain."

The brothers spread out side-by-side once they were over the bridge. They pulled to a stop in front of the gathered men.

"You have something to say?" Cordell challenged the group.

One man stepped forward. "All I've got to say is thanks for getting my horse back. He's got his faults, but I do favor him." He walked up and took the reins from Adam.

"I take it you don't have law in this town," Fallon said him.

The man laughed. "This here's Pecos country, son. The tail end of nowhere. We take care of our own problems and like it that way."

A man in the group called out, "We want to know why you shot that man."

Fallon answered for them. "That man murdered our ma and pa back in Tucson. We've been on him for the past week. He also murdered a miner and stole his horse. He's a bad outlaw and has never been anything better. We come for him and we got him."

The men all looked at other and exchanged comments. The man who asked the question answered, "Good enough for us."

"Do you have a doctor here?" Adam asked.

"My brother's been shot."

"No doc," the man answered, "but the barber does a pretty fair job of tending to injuries, broken bones, and gunshots"

"Thanks," Adam said. "Mind if we ride on?"

The gathered men parted to open the way. "Ride on," the man said.

They rode on to the depot then turned down the main street. They rode past the restaurant where the woman stood in the street watching them. "Guess you found him," she called out.

Cordell smiled at her, "We found him. When's supper?"

"Pretty quick now."

"We'll be back."

The woman smiled, "I'll be watching for you."

Fallon looked over at Cordell and shook his head without saying a word.

Cordell looked back at him and shrugged.

Adam shook his head and smiled.

They reached the barber shop where they dismounted and tied off the horses. They walked in to find the barber sitting in his chair talking politics with another man seated in a chair across from him.

Cordell held out his arm. "Hear tell you're the closest thing to a doctor around here."

The barber stood up and looked at the arm. "Come over here."

Cordell walked with him to the end of the room where a small table stood with an oversized wash basin on top of it. An assortment of medicines and surgical tools were on a shelf above it.

The barber asked, "You fancy that shirt?"

Cordell shook his head, "Not any more. Got a store where I can get a new one?"

"We do."

Cordell peeled off the shirt and dropped it on the floor.

The barber took a pair of scissors and cut the knotted handkerchief off and examined the wound. He squeezed the arm and looked it all over. Blood oozed out, the barber caught it with a clean cloth and wiped the wound lightly. "Gun shot?"

"Yup."

"You got a lot of dirt in that. It needs to be cleaned good or it'll infect. It's gonna hurt like sin. You game for it?"

Cordell was already gritting his teeth in pain from the rough examination. "Can't hurt any worse than it already does."

"Oh, sure it can. Hold your arm over the basin there."

Cordell held his forearm over the basin as the barber poured a diluted solution of carbolic acid over the wound letting the residue run off into the basin. He then took another clean cloth and began to scrub the dirt out of the wound.

Cordell let out an involuntary yelp of pain and clenched his fist. Sweat was pouring down his face leaving muddy rivulets through his whiskers. He clenched his teeth together and tried to think of something else as he stared up at the ceiling.

After what seemed like hours the barber declared the wound clean, poured water over it, and wrapped a bandage around it. "I suggest you take a bath and get rid of the rest of the dirt on you. You do that and then come back and I'll put another bandage on it."

"I don't need a bath," Cordell whispered through gritted teeth.

"Actually, you do. Not only is dirt unhealthy, but you smell like a gut wagon."

Cordell looked back at his brothers who both nodded their heads in agreement with the barber. "Fine, where do I find the baths?"

"Behind us, I run that too." The barber stepped back. "Okay, it's two dollars for the doctoring and fifty cents for the bath."

Cordell dug into his pocket and counted out the money to the man. He walked back to his brothers, "You could use baths yourselves."

"We intend to," Adam agreed.

An hour later the three were sitting in lukewarm water soaking two hundred miles of trail dust and baked on sweat off their exhausted bodies. The new clothes they had bought were on the floor beside them.

"What's the plan from here?" Adam asked.

"We ride back to El Paso," Cordell answered as he held his bandaged arm clear of the water and grimaced at it.

"Too bad that train doesn't run all the way to El Paso," Adam said.

"Wouldn't matter if it did," Fallon replied. "We still have the horses and that livery man probably thinks we've stolen them by now."

"Wouldn't that depot have a telegraph?" Cordell asked.

"No doubt," Fallon answered. Then he caught on to Cordell's thought. "I'll send a telegram to that livery man that we are on the way back with the horses so he doesn't set the law on us when we get back there."

"The law might already be waiting for us on account of that shooting in the Desert Rose," Adam said.

Fallon agreed. "We'll have to get in and out of there as fast as we can."

They were all silent for several minutes before Adam asked, "Have we all come to grips with Pa's history?"

"I have no problem with it," Cordell immediately answered. He looked at Fallon.

Fallon glanced back at him. "I understand a lot more now about why Pa did what he did. I only wish he were still alive so I could tell him that. I will always regret the way we parted and it was all me, my pride, my self-pity, my anger. It didn't have to end that way. Then again, I might never have figured that out if not for the murders and Leroy Jackson. I would still be in Austin harboring my resentment."

"You have to let it go, Fallon," Cordell said. "I understand why you felt like you did. No one can change the past, but we can make sure it doesn't become part of the future."

Fallon stared at the wall in silence for a moment then said, "Part of the future is making it up to Helen . . . if she will let me."

"She will," Adam replied. "You think any more about the sheriff idea?"

"Actually, I have. I'm going to try for it. Regardless of whether I get it or not, I'm moving back to Tucson."

Adam turned to face Cordell. "What about

you? Figure to stick around?"

"I don't know."

"There's a job for you out on the ranch if you decide to stay."

"Maybe." Cordell's lips curled in his impish grin. "Unless I run against Fallon for sheriff."

Fallon gave him an incredulous look.

"The ladies would vote for me."

"Woman can't vote," Fallon replied.

"Well, that's stupid. Probably a law written by lawyers to elbow out eligible scoundrel types from the contest."

"Probably."

"Think I'd have a chance?"

Fallon snorted. "When that desert freezes over and pigs skate on the ice."

"Yeah, that's what I thought."

Chapter 22

The brothers made a wide swing out and rode into El Paso from the north. They had followed the Texas and Pacific tracks until the steel rails ended in a railroad workers camp, from there they continued on due west to El Paso. They had held a steady pace making the ride in three days.

Now, back in El Paso they rode cautiously not knowing if Cain's corrupt lawman had been set on them. Except for Cordell's buckskin jacket, they were wearing different clothes then they wore when they assailed Cain's stronghold. Fallon had discarded the ruined suit and was dressed like a range rider with a canvas jacket. Adam wore similar, but in shirt sleeves having rolled his suit and tied it behind the cantle of his saddle.

Their first stop was at the depot to inquire as to the next train to Tucson. It was due in that afternoon so they purchased their tickets for it. They went on from there toward the livery keeping a close watch for the law. Arriving at the livery they dismounted.

The old balding hostler limped out and looked them over. "Well, glad to see you brought my horses back. What'd you do, ride clear to China and back?"

"Didn't you get my telegram?" Fallon asked.

"Yeah, I got it. Saved me a trip to the Marshal's office. I hate that man and wasn't looking forward to it."

"Sorry, things ran a little longer than we anticipated."

The hostler broke into a grin. "You the boys who turned the whorehouse upside down?"

All three men looked at him suspiciously.

He waved his hand. "I ain't said nothing to the marshal, although he did come nosing around here asking questions. That crook doesn't come around unless Winston Cain or that woman up there yanks his chain or whistles him up like a dog. I suspected it was you boys the way you flew in here demanding horses that morning."

"What's the word on the shooting?" Cordell asked.

"According to what I heard, three fellows went in there and shot the bejeezes out of the place. Killed four of their hired thugs and wounded two others while trying to kill Cain. He lit out and no one's seen him since." He grinned knowingly at the brothers.

"So, who'd the marshal say he was looking for?"

"Three young men, sort of matched your descriptions." He pointed at Cordell, "Especially him. They might have let it drop though since I hear tell that madam's running things in Cain's absence. She might not want to ruin her place by having him found or stirring up the pot. I wouldn't bet my life on it though."

"So, Cain hasn't come back?"

The old man grinned at Cordell.

Cordell grinned back at him.

Fallon looked around cautiously. "We might as well settle up on the bill and get a move on before someone spots us standing here."

The hostler pulled a folded bill out of his pocket. "Saw you coming in." He handed the bill to Fallon.

"How about a straight swap on that bill?" Cordell asked.

Looking at Cordell with his sharp blue eyes showing interest the hostler asked, "What you have to swap?"

Cordell pointed at the horse he had taken from Cain's stable. "He's a good horse. Could stand a decent feeding or two, but he's worth more than that bill is. Saddle included."

Rubbing his whiskered jaw the old man gave the horse a good looking over. He lifted the legs, patted the muscled hips, and checked its age by the teeth. He nodded, "He's a good horse alright. Got proof of ownership?"

"Seems I found him running loose. You might notice there's no brand or any such identifying marks."

"Found him, did yuh? Just wandering around, saddle and all?"

"Yup. He might have once belonged to Winston Cain, but he probably won't be back to say anything . . . from what I hear that is"

The old man nodded. "Must have took a long trip since he ain't been back."

"A one way trip south . . . from what I hear."

The hostler thought it over for several seconds then gently pulled the bill out from between Fallon's fingers. "It's a swap."

Fallon smiled. "Works for me."

They took the canteens. Adam removed his rolled suit from the saddle. They had finished the last of the food brought from Pecos Station so there was nothing in the saddlebags.

The hostler watched them as they filled the canteens at his corral pump. "Say, if you don't mind my asking, what *was* the shooting over anyway."

Fallon looked at him as he corked his filled canteen. "Cain murdered our ma and pa over a twenty year old imagined grudge."

"I see. Eye for an eye."

"No," Fallon replied. "Justice owed."

"Sounds like it. Well, I ain't seen yuh." He turned and led the horses into the barn.

As they walked away from the livery Cordell said to Fallon, "You get to buy me lunch."

"How do you figure that?"

"Because I saved you a small fortune on that rental bill."

"And here I thought you did it out of pure brotherly love."

"Nope, free lunch."

"Scoundrel."

"Flannel mouth."

They entered into the business area of the town losing themselves in the movement of people, freight wagons, and the general activity. Keeping a low profile they hoped to get on the train and be out of town before Cain's bought and paid for law spotted them. They needed to kill several hours before the train pulled in.

Stopping to look around Cordell studied his reflection in a store window. "I'm the most obvious one," he said.

"Maybe if you take off the jacket," Adam suggested.

"I need to do more than that." Cordell looked down the street and saw a barber shop sign. He walked toward it. His brothers followed him.

"What are you going to do?" Fallon asked.

"Make me less obvious."

Fallon looked at the barber's sign. "It's about time."

"You're getting your wish."

"You do realize it will destroy your scoundrel charm with the ladies."

"I won't be very charming if I'm decorating a hangman's scaffold." Cordell then broke into a roguish smile, "Besides, there's a lot more that's charming about me than my hair." He handed Fallon his canteen and walked in the door.

Fallon and Adam watched through the window as the barber greeted Cordell and had him sit in the vacant chair. They both sat down on a bench outside the barber shop to wait. Adam glanced at Fallon and could see a difference in him. He seemed unburdened and more relaxed. The friendly banter between him and Cordell was a pleasant change from their constant quarreling. He considered the guilt and frustration Fallon had carried all these years, keeping it all to himself, it must have been hard.

A half hour passed before Cordell walked back out carrying his jacket. Besides a haircut he had gotten a shave leaving only the mustache. Fallon whistled at his brother's freshly shorn head, "Well, I never thought I'd see the day."

"Don't get too excited, I intend to let it grow back out." He then swiped his finger back and forth across the mustache and said, "This maintains my scoundrel charm I believe."

"We certainly wouldn't want you to go completely scoundrel free now would we?" Fallon gestured down the street. "I see a café down that way, let's eat."

"You're buying me lunch," Cordell reminded him.

"As long as it isn't more than fifty cents."

"Oh, it will be. Then, you get to buy me a beer at the saloon afterwards."

Fallon lifted his right eyebrow. "Driving up the price? What next, you want me to carry you on my back?"

"Well, now that you mention it, my feet do kind of ache."

"Your skull will kind of ache in a minute."

"Cordell, I'd quit while I'm ahead," Adam warned.

'Alright, lunch and a beer. You don't have to carry me."

Fallon snorted, "Thanks."

They walked on to the café. After eating, they found a saloon close to the depot where they spent the early afternoon sitting at a dark corner table until it was time for the train.

Arriving at the depot ahead of the train's arrival time they decided it was safer to sit separately from each other in case the marshal came around looking for three men together. Fallon exchanged jackets with Cordell since their earlier descriptions were a blonde haired man in a buckskin jacket and a brown hair man in a suit. They wouldn't fit those descriptions.

As they sat on different benches the marshal made his way through and around the depot looking over the waiting passengers. He gave longer looks at Fallon in the buckskin jacket and then Cordell. He continued walking, leaving the depot and proceeding down the street.

Cordell stood up and casually strolled toward Fallon. He stopped in front of Fallon and said in a low voice, "He was looking."

"Yes, he was. Good thing you cut your hair."

"And swapped jackets," Cordell said as he turned and walked back to the bench he had been sitting on.

The train rolled in on time. As it braked to a stop with a whistle blast a railroad man walked onto the platform and called out that the train was now boarding for Benson and Tucson.

The brothers got up and followed the other people as they filed into the passenger cars. Adam and Fallon sat in the seats beside each other. Cordell took an aisle seat across from Fallon.

Fallon leaned toward Cordell, "This time when the conductor asks for your ticket just give it to him."

"What ticket?"

Fallon scowled at him.

The car was filling up when a young woman stopped and looked at the empty seat beside Cordell. Smiling at Cordell she asked, "Excuse me, is that seat taken?"

Cordell took off his hat and stood, "No, ma'am. You are welcome to it unless you would prefer to sit in my seat and I will move over."

"No. I would like the window seat so I can look out."

"Of course," Cordell replied. He stepped out into the aisle to let her move into the seat.

She smiled at him as she sat down. "Thank you sir, you are most gallant."

Cordell returned the smile and sat down.

Fallon looked at him and shook his head.

Cordell grinned at his brother and swiped the mustache. He mouthed the word, "Scoundrel."

Fallon rolled his eyes and tipped his hat over his nose as he settled back into the seat.

Chapter 23

The train rolled on through the night stopping only for water refills. It pulled into the depot at Benson in the morning, then continued on to Tucson arriving there two hours later. The brothers climbed down the train car steps at the depot they had departed from over a week before. They had no idea what lay before them or what changes would take place in them all as they had boarded that morning.

Adam was suddenly very tired. He looked at his brothers, even Cordell was showing the strain of the past days although he would never admit it. Fallon held the stoic countenance of the elder brother, but the trek had taken a physical toll on him as well.

"We're all still wearing the trail dust from Pecos Station. We look a sight," Adam said.

Fallon gave himself a look over. "I like it." Then, with a hint of pride he added, "I feel like I've done something worthwhile for once in my life."

"You did," Cordell remarked. "We all did."

Adam looked toward the expanse of the growing town. "I'll bet Laura, Ruth, and Elwood are

254

worried sick. I never thought to send them a wire from Pecos Station."

"We probably should have, alright," Fallon agreed. "Too late now, we'd best go face the music."

They walked on to Elwood and Ruth's house. Stepping up on the porch Adam looked them over. "We're a mess."

"You're a rancher," Cordell chided him, "you've never been dirty before?" He knocked on the door.

Adam smiled, "Just wanted to make a good impression, but you're right, Laura has seen me dirty before."

Footsteps sounded from inside the house, the door knob turned, and the door swung in and open. Ruth stood transfixed for several seconds as she stared at them. She then burst out, "Praise the Good Lord. We did not know what had happened to you boys."

Cordell grinned, "Can we come in?"

"Oh, of course, I was simply taken aback for a moment." Ruth stepped back and called into the house. "They are back, thank heaven."

A rush of footsteps broke into the room as Laura ran up to Adam and threw her arms around him. "We were so worried," she whispered.

"I'm sorry," Adam apologized. "We should have wired, but it was a frenzied and tense several days."

Elwood walked into the room to see Ruth making a fuss over the boys. Cordell was the first to see him. He walked up to his uncle and extended his hand. "Feeling better, Uncle Elwood?"

"Yes, much. Thank you."

Adam and Fallon then acknowledged their uncle.

"I'll bet you boys are hungry," Ruth said excitedly.

"We are that," Adam agreed.

"I have coffee on, come in the kitchen and sit." Ruth hurried to the kitchen ahead of them.

Elwood smiled at his nephews. "Coffee is the strongest thing you will find in this house from now on. I am still ashamed of my earlier behavior."

Cordell put his hand on Elwood's back and gave him the imp smile. "We won't tell."

"If you do, I'll deny it," Elwood laughed. Elwood stared at Cordell with sudden realization. "Your hair . . . you got a haircut."

"Had to, but that's part of a long story."

Elwood's expression turned serious as he met the eyes of each of his nephews. "Did you find him?"

"We did," Cordell answered.

"Is he?"

"He is."

Elwood nodded. "Long overdue. Too bad it didn't happen twenty years ago."

"If it had there would still be a lot unsaid and unresolved," Fallon said. "There is a lot we now understand and it's good that we do."

Elwood met Fallon's eyes. "The truth should never have been kept from you boys. I never agreed with it. I didn't care for Beau for a long time, but then when we became friends, I felt he should come clean with you boys. He and Tessa didn't want you to know that there had ever been a Beau Whitlock."

"Except, now we know. It's water under the bridge, though."

They all walked across the room and into the big kitchen where they all sat around the table. Ruth served coffee.

Laura sat next to Adam simply feeling the relief of his being back safely. Adam smiled at her, "I'm a little dirty."

"I don't care," she replied. "You are back. That is all that matters."

"Did you stay here the whole time?" Adam asked.

"Yes. I did not want to make the long trip home by myself, but mostly I wanted to be here when you returned. Pa came down once to check on us and I told him everything and what was happening. He wished you well."

"Things went a lot different than we had expected."

Laura hesitated for a second trying to form the words. "Did you kill Winston Cain?"

Adam searched her brown eyes for an indication of her mood as she had been set against their actions at the start. He nodded his head slowly.

"Pa said you were right in doing what you did. He said if he were in your place he would do the same thing."

"I'm glad he understands."

Ruth listened as Adam and Laura talked and then asked, "You were gone so long, what happened?"

"We had to chase him," Cordell answered.

"To where?"

"Pecos."

Elwood's eyebrows lifted. "The cattle crossing on the Pecos River?"

"It's called Pecos Station now," Adam said. "The railroad is running through it."

"You chased Cain for hundreds of miles?"

Fallon glanced at Cordell with an approving smile. "Little brother did. Cordell tracked him from El Paso to Van Horn Wells, and then to Pecos. He's everything Pa was."

Cordell smiled at the shocked faces around the table. It was clear they were surprised by Fallon's change of attitude toward him. "Fallon and I have come to understand each other a little better."

Ruth broke into a smile. "I am so happy for that. Brothers should get along."

"Okay," Elwood began, "if you left here on the train how did you follow Cain across the country?"

"We rented horses and set out after him," Adam answered.

Elwood looked at him. "There seems to be a lot to tell about this adventure. Why don't you boys get cleaned up while Ruth makes some lunch? We can talk about it after."

Cordell slid up the sleeve of his jacket and shirt to reveal the soiled bandage around his arm. "Do you have some clean bandage for this?"

Ruth looked at the dirty cloth and dried blood that had soaked through it. "My goodness, what happened to you?"

"Cain got off a lucky shot."

"You were shot!"

"Just a little Aunt Ruth, it's not a big thing. I just figure I should put something clean on it."

"I will get something right away." Ruth rushed out of the kitchen.

"I have got to hear this story," Elwood said.

An hour later with the brothers washed, clothes brushed, and guns put away they sat down for lunch. They made small talk as they ate, not wishing to upset the meal with the sordid details of their encounters while hunting Cain down. At the end of the meal they all moved to the sitting room to listen.

The brothers took turns telling the story, skimming over the more gruesome points. Laura sat nervous and tense in her chair as she realized the danger her husband had been in. Although Ruth and Elwood had filled her in on the background of her in-laws, and the part Winston Cain had played in their problems, it wasn't until the brothers told the full story that she fully comprehended the wretchedness of the man.

When the men concluded the telling Laura slowly shook her head. "How could one person be so vile and evil?"

"It was a shock for me too," Adam said. "I guess . . .," he stopped short and cast a quick glance at Cordell who gave him a knowing look back. Adam began again, "You and I have been pretty sheltered from a lot of the bad people and the violence in this world around us. Fallon deals with it in court and Cordell has seen far more of it than any of us ever have. It was eye opening and educational for me."

Cordell glanced from Adam to Laura. "That's why Cain had to be stopped and, in my experience, a bullet is the surest way to keep a cold-blooded murderer from killing again."

"It all sounds so wrong," Laura said, "however, I now understand." She looked at Fallon. "The law and courts could never have done anything could they?"

Fallon shook his head. "No. There was no evidence to arrest him on and even if he was he would have easily beat a trial and walked away victorious in his crime."

"When we first encountered him in El Paso," Adam put in, "he admitted to having killed them."

"We will all keep this little affair under our hats," Elwood said firmly.

They all nodded in agreement.

"No one has to know that Ryan and Tessa had ever been anything other than the Monroes who ran a store," Ruth said.

"Some things are best kept in the family," Fallon added.

Elwood looked at Fallon. "What now Fallon? Will you be returning to Austin and will it be another three years before we see you again?"

Fallon surprised them when he answered, "No. I will be coming back to Tucson."

"Will you open an office here?" Ruth asked.

"I'm through being a lawyer."

"My goodness. Why?"

"I hate being a lawyer. I never wanted to be one."

Ruth's mouth dropped open in shock.

"I know," Elwood said. "You were forced into it."

Fallon gave his uncle a look of surprise. "How did you know?"

"Because I saw it in your eyes, and your mood, when you left home for Baylor in Waco. I talked to Tessa about it, but she and Ryan insisted that you had to make a name for yourself. I believe they feared you would go the way of Beau Whitlock if you didn't or they wanted to clean up the family name by having a son who represented the law. Which I'm not sure, but I thought they should let you choose your own way."

Fallon fought back the anger he was determined to bury. "I was never given a choice."

"I had no idea," Ruth said. "What will you do instead?"

Fallon grinned, "I had considered becoming a scoundrel."

"*What?*" Ruth spit out. "You want to be a scoundrel? My goodness why?"

Fallon glanced at Cordell. "But, that job's already taken. I don't want to copy."

Cordell burst out laughing. As did Elwood and Adam.

Ruth smiled as she caught onto the joke. "Yes, Cordell mentioned earlier that the two of you have come to understand each other."

Fallon laughed lightly. "We were ready to kill each other. In fact we almost did until Adam said something that woke me up. After I dwelt on it I knew I was the one at fault. We all had a good talk out there under the stars and we came to understand a lot more about each other. Cordell and I buried the hatchet."

"What are your plans, Fallon?" Laura asked.

"I'm going to run for Pima County Sheriff. Adam thinks I've got a good shot at it with my law background and he said Red had connections that could help."

Laura smiled. "Yes, Pa knows everyone. I think that is a splendid plan."

Fallon replied, "First, I have a lot of making up to do for someone."

"Helen?"

Fallon sighed as he looked at Laura. "Yes. If she will give me a second chance."

"Helen and I are friends. She has spoken of it to me. In fact I have seen her several times since you have been away and she said that you were coming back to talk. I believe she is hopeful of a reunion."

"Did you tell her where we went and why?"

Laura shook her head. "Only that you were away with your brothers."

Fallon's face brightened. "Thank you. I will explain it to her. Better she hear it from me."

Ruth looked at Cordell. "How about you young man? You got your hair cut and are looking respectable now, ready to settle down?"

"Probably not."

"Are you leaving again?"

"I'm too restless to stay in one place for long."

"Like I told you before, I have a job for you if you want it," Adam said to him.

"Maybe one day." Cordell smiled lightly. "You never know what might make me want to stick around."

"Charlotte seemed smitten with you," Fallon said stifling a grin. "Seems that would be worth sticking around for."

"Girls like a scoundrel, what can I say?" Cordell returned.

"Her father hates you, of course."

Cordell broke into the impish smile. "How about that."

Fallon stood up. "Well, there's no time like the present to start mending my fences. If you will all excuse me, I believe I will walk on into town. I have a sudden taste for a freshly baked loaf of bread."

Fallon began to walk out of the house when he felt an urge to wear his gun. He didn't feel the need to pack a gun to see Helen; however, he knew well that danger lay in wait for the unarmed man. The dead miner came directly to mind. He walked back into the bedroom and pulled his holstered gun from his bag and buckled it around his waist letting his jacket fall over it.

Fallon had been gone for half an hour when Cordell said to Adam, "We should go look up Leroy and tell him what happened."

Adam agreed. "We owe him that. If not for him we would be none the wiser for what really happened. I'm sure he would also like to know he doesn't have to keep watching for Cain anymore."

"He was Pa's best friend, he might as well be our friend too."

"Leroy's probably at the Congress." Adam turned to Laura, "We're going to walk on into town and look up Leroy to tell him how this all came out."

"Alright. Will you be back for supper?"

"Yes. We won't be that long."

As they walked out of the room Cordell headed back for the bedroom.

"Where are you going?" Adam asked.

"To get my gun."

"Do you really think you need it here in town?"

"I always think I need it, that's why I'm still alive."

Adam nodded, walked back into his and Laura's room and put on his gun. He shook out his wrinkled, dirty suit coat to cover the gun and went back out to the hall.

Cordell slipped on his buckskin jacket. "Okay, let's go find Leroy."

Chapter 24

Fallon stopped in front of the bakery and took a deep settling breath. He opened the door and walked in. Helen was behind the counter. She looked up at the tinkling bell and smiled at him. The smile was a promising sign, he thought.

Fallon moved up to the counter and smiled in return. "I'm back, like I promised."

Helen continued to smile warmly at him. "Laura said you and your brothers were still away."

"Yes, our business ran longer than we expected."

Helen turned to the lady who owned the bakery. "Mrs. Walters, would it be alright if I left a bit early today?"

Mrs. Walters looked at Fallon and smiled. "Certainly."

"Thank you." Helen took off the apron she was wearing and hung it on a peg. She then followed Fallon out of the store.

"Would you like to go to the café and have a cup of coffee?" Fallon asked.

"Yes. We can talk."

Fallon nodded. "There is much I want to tell you."

They began to walk toward the café.

Helen glanced at him with nervous eyes. "Are you going back to Austin?"

"No. I'm coming back home."

Helen stopped as her eyes opened wide in surprise. "You were serious then about leaving Austin?"

"Yes. I don't want to be a lawyer. I never did."

Helen's mouth opened to speak, yet no words came out for several seconds. Finally she said, "I do not understand. Why did you go off to law school if that is not what you wanted?"

Fallon sighed. "It's a long story. To answer your question in short, it was my parents who insisted I become a lawyer. They meant no harm, they thought they were helping me to make something of my life." He paused looking at the boards under his feet. "I have learned a lot about myself recently . . . much of it unpleasant."

"Self-examination?"

Fallon nodded feeling shame. "I was filled with anger and self-pity. I had a fight with my father and . . . ," he couldn't finish.

"And you never came back," Helen finished the sentence for him.

Fallon nodded as he continued to look at the ground. "And you suffered for it." He looked back up at her holding her brown eyes with his. "I am so sorry. I want to make it up to you, for us to begin again."

Helen slipped her hand into Fallon's. "I want that, too."

A smile filled Fallon's face. "How about that coffee?"

They walked on and into the café.

Cordell and Adam walked down Congress Street headed for the Congress Hall Saloon. Before they reached it Cordell stopped and looked down the street.

"What are you looking at?" Adam asked.

"I just got to thinking about my horse. I paid for two days board thinking I'd be back. Now, I'm worried about him. I hope Faust didn't sell him, thinking I had abandoned him there."

"My horse and buggy are there too. Faust wouldn't sell your horse any more than he would mine. We'll get the bill squared with him."

Cordell scowled. "He knows you, he doesn't know me all that well, and what he does is probably all bad. He might not sell yours, but he would mine. I'm going to go see."

"I'll go with you."

"No. Go ahead and find Leroy before he takes off. I'll only be a bit, then I'll join you, providing Faust hasn't sold my horse."

"Okay. I'll meet you at the Congress."

The brothers parted walking in opposite directions.

Cordell walked until he was out of the business district and to the end of the street where the livery stood. As he drew closer to the big barn and corral behind it the hair on the back of his neck began to bristle. He stopped and studied the layout. He didn't see anything out of place, but something had him nervous. He slipped the loop off the hammer of his Colt and continued on to the open doors of the barn.

He walked into the barn with the smell of hay, horses, and dust strong in the air. He looked up and down the aisle between the gateless stalls. The double doors on the opposite side of the barn were open. Horses were tied in most of the stalls. Some were asleep while others turned their heads back to look at him. In the end stall he saw his horse and felt relief that he was still there.

"Mr. Faust," Cordell called out.

A shuffling of feet in the loft above him drew his attention, but no one descended the inside ladder. A filtering of dust and bits of hay shifted through the cracks floating down to the ground reflecting in the light. He looked around feeling that something was amiss. Then Faust appeared from his back office and walked up to him.

Cordell nodded toward him. "I've come to settle my bill and take my horse."

In his broken English Faust said, "Yes. I thought you had deserted him. You said two days."

"I know. Our business ran longer than expected."

"And your brother's horse and buggy?"

"He will be along to settle with you on it."

Faust nodded his acceptance. "Let me find your bill, I will return." He walked away toward his office.

Hearing a steady squeaking sound from outside Cordell glanced up at the loft again. He called after Faust, "Do you have an outside ladder to the loft?"

Faust turned around with a confused look. "No. Only the pulley rope outside the upper loading door. Why?"

"Just wondering."

Faust shook his head and continued on.

Cordell walked out the rear doors of the barn where the rope hung outside the open loading door in the loft. The rope was swaying slightly and there was the distinct smell of stirred up dust. He looked up the two ropes to the steel pulley at the top. He pulled the rope through the pulley, it made the same squeaking sound he had heard.

There had been a man in the loft. Why would he shinny down the rope when he could have used the ladder inside? Cordell whispered, "Because he didn't want me to see him."

The sound of boots on hard ground, jingling spur rowels, and the swishing made from pants legs rubbing together approached from behind him. He turned around to see four Mexicans spreading out from each other as they marched a beeline directly toward him. He knew banditos when he saw them. He immediately thought of the two banditos he had killed down on the border.

Adam stepped into the Congress Hall and looked among the crowd for Leroy. He spotted him sitting at the same table as before facing the door. He was reading a paper with a half empty beer glass in front of him. Leroy appeared to be reading, but he knew the old outlaw was seeing every man who walked through the door. He crossed the room to where Leroy sat.

Leroy lowered the paper eyeing Adam over the top of it as he reached the table. His eyes flicked around looking for Cordell. "I see you got back in one piece."

"We wanted to come by and tell you that we got Cain."

Leroy nodded. "Good. Where's Cordell?"

Adam jabbed a thumb over his shoulder, "He went to the livery to check on his horse. He'll be here pretty quick."

Leroy threw down the paper and jumped up from his chair. "Come on, we need to get to the livery fast."

"Why?" Adam asked suddenly alarmed.

"There's four Mexicans laying for Cordell over at that livery." He rushed across the saloon floor with Adam following.

As they cleared the door Leroy snapped out to Adam, "I hope you have a gun on under that coat."

"Yeah, I do."

Leroy jumped into the street to avoid the human traffic on the boardwalk. "Come on, run."

As they ran down the dirt street toward the livery Adam spotted Fallon coming out of the café with Helen.

Fallon looked up to see his brother and Leroy running. As the two men ran past him he shouted, "What's wrong?"

Adam shouted back, "Cordell's walking into an ambush at the livery."

Fallon said quickly to Helen, "I'll be back." He ran after Adam and Leroy.

Helen stood in startled surprise at the sudden

rush of the men and Adam's statement. She knew Cordell, not well, but he was Fallon's youngest brother and was considered a gunfighter and trouble by many. It sounded like men were going to kill him. She turned and hurried toward Clay Scott's office.

Silvio grinned with triumph as he kept his cold brown eyes on Cordell. Monolito had run the short distance to his house to tell them that he was at the barn. "*Hola*, Cordell Monroe. We have ridden a long way to find you."

Cordell didn't answer. He knew men like that one liked to talk it up before actually getting into action. He wasn't of that frame of mind. He knew by the way the four were spread out it was coming down to shooting time.

He took in the dress of the men. Boots, big spurs, cartridge belts, double revolvers. It wasn't any of them that rode that rope down, which meant there was a fifth man somewhere unseen.

"You killed my cousins down in Black Water," Silvio called across the fifty paces that separated them. "That was a very big mistake for you."

Another set of steps and Silvio put his hand on the butt of one of his guns.

That was enough for Cordell. His hand flashed down for his Colt, he brought the barrel up level while snapping back the hammer. The first .45 slug took Silvio just above the belt buckle. The Mexican jerked back and his feet went out from under him.

The other three Mexicans drew and began hammering shots at Cordell.

A sledgehammer blow hit Cordell in the thigh while another painful stab of fire burned through his left side. He returned shot for shot dropping a second attacker as he fell to the ground. His five shots were spent.

He was on the ground ramming the spent brass from the Colt's cylinder and shoving live cartridges in their place. He was going to die, but not alone. The remaining two Mexicans had flattened out on the ground giving him a chance to reload. Then, they rose to their feet aiming at him as he slipped the fourth cartridge into the cylinder. A rapid succession of pistol shots came from behind him. The two Mexicans fell like pole-axed steers.

Filling the cylinder, Cordell slapped the Colt's loading gate shut and lifted himself up on his elbow staring at the spot the Mexicans had been standing a moment before. The leader he had first hit rose up on his knees firing a shot at a point past where he lay. He shot into the Mexican a half second before the impact of several bullets slammed into his body and he crumpled to the ground.

In the confusion of the fight Monolito had snuck around the barn and entered the front doors with a rifle. From inside the barn he had a clear view of Cordell on the ground propped up on his elbow. He shouldered the rifle and took aim at Cordell.

Fallon ran into the barn. He looked down the aisle between the stalls and out the rear doors. He could see Cordell on the ground and a man standing in the aisle between him and his brother. With the man's back toward him it took Fallon a second to realize the man was pointing a rifle at Cordell.

Fallon pulled his gun at the same time

shouting, "Drop the rifle!"

Monolito turned his head around with a flash of rage in his eyes. He swung the rifle toward the man coming up behind him.

Fallon fired three rapid shots at the man causing him to drop the rifle and grip his side after the third shot. Falling to his knees he clumsily grabbed for the rifle. Fallon took aim and shot him in the head.

Adam and Leroy ran into the barn to see the fifth man dead and Fallon walking toward them reloading as he did.

Faust ran out of his office chattering incoherently in German. He had walked out just as the shooting began and then ducked back into the office for safety.

Cordell fell back to the ground and lay still.

Fallon kept moving toward Cordell. "Cordell," he called out. He felt panic well up inside him. He couldn't lose his brother now. Not after they had made amends.

Adam and Leroy turned and left the barn beside Fallon. The three came together hovering over Cordell who looked up at them. He forced a grin, "Jeez, this hurts."

Fallon let out the breath he had been holding. "You little scoundrel. You scared ten years out of me."

Cordell grimaced around the grin. "Scared me a little too."

Fallon knelt down, opened Cordell's shirt and looked at the wound. "Boy, that's ugly."

"Thanks. I feel much better now. Got one in my leg to match it."

"Show off," Fallon sniped back.

Adam ran off for the doctor. He ran into Scott half way back to the main part of town.

"What's going on?" Scott demanded.

"Back at the barn. Four Mexicans ambushed Cordell."

Scott paused for a moment. "Is it over?"

"Yeah, they're all dead and Cordell has been shot at least twice."

Scott cursed to himself. That meant Monroe was still alive. "I'd best get over there." Scott hurried along his way.

Adam continued on to the doctor's office and burst in the door. "Doctor!" he shouted in the little waiting room.

Doctor Smith hurried out of a back room. "What's all the commotion?"

"There was a shooting down at the livery. My brother's been shot, he needs you."

Charlotte rushed out of the backroom wearing a white nurse's smock. "Which brother?" she demanded anxiously."

"Cordell."

"Oh, my goodness," she gasped. "How bad is he?"

"I don't know, he's alive though."

Smith disappeared into the back room and ran back out with his bag. Take me there quickly.

"I am coming to help," Charlotte told Smith as he rushed by.

"Yes, hurry."

They all ran out together following Adam to the livery barn. When they reached the scene of the fight Smith was taken slightly aback at the presence of the four dead men sprawled out on the ground and Cordell being hovered over by Fallon and another man he didn't know.

Several men and boys had crowded around to gawk at the results of the fight. Many had heard the shooting, others had learned of it as the word quickly spread through the town. Faust was walking with and talking to Scott as they made their way around looking over the bodies.

Smith and Charlotte knelt down to either side of Cordell. Cordell grinned at Charlotte, "Evening, Charlotte."

"Hush now," she replied. "Let Dr. Smith check you."

Smith made a quick survey of Cordell's wounds. He looked up at the men around him. "Someone get a wagon so we can bring him back to my office."

"How bad is he?" Adam asked Smith.

"I don't think any vital organs were hit. I will have to check more closely in a cleaner environment though."

Scott finished his check of the battle scene then walked over to where Cordell lay. He scowled down at Cordell. "Mr. Faust told me these men came after you and you defended yourself."

Cordell replied in a low voice, "They came out of nowhere."

Scott held the scowl. "You're riff-raff, Monroe. Always have been. Trouble follows you like coyotes follow sheep."

Charlotte snapped at him, "Why do you always have to act like that, Father?"

"Because he's a no good outlaw and trash,

Charlotte, and it's high time you realized it. He's scum."

The last word was barely out of Scott's mouth when Fallon's fist slammed it shut. Scott fell on his backside with a look of shock.

Scott wiped the blood from his mouth as realization came to him that Fallon Monroe had struck him. He glared up as his split lips twisted in rage. "You're under arrest Monroe for attacking an officer of the law."

"You have bad mouthed my brother for the last time. I'm an officer of the law too, get up so I can knock that empty head of yours off. If you're going to arrest me I want it to be worthwhile."

The men standing around stared in surprise at the sudden action.

Scott cast his eyes around the crowd, then back to Fallon. He slid his revolver out of his holster. "You're under arrest." He pointed the gun at Fallon.

Adam stepped forward and kicked the gun out of Scott's hand. Scott grabbed his hand and screamed up at Adam. "You're under arrest too."

A man drove a wagon around and stopped next to where Cordell lay. Smith stood and instructed several men to lift Cordell into the wagon and take him to his office. The men did as instructed with Cordell.

Smith calmly looked down at Scott who was still sitting on the ground. "Marshal Scott, you were once a fine officer of the law, but over the years you have become a bully. If you arrest these men I will personally testify that you instigated your punch in the mouth, that I may add you deserved, for your insults to the Monroe family. Personally, I believe it is time for a new marshal in this town. The Mayor is my close friend and I will be talking to him about it."

Smith turned and climbed up into the wagonbed. Charlotte was already up in the wagonbed and kneeling beside Cordell.

Scott sat in shocked rage at Smith's diatribe against him. He struggled to his feet glaring at Fallon and Adam. Taking a quick scan around him at the gathered townsmen he saw only unfriendly faces looking back at him.

Scott then saw his daughter in the wagon. With a growl of fury he shouted at her, "You get out of that wagon this instant, you aren't going with him."

"I am Dr. Smith's assistant!" she snapped back at him.

The wagon pulled away leaving Scott glowering after it with a deep scowl pulling down his bloody mouth.

Fallon stepped up and looked Scott directly in the face. "I agree with Dr. Smith, I think it's time for a new marshal in this town."

Scott turned his infuriated eyes on Fallon and barked a humorless laugh. "Who's going to replace me? I've held this position for eight years. I'm in good here with the citizens and the town council."

"No, you are not," a voice came from the crowd.

A man stepped forward. The townsmen knew him, it was Simeon Nader of the city council. "I am a witness to your unprofessional display, Marshal Scott. I also agree with Dr. Smith's observations in regards to you. There will be discussion at the next meeting about replacing you."

Scott's mouth dropped open. Then, he

slammed it shut. "Well, these two are under arrest all the same."

"I think not," the councilman said. "If you had said about my brother what you said about Mr. Monroe I would have punched you in the mouth too."

Leroy spoke up, "Mr. Nader, you might also be interested in knowing that the marshal knew these outlaws were in town gunning for Cordell and didn't do anything about it. In fact he encouraged them to follow through with killing Cordell."

Scott glared in a threatening manner at Leroy, who boldly returned the look.

"Really?" Nader replied. "Please elaborate."

Leroy gestured with his chin toward Scott. "He was talking to them. They were asking him about Cordell. I overheard the whole conversation. He told them how he didn't like Cordell and "accidents" could happen. I knew right off they were south-of-the-border banditos on the hunt. They were heavily armed and Scott let them parade around at will. They have been hanging around the livery for the past several days. I've been keeping an eye open for Cordell to warn him."

The townsmen moved in closer to listen to the accusation against Scott.

"There's no law against them being in town," Scott justified angrily. "And, I don't know what you *think* you heard, but I never said no such thing."

Leroy stepped up to Scott and looked him directly in the eyes. "I know what I heard."

"That is a serious charge, Marshal," Nader stated flatly.

Anxious to avert his eyes from Leroy's, Scott

looked at Nader. "It's his word against mine."

Nader agreed, "True; however, your behavior here today and the growing distrust of the citizens of Tucson toward you is warrant enough to replace you. Remember, you serve at the will of the citizens, town council, and mayor, not yourself."

"How was I supposed to know what they had in mind?" Scott shouted at Nader.

"It's your job to know!" Nader shot back. "Four heavily armed men walking freely about town, clearly not citizens lightly armed for self-defense, and you do not see a problem in that? They were a threat to every citizen in this town! You should have sent them packing the day they got here."

Scott growled, "What do you know about it anyway?"

Nader's temper was escalating by the second. "I know you are fired as of this moment. Report to the mayor's office immediately."

Scott stepped up to Nader in a threatening manner. Several men, including Leroy, Fallon, and Adam closed in on him.

Scott hesitated. Nader reached out and removed the badge from Scott's shirt. Scott stood in amazed silence.

Nader looked at Fallon. "Mr. Monroe, you are an officer of the court. I appoint you as temporary City Marshal until the city council hires a new marshal." He handed the badge to Fallon who pinned it to his shirt.

Scott ground his teeth as he glared at the accusing faces around him. "It doesn't matter. I'll be the new Pima County Sheriff by the first of the year and then you'll all be sorry."

"You have to win the election first," Fallon said.

"I'll win it."

"No, you won't, because I'm running and I intend to win it."

Scott snarled, "We'll see about that."

"Yes, we will," Fallon replied.

Fallon, Adam, and Leroy walked away from the barn leaving Scott surrounded by a large number of townsmen demanding an accounting from him over the shooting and what they had heard.

Chapter 25

Helen had been watching the rush of people and the excited talk about a gunfight at the livery. That was what Adam had shouted to Fallon and where they had run to. She had seen the wagon roll by with Charlotte Scott in the back looking over someone who was apparently lying in the bed. Then, she spotted Fallon walking toward her with Adam and the other man he had been with.

She hurried toward Fallon who stopped near her. Her eyes momentarily fixed on the badge and then lifted to Fallon's face. "What happened?"

"There were five outlaws waiting for Cordell down at the livery. Cordell has been shot."

Helen put her hand over her mouth, "Oh, no. How is he?"

"It doesn't appear to be life threatening. We're headed for the doctor's now."

"I will come with you." Together they followed Adam and Leroy.

Helen said in a low voice, "I heard what your brother said and then I heard the shooting. I went to

Marshal Scott and told him."

"He showed up and went to calling Cordell names and blaming him for the fight."

"Why, would he do that?"

"He's got a burr under his saddle for our family, especially Cordell, always has. It seems he knew the outlaws were in town gunning for Cordell and did nothing to prevent it. In fact, according to Leroy Jackson, he overheard Scott encouraging them to kill Cordell."

Helen gasped, "That's *horrible!*"

"Simeon Nader was there. He and Scott got into it and Mr. Nader fired him on the spot."

"I have heard a good deal of talk, people are quite unhappy with Marshal Scott."

"He's gone now. He indicated the badge on his jacket. "Mr. Nader appointed me temporary City Marshal."

They arrived at Dr. Smith's office where a group was gathered outside.

Cordell had been rushed into the doctor's examination room with the assistance of several men. Leroy stood with Adam outside the office as he thanked the men for helping his brother. Fallon and Helen moved up beside them.

The four entered the office and waited. An hour passed before Dr. Smith came out of the backroom. They all looked at him anxiously.

"He is a very lucky young man," Smith began. "He will live, but will require several weeks of healing time. The bullet that could have done extensive internal damage broke the third rib and deflected back out causing a long ragged wound, vicious looking, but not life threatening. The second bullet damaged the thigh muscle and chipped the leg bone."

They all smiled relieved at the good news. Fallon laughed, "Knowing Cordell he won't stay down three days."

Smith smiled, "He wants to get up already. You may have to tie him down to recuperate."

"Can we see him?" Adam asked.

"Yes, for a few minutes."

"You go ahead," Helen said to Fallon, "I will wait here."

The men went in to find Cordell on a bed with a blanket over him. Charlotte was sitting next to him. His face was drawn and pale. The pain of his wounds showed in his eyes, but he was demonstrating his good humor all the same.

Charlotte stood up as they walked in. "He is doing well," she smiled down at Cordell.

"Well, that's good news," Adam said.

Cordell looked up at Adam and grinned. "I'd say you earned your eagle feather. Still feel sheltered?"

"Not anymore."

"How did you all know to come and help me?"

Adam tipped his head toward Leroy. "Leroy knew that bunch was in town gunning for you and hanging out by the livery. He was keeping an eye out for you to warn you. When I found him he wanted to know where you were. I told him you had gone to the livery and the race was on."

Cordell reached his arm out from under the blanket and extended his hand to Leroy. "Thanks."

Leroy shook his hand. "It's the least I could do for my old pard's son."

"Hope you don't plan on remaining a

stranger."

"I'll be around."

Cordell shifted his eyes to Fallon. "Some fun, huh? Hanging around me is more exciting than some stuffy old courtroom isn't it?" His eyes then narrowed, "What's with the badge? Sheriff already?"

Fallon glanced at Charlotte. "I'll tell you about it later."

"My father was fired for his bad behavior, wasn't he?" Charlotte asked.

Fallon shifting nervously, "Yes. I've been appointed temporary City Marshal."

"Oh, he should be in a fouler mood than usual." She then let a small smile slip, "Mother will settle him down though."

"With a brick?" Cordell mused.

"If necessary," Charlotte grinned.

Fallon wanted to change the subject. He gave Cordell a mock look of disappointment. "How come you keep getting shot at these things? I thought you were supposed to be some kind of gunfighter?"

Cordell made a soundless laugh. "I got the first two, didn't I?"

"I have to say, I'm really disappointed in you little brother." Fallon winked at Charlotte to show he was only teasing.

"I'll try and do better in the next one."

"Yeah, you need to work on that."

"Doctor Smith says you're going to be down a while." Adam said to Cordell.

"A day or two."

Charlotte dug her fists into her sides. "A day or two my foot, Mr. Monroe! You will stay abed until you heal. Doctor's orders!"

Leroy laughed, "Better watch out, her mother may lend her that brick."

"This is going to delay your leaving town you know," Adam said with amusement in his eyes.

Cordell smiled, glanced at Charlotte, then back to Adam. "About that . . ."

"Yeah?"

"That job you said you had for me?"

"What about it?" Adam said stifling a smile.

"Think I'll take it."

"I thought you were too restless to settle in one place?"

Cordell turned his face toward Charlotte and winked at her. "Like I told you once, you never know what might make me want to stick around."

Adam smiled at Charlotte as she blushed red. "Can't say I blame you. The job is yours, just get healed.

Fallon shook his head. "Girls really do go for scoundrels don't they?"

"It's part of my charm," Cordell replied with an impish grin.

"If I'm not mistaken," Adam grinned. "Weren't you the one who chased Charlotte with a snake back in fifth grade and put a lizard in her lunch pail in sixth?"

"It was just a little lizard," Cordell replied.

Charlotte laughed, "It was huge to me. You were such a little rascal Cordell Monroe."

"I promise not to do it again."

"However, I do recall you beating up Billy Ekers when he pushed me down and made me cry. You were my knight in shining armor that day."

Dr. Smith stepped into the room. "Cordell

Dave P. Fisher

needs to get some rest now."

The men said their good byes to Cordell and filed out of the room.

"How is he?" Helen asked Fallon.

"He'll be fine."

"I am glad to hear that."

They all walked out of the office and into the street where they stood together in silence.

Leroy put his hand out to Adam. "Think I'll go on home."

Adam shook his hand. "Thanks for everything."

"No problem." Leroy extended his hand to Fallon who took it. "One of you want to fill me in tomorrow?"

"I will," Fallon replied. "I'm sure Adam has a lot of work waiting for him up at the ranch."

"Good enough. I'll see you then." He tipped his hat to Helen, "Evening, ma'am."

Helen tipped her head toward Leroy in return.

Leroy then pointed to the badge on Fallon's jacket, "Looks a lot better on you." He turned and walked away.

As Leroy walked away Helen asked Fallon, "Who is that man?"

Fallon watched Leroy's back growing smaller in the distance. "An old friend of the family."

Helen glanced from Fallon to Adam and back to Fallon. "I am sure you and your brother would like to talk alone. I am going to go home and clean up a bit. Can we meet for dinner?"

"Yes. I will knock on your door in an hour."

Helen smiled. "Until then." She walked away down the boardwalk.

"Let's take a walk," Fallon said without looking at his brother.

Together they walked into the residential area until they came to the burned out remains of the house their parents had lived in, and they had as well for several years. The debris had been cleaned up and hauled away. All that remained on the charred sand was part of the foundation and the hole of the cellar.

They studied the site in silence for a moment.

"It's been a crazy two weeks," Adam said softly. "The fire, the folks murdered, learning the truth about Pa's history, Cain, killing Cain, this business today. Lord, it's enough to make a man dizzy just thinking about it."

Fallon continued to look over the burned ground. "It's a blur alright. I haven't had time to put it all in some semblance of order."

"I'm not like you Fallon, and I definitely don't have the same makeup as Cordell. I remember when we first moved here, I was twelve, you were fifteen, and Cordell ten. In the three years I was in this school I was in one fight. You were only in it a year and had a couple right off. Cordell. Cordell was in so many fights by the time he got out of school I can't even count them all."

Fallon nodded. "No one pushed Cordell around."

"I was the quiet one," Adam admitted with a hint of embarrassment. "I wasn't a scrapper like the two of you. I took the job with Red, married Laura, and settled right down. My life was pretty mild and my world small."

Fallon glanced at Adam, "What's your point?"

"I was naïve to the world around me,

especially to the violence and men like Cain, and now I feel like that world has come along and smacked me up the side of the head. I've had an awakening to a bigger sphere."

"You have that alright."

Adam hesitated, then said. "I feel like I've earned a place beside my brothers. I've caught up with you."

Fallon huffed a small laugh. "Neither one of us will ever catch up with Cordell though."

Adam shook his head. "No."

Fallon stared out over the burn. "I wouldn't be standing here right now if Cordell hadn't pushed me out of that saloon door. I had no idea what was up, but he did. He knew and read it. You don't learn that in law school."

"He saved me in the Desert Rose. I was busy trying to go easy with that woman and had no clue she was about to shoot me."

"She was?"

"Cordell knocked her aside and she dropped the gun. A little derringer."

"We both owe him."

"You saved him today though."

Fallon shrugged. "Maybe. That man might have missed him.

"Or not have missed him. It's what brothers do for each other."

"Yeah. I forgot that for a long time."

Adam was silent for a minute as he looked over the scorched ground and pictured where everything had been in the house. He could see their mother and father in the house. "This is where it all ended." He let out a sigh.

"No." Fallon slightly shook his head. "This is where it all began."

Adam gave him a curious look. "Began?"

"The beginning of the truth. The beginning of knowing our real family history, our real names. The beginning of my return from self-exile and the beginning of family healing."

Adam thought on that for a second. "That's a good way to look at it alright."

They stood in silence for another minute before Adam asked softly, "Were we right?"

"About what?"

"Killing Winston Cain."

"Was Cain right to murder Ma and Pa? Shoot them down like he did? Burn the house down? Was Cain right to murder that miner? From what Leroy was saying he executed other people and I'm sure they were unarmed and defenseless." Fallon turned his head to look at Adam. "Is it right to kill a rabid dog?"

Adam met his brother's eyes and then looked back out over the burn. "Two weeks ago I had my doubts about our right to do this when Cordell challenged us to find the killer. I went along because I felt it was my duty."

"But now?"

"I see things a lot differently. You said it back in Pecos, 'justice owed.' Cain was owed a bullet for his crimes."

"And he paid his dues in full. I have no regrets," Fallon said flatly.

"Me either. Not now, not ever," Adam said with feeling.

"Only a few will ever know what we did

anyway."

Adam's eyes scanned over the burn. "Looks like we will have our own family secret."

Fallon nodded. "A family tradition that I hope ends with us. You should go and tell Laura, Elwood, and Ruth what happened. They probably haven't heard about Cordell yet."

"I will. You're going to meet Helen?"

"In a bit. First I need to put some ghosts to rest."

Adam patted his brother on the back. "See you later."

Fallon nodded without a response.

The sound of Adam's boots faded away leaving Fallon standing in silence. He walked into the charred square, moving slowly through it, remembering. Remembering the good times spent in this house, and the fight that ended it. The fight he so sorely regretted.

Now, because of the sick and twisted mind of Winston Cain, he could never reconcile with his father. Never apologize to his mother for leaving the way he did. Then, to add misery on misery, Cain burned the house down so there was nothing left of them but memories.

His boot toe kicked into an object lightly covered by the blackened sand. He reached down and picked up a metal photograph frame. He remembered it well. It had rested on a shelf holding the only photograph ever taken of their parents. All that remained of the photograph now, like everything else, was a memory. The thought made him angry.

He knocked the dust off the frame and cleaned it carefully with his fingers. Looking the simple metal square over he repeated Adam's question to himself, 'were we right?'

"Yes, Adam we were," he said out loud. Then in a burst of anger he snarled, "Beau Whitlock's boys, by God, *made it right*."

He walked out of the burned square carrying the last remnant of his parents so he could always look at it and remember why they were right.

About the Author

Mountain men and explorers make up the branches of Dave's family tree. His mother's side was from Canada where the men plied the fur trade, venturing into the Rocky Mountains during the beaver boom in the 1820's.

His grandfather was Blackfoot born in a tepee on the reservation in Montana. He was a hunter and horseman who brought a great deal of Old West influence into the Fisher family. His father was born in 1905 and saw the last of the Old West. From them Dave heard the stories of the West that was.

A life-long Westerner Dave inherited that pioneer blood and followed in the footsteps of his ancestors. Originally from Oregon, he worked cattle and rode saddle broncs. His adventures have taken him across the wilds of Alaska as a horsepacker and hunting guide, through the Rocky Mountains of Montana, Wyoming, and Colorado where he wrangled, guided and packed for a variety of outfitters and the National Park Service.

Dave weaves his experience into each story. His writing, steeped in historical accuracy and drawing on extensive research, draws his readers into the story by their realism and Dave's personal knowledge of the West, its people, and character.

He has near to 500 fiction and non-fiction works published. Included are 20 western action/adventure and outdoor novels and short story collections, 70 short stories, and inclusion in 18 anthologies. He is the first, and currently the only, writer to win the *Will Rogers Medallion Award* three times. In 2008 for Best

Western Fiction, in 2013 for Best Western Humor, and 2014 for Best Western Novel. Nine of his short stories have earned Reader's Choice Awards.

You can learn more about Dave's background and writing at his website: www.davepfisher.com

From Double Diamond Books –

Dave P. Fisher

The
Outlaw Hunter

Eli Warren didn't consider himself a bounty hunter. He hunted outlaws like some men hunted wolves or mountain lions. The bounties he collected were simply payments rendered to a workman, and he was a man good at his work.

Under Eli's flint-hard exterior, that was merciless to outlaws, ran a wide streak of kindness that showed itself the day he picked up a starving orphan in Dodge City and took him along. He soon learned that the twelve-year-old Rob Slater harbored a common intent with him – to run down the elusive Parson gang. He for the $10,000 reward, and Rob, because Jude Parson had murdered his folks. Rob asked Eli to teach him the trade so one day he could look Jude Parson in the eye and square things with the killer.

Under Eli's tutorage the two came to turn the outlaw world on its ear until the day Eli honored his brother's dying request and took his young daughter into his care touching off a series of unexpected changes that would forever mold their futures.

From Double Diamond Books –

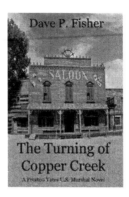

Copper Creek rested quietly in the Nevada desert, peaceful on the surface, but churning with corruption and violence beneath. Run by The Council, it was ruled with an iron fist and hired guns. In a move to control the entire region when gold was discovered The Council, a secret organization of men who had built the town around a copper mine and on the graves of those they had murdered, began to eliminate neighboring prospectors and settlers.

The settlers, miners, and ranchers fought back. The winning cards all belonged to The Council until one of the miners, the father of U.S. Marshal Preston Yates, sent a wire to his son asking for his help and the authority of his badge.

Shortly after Preston Yates rode into town the battle for Copper Creek began. Will the solid citizens of the area prevail against the murderous Council and their hired thugs, or will The Council once again have their own way?

From Double Diamond Books –

In the tradition of yesterday's story masters
Outdoor Sporting Fiction is back.

COLD BLOWS THE TUNDRA WIND – A contemporary crime story set against the backdrop of the Alaska wilderness in the tradition of Jack London and James Oliver Curwood.

Just as hunting season is about to start, Master Guide John Forester goes up against outlaw guide and poacher Dirk Benedict, and an Alaska Wildlife Trooper on the take only to find himself behind bars when they set him up. With Forester out of the way and the trooper in his pocket, Benedict has free run to conduct his business while John's wife and 18-year-old son Lee face financial ruin and fears for John's long-term imprisonment.

While Lee, an Assistant Guide who cannot legally guide alone, works to hold everything together, Parker Raines, a Registered Guide and a stranger to them all, steps up to accept the job of guiding in John's absence. Teaming up with Lee, things are looking up for Johnson Creek Outfitters and the family, until Lee discovers Parker associating with Benedict, leaving him and his mother to wonder about Parker's real intentions. Did Parker work his way into the operation to serve his own illegal agenda or is there more to the mysterious guide than meets the eye?

From Double Diamond Books –

Second in the new line of Dave P. Fisher's contemporary Outdoor Sporting Fiction

A strong-arm mining company, a boy running from killers, and an attempted kidnapping of his daughter brings Jason Donnelly out from under his Alaska cover to fight the crime family who thought they'd killed him twelve years before.

Jason Donnelly thought he was a high level body guard for VIP's until he found out the people he worked for and guarded were the leaders of the Clemente crime family. Once in, you didn't get out. Determined to break away he is betrayed by his brother, resulting in his wife's death from the car bomb meant for him. Taking his four-year-old daughter Jason escapes back to his native Alaska, adopts his old nickname of Duke, and takes up a gold claim in the bush.

Duke realizes his cover has been blown when he learns that the mining company trying to push him out belongs to the Clemente family who are making a move for the Alaska territory. He has two choices – to leave everything and run again or stand and fight. Jason Duke Donnelly makes his choice – he's done running.

Made in the USA
Middletown, DE
19 January 2018